If
I
Should
Speak

A Novel

By Umm Zakiyyah

If I Should Speak
A Novel

ISBN: 0-9707667-0-X

Library of Congress Control Number:
2001129076

Copies of this book can be ordered online at
www.al-walaa.com
or by calling Toll-Free 1(866)550-7839

Published by:
Al-Walaa Publications College Park, MD USA
Printed in the USA

*All characters and events in this book are fictional, and any resemblance to
real persons or incidents is coincidental.*

All quotes from real people or books have been cited in the footnotes as such.

Dedication

*For all who have open minds and hearts and ever tread
the path of life as students.*

"What is the life of this world but amusement and play?
But verily the Home in the Hereafter—that is Life indeed,
If they but knew"[1]

---

[1] The Holy Qur'an; *Al-'Ankaboot*, 29:64

Chapter One

"I'm tired of this!" Tamika kicked her dormitory room door closed in disgust. Her roommate's clothes were thrown carelessly about the room. A pair of shorts still lay untouched on her roommate's desk. They had been there for two days already. Blond hair strands had begun to gather into dust balls under Jennifer's bed.

Angry, Tamika stormed out of the room, marching down the hall to the resident advisor's (RA) room to get the vacuum cleaner. She was pounding impatiently on Mandy's door before she realized it.

The RA quickly opened the door. "What's wrong?" She gasped, thinking the matter to be an emergency. Her red hair was disheveled, and red imprints stood out against her pale skin. She had been sleeping.

"Sorry to wake you," Tamika apologized in a calmer tone than her knocking had suggested, "but I need to borrow the vacuum cleaner."

Mandy rolled her eyes and sucked her teeth, upset for having been disturbed for such a trivial matter. She rolled the vacuum into the hall, and she slammed the door in Tamika's face without a word. Mandy was so angry that she did not even remember to take Tamika's student identification card as collateral.

Tamika shrugged, too upset with Jennifer to allow the RA's rudeness to bother her. Sighing, she rolled the vacuum down the hall. In her room, she took one last look at the disastrous mess before she began cleaning.

Tamika had heard horror stories from her friends who had experienced strenuous roommate situations, but now she was experiencing it first hand. She had been lucky the year before as a freshman, when she was placed with her now best friend Makisha. However, Makisha now had a single, no roommate, a situation of which Tamika could only dream.

As she vacuumed and organized the room, Tamika thought of Jennifer's forever broken promises, swearing that she would clean her side of the room. Tamika would usually keep both sides tidy, but Jennifer would complain, stating that it made her feel guilty and promising that she would clean her side from then on.

Today, the two had discussed the uncleanness of the room, and Jennifer had promised that her side of the room would be clean before Tamika returned that afternoon. However, Jennifer was nowhere in sight, and half of the room was untouched, unkempt for yet another day.

Just as Tamika turned off the vacuum, the door opened.

"Oh my God!" Jennifer was saying to her friend Christina as they entered the room. "You've gotta be kidding!"

Before Christina could respond, she and Jennifer's eyes caught Tamika's icy glare. Jennifer's dark blue eyes slowly traced every inch of the room, and Tamika's gaze remained fixed on Jennifer, whose blond hair was pulled casually back in a ponytail and hung just above her shoulders. She was dressed in a navy blue sweatshirt and matching pants and was wearing running shoes. Jennifer's face was slightly reddened and moist with perspiration, indicating to Tamika that her roommate had been exercising— Jennifer had been relaxing and enjoying herself while she cleaned the room.

"Oh my God," Jennifer said, cupping her hand over her mouth, remembering just then. "I'm so sorry, Tamika." She smiled uneasily. "I totally forgot. Oh my God."

"Yeah," Tamika agreed sarcastically. "'Oh my God' is right." Her stare did not leave her roommate's face.

"Okay," Jennifer defended, "I forgot, okay?" She rolled her eyes and waved her hand at Tamika. "Don't make such a big deal, gosh."

"I better go," Christina announced, leaving the room and closing the door without waiting for a reply.

"A big deal!" Tamika exclaimed impatiently.

"Calm down, for God's sake. I forgot."

She felt herself becoming hot with anger. "Calm down!" She let her voice descend to a lower tone. "Calm down?" she whispered in disbelief. She held the handle of the vacuum and shook the machine in her tight grip. "You see this, huh? Miss Forgetful? Do you?"

Silence.

"Well, *this* is what I've been doing for the last forty minutes." Tamika shook her head at a loss for words.

"I told you I'd do it," Jennifer retorted.

"But did you?"

She rolled her eyes and shoved past Tamika with her shoulders, throwing Tamika off balance momentarily. Jennifer collapsed in her desk chair and groaned, furiously pulling the ponytail holder from her sweat-dampened hair, letting her hair fall comfortably over her shoulders. "I don't have time for this. I have studying to do." She opened a book, fumbling through the pages nervously.

"Don't you *ever* put your hands on me again," Tamika hissed through gritted teeth, struggling to calm herself.

"My *hands* didn't touch you," her roommate corrected, still facing her book.

"Don't be funny with me girl. You know exactly what I mean."

"Okay," Jennifer said, fed up, abruptly turning in her chair to face her roommate. "Is this about the room or what?"

"No," Tamika replied, fuming. "This is about your junk everywhere and how I'm tired of you playing Miss Innocent whenever I bring it to your attention."

Her roommate opened her mouth to say something.

"Don't say another word to me," she stopped her. "I don't wanna hear 'I'm sorry' or 'Oh my God' come outta your mouth again."

Frustrated, Jennifer stood, tossed her hair, and picked up the receiver to her phone that sat on a nightstand next to her bed. "I'm calling my mother," she announced, obviously hurt and upset. Her face grew red, and her eyes began to water.

Annoyed, Tamika dashed over to her roommate and slammed the receiver down before Jennifer could finish dialing. "Oh no you're not," she protested. "Not this time." Her hand was on top of Jennifer's, pressing forcefully.

Jennifer threw Tamika's hand off of hers, snatched up the receiver and began dialing again. Tears were now streaming down her cheeks. She hissed the word under her breath, but Tamika had heard.

"What did you say?" Tamika asked incredulously in a whisper. "What did you say?" The question now became a dare.

Her roommate proudly flipped her hair and turned her back to Tamika, intentionally ignoring the question. She carried the entire phone to her bed and held the receiver between her shoulder and ear. "Mom?" she whined into the phone. "Nothing," she lied to her mother after an inquiry as to what was wrong. "I mean," she corrected then whispered as if it were an evil word, "*Her.*" As her mother comforted her, her crying became uncontrollable, and she sobbed, unable to speak intelligibly.

Tamika did not blink as she stared disbelieving at Jennifer, the filthy word still stinging her ears. Rage built up inside of her, and she struggled to control herself. Never in her life had she heard such a word come out of a white person's mouth except while watching an old movie—until now.

Before she could even consider the repercussions of her action, Tamika yanked Jennifer's phone cord from the wall in her frustration and held the end tightly in her fist.

"Mom? Mom?" Jennifer pressed the button on the phone repeatedly. Panicked and immediately realizing what had happened, she jerked around to face Tamika, whose glare was cruel and unmoving.

"What did you say?" Tamika demanded louder than before, now that she definitely had her roommate's attention.

Jennifer's shock interrupted her crying, and she slowly set her phone down, staring at her roommate, livid. "That was my mother," she hissed.

"I asked you a question," Tamika reminded her. The cord's end was now causing her palm to sweat with the tight grip.

"That was my mother, you—!" Infuriated, Jennifer was now on her feet, arms swinging wildly at her roommate, her obscenities flying almost as quickly as her arms.

Before Jennifer could take hold of Tamika's hair, Tamika dropped the cord and caught her roommate's arms. She then thrust Jennifer away from her in a desperate attempt to protect herself. Jennifer fell into the bed with such force that the bed moved several feet as her heavy body crashed into it. Jennifer let out a scream and again began to shout offenses at Tamika, calling her every accursed name she could think of. A second later, she was on her feet again, charging at Tamika, who again tried to catch her arms, but this time unsuccessfully. Instead, the two fell on the floor, Jennifer on top, pulling and yanking at Tamika's hair. Somehow Tamika managed to overcome her. Now on top, Tamika pinned Jennifer down, pressing her arms against the floor forcefully to restrain Jennifer's flying arms.

"Get off me! Get off me!" Jennifer hollered as she realized her defeat, hoping someone would hear.

The sound of a phone ringing came from Tamika's desk.

Jennifer's mother.

But no one seemed to hear it.

"Get off me!"

A moment later the door swung open, and Mandy stared at the roommates, stunned. "What on earth is going on in here!" Two other residents rushed into the doorway, panting. "Go call security!" Mandy instructed desperately, her eyes glued to Tamika. Both residents ran in obedience.

The ringing ceased.

Jennifer began to cry again, and for a moment all that could be heard were her sobs and sniffles.

Sensing how the scene must appear to the RA, Tamika slowly removed herself from Jennifer and stood several feet from her roommate.

Mandy quickly ran to Jennifer and knelt beside her, gently holding her hand to help her get up. "Are you okay?"

Sniffling, Jennifer nodded, unable to speak.

Mandy glared at Tamika, her green eyes scolding, shaking her head as if it were a shame as she helped Jennifer to her feet.

"You're hurt!" Mandy cried as she saw blood on Jennifer's hand.

Jennifer touched the back of her head again and glanced at her fingers. She *was* bleeding! "I, I," she started to say.

"Don't worry," Mandy consoled her, glancing disapprovingly at Tamika. "You can tell security." She paused, looking at both roommates and said, "But now, both of you need to come with me."

An hour later, Tamika found herself with a conduct charge of physical assault, a Conduct Board hearing the following evening, and a room to herself for the night. The campus security had asked Jennifer if she wanted Tamika moved to another room that night, but Jennifer declined the offer, stating that she would rather stay with a friend, because she felt unsafe in a room to which Tamika had a key.

Unsafe.

The word echoed in Tamika's head. Unsafe. *'Really?'* she asked herself as she recounted the entire incident and the conversation with the campus security that had followed. The security personnel had allowed Jennifer to tell an exaggerated version of the story, with no interruptions from Tamika. In her story, Jennifer told of Tamika's alleged prior intimidation and the feeling that at any moment, Tamika would become violent. Whenever Tamika had tried to interject and correct her, she was told, "Quiet, please," by the security officers, who were taking notes on Jennifer's statements. Of course, Mandy's presence made the situation no better.

Mandy explained how she found Tamika on top of a bleeding, screaming, and helpless Jennifer. The RA's vivid recap of the scene rendered even Tamika speechless. Mandy had no idea what had been going on in the room, yet she had much to say. It seemed no one cared to hear Tamika's side of the story. However, they did pretend to listen when the officers asked her to recount her side, a gesture that Tamika sensed was based more on routine than sincere concern for the truth. The blank stares and mechanical nods made it clear to Tamika that the interest was feigned. And despite the sound of pen strokes whistling across the pages of the officers' report as she spoke, it was clear she was talking to herself. It was no use trying to expound upon her version of the incident. She was already guilty in their minds, and her carrying on, as she had started to do, only made her case worse. So she had decided to just call it a night, and she went back to her room.

Presently, Tamika lay in her clean room, staring at the water stained ceiling. The vacuum cleaner stood next to her desk. Its plug was still in the outlet. She sighed out of frustration and got out of bed. She pulled the plug from the wall and wrapped the cord neatly on the vacuum. She then pushed the vacuum to the corner of her room, deciding that she would return it in the morning. She doubted that she could stomach the sight of Mandy again that night.

As she situated the vacuum in the corner, her eyes grazed her reflection in the mirror. For a second, she barely recognized the young woman who stared back at her. The once meticulously sculpted mascara now created dark, ominous shadows around her eyes, making her appear almost ghostly in the glass. Her almond brown eyes were usually bright, almost jovial, but they now sat behind the shadowy gloom, hidden and distant, their kindness concealed by the stress that had greeted them, suggesting that beneath them was irrational emotion— anger waiting to unleash itself. Thin red welts swelled from her cheeks, likely the result of Jennifer's irate fingernails scraping her skin, and although their presence should have suggested that she had been a victim, the blood stained scrapes instead made her appear almost vicious, intimating more a brutal branding than an injury. The honey brown of her face, normally smooth, seemed rough at the moment, her tightened, angry jaw only exacerbating the ferocious appearance. Fistfuls of permed hair protruded awkwardly from one side of her head, an unwanted complement to the now unkempt, loosened bun at the back of her head.

Had this threatening person who now stared back at Tamika been the young woman the security had seen and with whom they had spoken? Had she been the young woman with whom Jennifer had lived? If so, then perhaps Tamika could see how a misunderstanding could have brewed.

Unexpectedly, her reflection blurred, and before she could stop them, the tears fell, sliding slowly, then quickening, down her cheeks. Ashamed, she covered her face with her hands and let herself sob, her shoulders shaking with each cry, at that moment wishing she was anywhere else but school.

***

Tamika sat in the lobby of Streamsdale University Student Center at 6:45 the next evening. Her Conduct Board hearing would begin in fifteen minutes. She had opted to attend the hearing without a Faculty Advisor, who would act somewhat like a lawyer for her. She would have laughed at the security officers' suggestion, except they were serious. The entire hearing was a joke to Tamika, and the idea of a "lawyer" seemed ludicrous in light of the trivial altercation with her roommate. She had simply told the officers, "No, thank you," when they offered her to submit a faculty member's name, wondering who on her earth could testify on her behalf. Besides, who had actually witnessed the incident?

Glancing at her watch, Tamika groaned. It was 6:59. She stood, and unexpectedly, her heart began to pound. *Why am I nervous*, she wondered, as she opened the door to the room in which the case would be held.

The room was set up similar to a courtroom, except the university's desks, tables, and chairs were being used for the effect. She smiled uneasily as she glanced across the room at the Conduct Board members, who were mostly students, seated at a long table facing her. There were two college professors on the board, and one was Dr. Sanders, her Religion 150 professor. Instinctively, she waved at him, momentarily forgetting where she was. Immediately, she was ashamed, realizing that she had done the wrong thing, which was confirmed by the uncomfortable expression on Dr. Sanders' face after the friendly gesture, his eyes quickly glancing away from her, now looking at the pen and paper before him.

Tamika was directed to sit down in a chair in front of everyone, and the hearing began. A student introduced herself and read Tamika what she thought would be her rights. But instead, the student explained that Tamika was under Streamsdale University's Honor Code and would be held accountable for any false testimony. She went on to tell Tamika that the case could not be discussed with any member of the board outside the room, and Tamika was forbidden to approach any of them concerning the hearing.

"Do you have any questions?" she asked Tamika.

She had to ask Tamika twice before receiving a response, which was more a mumble and a shake of the head than it was a clear answer.

"You, Tamika Douglass, have been charged with the physical assault of Jennifer Mayer," she informed her. "How do you plead?"

Physical assault? How do I plead? This all had to be a joke. These students could not be serious.

"How do you plead, Miss Douglass?"

So they were serious. "Not guilty," she replied.

The student directed Tamika's roommate to sit in the desk that was about three feet from where Tamika sat. "Jennifer," she began, "tell the board exactly what happened last night."

Jennifer began uneasily, but minutes later, she articulately described the incident, recounting how she had tried to call her mother when Tamika violently punched her hand into the receiver. She further explained that after she asked Tamika why she had done it, Tamika shoved her into the bed, injuring her head. Afraid, Jennifer explained, she tried to fight back, but to no avail. That was when Mandy came in, *thank God,* before Tamika was about to hurt her any further. Mandy testified next and told the board what she had seen. She carried on dramatically, and Tamika was amazed at how Mandy's three minutes at the scene had turned into nearly thirty minutes of expressions, gestures, and reenactments.

Tamika stared at the table as Christina took the seat in front of the board, recounting what she had seen. She told them that she had left the room out of fear for her safety, afraid that Tamika would attack her. Next, the two residents who had fetched security testified, and they too recounted the "terrifying" scene. Tamika began to feel overwhelmed, now wishing she had opted to have a Faculty Advisor by her side, not so much for her defense but for comfort and support. However, she had no one, leaving her feeling isolated and alone as she was painted a villain. The room harbored an unfriendly atmosphere that she could not break. She imagined that it would not matter what she said at that point, and she was certain that she had lost the case.

She stole a quick glance at Dr. Sanders, who listened intently to the witnesses. He had not even as much as looked at Tamika since she had unwittingly waved to him.

Tamika's stomach began to knot, and her head ached. She swallowed. She wanted nothing more than to just get up, leave, and never come back. But there was no escape. Her hands that were folded neatly in front of her began to shake. She quickly removed them from the table and onto her lap, where her palms began to sweat. The voices in the room were far away now, mere whispers in the background, and Tamika's mind drifted to her first day of second semester the year before, when she had first met Dr. Sanders.

After class, she had eagerly introduced herself to the first African-American professor she had had since enrolling as a freshman.

"Hi, Dr. Sanders," she greeted him that day. "I'm Tamika Douglass."

"Well, hello, Miss Douglass," he returned the friendly greeting with a smile. "How are you?"

"I'm fine, and you?"

"Just fine. And where are you from?"

"Milwaukee."

"Wisconsin?"

"Yes."

"That's quite a ways. I hear it's cold up there."

"It is, but it's beautiful in the summer."

"I hear that too," he replied, stacking papers and putting them into his black briefcase. "So what brings you to Georgia?"

"Streamsdale."

"The university or the town?"

She shrugged. "Both, I suppose. But I guess the university more than the town." She paused then confessed, "They gave me the most money."

He laughed. "Well, that is important," he admitted. "I'm still paying off my student loans."

"Where are you from?"

"Tampa Bay."

"Florida?"

"Yes, I guess I was a Southern boy, as they say."

The conversation had been nice and easy-going, and he proved to be amicable, even as a professor, which was why Tamika enjoyed his class a lot. He also had a sense of humor that gave the class a relaxed atmosphere. She had never been one to study world religions, but after having Dr. Sanders for Religion 101, her interest was sparked in the subject. And she had actually begun considering declaring Religion her major, which was why she enrolled in the 150 course this year.

"Tamika?" the student who headed the Conduct Board repeated.

"Oh, um, yes?" Tamika had unintentionally shut out her surroundings.

The student blinked, and again inquired, "Do you have anything to add to the testimony?"

All eyes fell on Tamika. The student and faculty board members shifted uncomfortably in their chairs. Even Dr. Sanders stared at her now, anticipating a response. "Um, no," she answered finally without thinking.

"No?" the student repeated, disbelieving. "Are you sure you've nothing to add?" She waited for a response. "This is your time to speak, Tamika," she reminded, "without interruption."

Tamika glanced nervously about the room. Everyone was waiting on her, focusing on her. How could she tell her side of the story when she had tuned out the majority of the other side? She wanted to argue her case, but for or against what would she argue? Without realizing it, she looked desperately to Dr. Sanders, pleading. He quickly looked away and began toying with his pen.

"What happened last night?" a student board member encouraged.

"Did you shove Jennifer into the bed, causing the head injury?" another asked.

"No," Tamika managed to mumble loud enough for the board to hear. "I was defending myself," she said louder.

"So are you saying Jennifer hit you first?"

"Yes," she answered more assertively, lifting her head to face the questioner. "She came at me, trying to hit me, so I pushed her away."

A million questions seemed to come to her at once, but amazingly, she managed to answer them all. When they had run out of questions, Tamika was allowed to leave.

"You can call Dean Floyd's office in the morning for the Conduct Board's decision. You are excused," the student dismissed her.

***

Friday afternoon, the day after she attended her board hearing for the charge of "physical assault," Tamika stood removing clothes from her closet, eyes watering from anger. She was angry with herself and the entire Conduct Board, particularly Dr. Sanders—angry with herself for not being more wise in building an irrefutable defense and angry with the board for being so unfair. How was it that she had been found guilty of such an outlandish charge due to some meaningless squabble with Jennifer? Wednesday had not been the first day they had argued, although it was the first time they had ever physically clashed. But still, Jennifer was the one who had attacked her, and

Tamika was only defending herself, having done nothing other than pushed her roommate away from her and held Jennifer's arms to prevent Jennifer from hurting her. How was it then that she had on her college conduct record the charge of "physical assault"? Assault! She had not assaulted anyone! Then why was she being punished by having to move out of the room—now Jennifer's room—by Monday morning?

Her mother often told her of the injustice of the so-called "justice" system of America. But Tamika had not expected to deal with this in college, not in this manner anyhow. And Dr. Sanders. She would have never expected that she would lose any case with him on the board. But she had. How could he? Guilty? He knew her better than that. She was not the type of person to assault someone. But apparently, she had expected more of him than he would give. Perhaps, he was afraid of losing his job if he stood up for her. How petty and inconsiderate.

She skipped her Religion 150 class that day, too upset to even look at Dr. Sanders, let alone listen to his voice for fifty minutes, constantly being reminded of the night before, when he had pretended as if he did not even know her. Besides, she did not feel like telling him again that she had not yet selected a topic for her religion paper, especially since she could not even think about a paper right now.

Tamika knew she should have turned in her topic two weeks ago when everyone else did, but she was too indecisive. Every subject seemed so boring to her. She had half a mind to just tell him Christianity would be her topic, but she knew he would not fall for that one, given that she was supposed to select a religion with which she was unfamiliar. Buddhism, she had considered, but she could not bring herself to conduct an extensive research on a religion that seemed to be made up primarily of meditating and the "inner self." It reminded her too much of the karate movies she could not stand when she was younger, and she could not even feign interest, definitely not for twenty pages—minimum. The project was beginning to make her reconsider religion as a major. Perhaps, she was not cut out for this after all. Maybe she should just drop the class. Maybe she should just drop out of school.

She was being irrational.

There was a knock at the door, and before Tamika could respond, the door opened.

"What's up!"

It was Makisha, lively as usual.

Tamika forced a smile. "Nothin' much."

"Heard you beat up your roommate," her best friend teased her, laughing and closing the door behind her. "Finally!" Makisha's large, silver loop earrings moved as she threw up her hands playfully, causing the smell of her perfume to drift in Tamika's direction with the motion.

Tamika chuckled. "Girl, you're crazy."

"But you gotta tell me everything."

She wrinkled her forehead. "It ain't nothin' to tell."

"What are you doing?" Makisha asked suddenly, noticing the piles of clothes on her friend's bed.

"Moving."

"Moving?" she asked in surprise, her dark brown forehead creasing in confusion. "Why?"

Tamika shrugged. "I don't know. Ask the Conduct Board."

"What? They're making you move?"

She nodded, sighing.

"Girl, you betta fight that."

She forced laughter. "Yeah, right. They think I 'physically assaulted' that girl. How am I gonna fight anything?"

"Physically assaulted her?" Makisha repeated in disbelief, taken aback by the extremity of the charge. "You serious?"

Tamika nodded.

They were silent for a few seconds.

"You okay?" Makisha inquired, now concerned as she noticed the distant expression on her friend's face.

Tamika shrugged, feeling as if she was going to cry, but she stopped herself, ashamed. "Yeah, I'm fine."

"When do you have to move?"

"By Monday."

"By Monday! That's crazy."

"I know," she murmured, laying her last outfit from the closet on her bed, then opening her drawer.

"So you ain't goin' out tonight?"

Tamika shook her head. "But I don't feel like it anyway."

"Girl, you need to get out!"

She sighed. "I need to sleep. I've been up doing this most of the morning."

"You didn't go to your classes?" Makisha inquired, stunned, her tone reeking of disapproval.

Oh. Tamika had told on herself. "No, I didn't feel like it."

"Girl," Makisha warned, concerned for her friend, "you better watch it. Your grades might fall."

Tamika shrugged. "I know."

"You wanna go shopping with me?" Makisha offered with a grin, her maroon lipstick accenting the whiteness of her teeth, which seemed to glow each time she smiled.

Tamika shook her head. "I have too much to do."

Makisha sucked her teeth. "You're a party pooper, girl."

Tamika waved her hand at her. "Whatever."

Makisha started to open the door and turned to her friend, unconsciously tossing the thick synthetic braids that hung just below her shoulders. "Well, I gotta go pick up some things, but I'm gonna try to come back to help you."

"Don't worry about it."

"Girl, you gonna need all the help you can get. You got boxes?"

"Not really."

"Well, I'll ask Dante to see if he can get some for you."

"Thanks."

"Girl, it ain't no problem," she told her with a wave of her hand, revealing the maroon polished nails that matched her lips. "But I probably can't bring 'em till Saturday or Sunday, 'cause," she nodded, smirking, "you know, I gotta go partyin' tonight." She moved her shoulders playfully imitating a dance move, and Tamika chuckled.

"Sorry I can't join you."

"Don't worry," she joked, "I'll make you feel *real* bad, telling you all about it."

Tamika smiled and nodded, at that moment noticing Makisha's large sweatshirt and blue jeans, a casual outfit that somehow looked exceptionally good on her. "I'm sure you will."

"Anyways, I'll be seein' ya!"

"Bye."

"Bye!"

The door shut, and the room suddenly grew still. Tamika sat down on the edge of her bed and lowered her head. A moment later, she began to cry, which she found herself doing a lot lately. She felt as if everything was coming down on her at once. She doubted if she could take anymore. She was barely into the second semester of her sophomore year, and already, she was overwhelmed by the demands of college. She had not even declared a major yet, and if she went on like this, it was doubtful, at best, if she would graduate.

Tamika never wanted to go to college in the first place, desiring to pursue a career in the music industry as a recording artist, hoping to become a famous singer. But her mother thought she was crazy. Sometimes she wondered if she actually was, but that did not decrease her love for music. But, she had to admit, there were many who dreamed of being famous singers and never made it. So she decided that college was not such a bad idea after all. Besides, no one in her family had a college degree, and her mother thought her insane to turn down such a golden opportunity as higher education, especially to pursue an "impossible" career like singing. Her older sister had begun college but was unable to finish due to pregnancy, which was the same thing that prevented their mother from going to college in the first place.

Tamika had done well her first year in college, averaging a 3.4 grade point average, but this had been because she had thrown herself into her books, determined to make her mother happy, even if she herself was not. But even then, she had good days and bad days, but she was grateful that the former occurred more often. However, her sophomore year had begun slowly, and her course load was heavy and demanding. She had been forced to take high level science and mathematics courses, which were required for graduation, and she was lost. She often spaced out in class, unable to focus on what her professors were saying, and she was too shy to ask questions for fear they would think she was stupid. She had already been made to feel like a fool the previous semester, having been shot down by one of her classmates for misunderstanding what the student felt was "basic information" for the chemistry course.

She hated to be another statistic, despising the idea of a minority student falling through the cracks. But at that moment, Tamika couldn't have cared less. She was tired of seeking to prove the world wrong on things they would believe no matter what she did. If she were to do bad, they would think it normal. If she were to do well, they would think she was an exception. It was exhausting trying to even keep up with what she had to prove. If she were not trying to prove that she was just as intelligent as the next person, she was trying to prove that she was not a sex object. If she were not trying to prove that she was just as capable of the job as the next person, she was trying to prove that she was unique. It was draining, all the battles she had to fight. At times she just felt like relaxing, forgetting about it all, but she could not. Her mother, other family, and friends were cheering her on, encouraging her to be the person they were unable to be—even if she did not want to be that person, and even if she was not cut out to be her.

And then there were the pressures of society, the necessity to find a job, get married one day, and buy a home and car. She did not feel like fighting the battles of the workplace, with its pervasive racism and sexism. For her, the workplace would be less a means to earn money than the grounds for yet more battles she was unequipped to fight. She had had a job all through high school, and it frustrated her how unfair everything was. She had watched white people pass her up after working only six months, while she was still in the same position after two years. They often became her manager although they were not even employed when she began working there. She would come home complaining to her mother, who would simply say, "That's just how it is."

Her aunts and uncles felt she could be a senator one day, capable of changing everything. Her mother thought perhaps she could be a lawyer and fight for minorities' rights. But Tamika, who was barely driven to even vote, feeling it a futile gesture in truly changing anything—in that century anyway (if any others), wanted nothing other than to go to the farthest corner of the room, away from everyone, and write a poem, which would turn into a song. Paper and pen were dearer to her than gold at those moments. The lyrics would come to her, and she would frantically write, hoping the words did not escape her mind before the pen could catch them. Sometimes she would recite the poem or sing it to her family, and they always enjoyed it, showering her with praise for her talent. But they did not believe in her beyond that.

"You gotta get an education if you wanna be anything," her mother would tell her.

But Tamika dreaded the idea of sitting in classrooms, taking tests, and stressing over grades for four years, after which she would have to spend several more years doing the same thing—only it would get worse in graduate school. She felt that her poetry and songs were as good as anybody's, if not better, so why couldn't she make it like others had? Her family just had no faith. She would prove them wrong. She would be famous one day. She knew it—even if they didn't. But one day they would know—when she did make it. Perhaps, they would find out after turning on the radio one day and thinking, gee, that voice sounds familiar.

They say be strong,
But what if I'm weak?
They say stand up, speak out
But what if I'm meek?
They say fight hard
But what if I've no hands?
They say it makes sense
But what if I don't understand?
They say be like this
But what if I'm like that?
They say hit hard
But what if I've no bat?
They say choose this
But what if I've no choice?
They say tell 'em this

But what if I've no voice?

The words had not escaped her mind before she was able to write them down, and for that, Tamika was grateful. It was short, she knew, but sometimes that was enough, especially for journal entries, which she wrote whenever she felt like it. This one had come to her that night before going to bed. And as usual, it calmed her to put her thoughts on paper, and she was finally able to sleep.

Chapter Two

After having finished moving out of her room, Tamika was grateful to Makisha for assisting. The actual packing and moving things back and forth took more time and energy than she had anticipated. She also appreciated the campus security unlocking the door to her new building and helping her move during the weekend. However, since the room was not officially hers until Monday, they could not permit her to do anything aside from set her belongings in the front lobby of the building and leave them there. But from there, they had taken her things to the room.

Sunday night she had slept in her old room, which appeared awkwardly bare after the move. It was strange to go to sleep one night in her old bed and wake up knowing it was no longer hers, could no longer be hers. It made her feel somewhat sad, but Tamika could not explain this feeling, for she had no desire to live with Jennifer any more than Jennifer had to live with her. And there was nothing particularly special about her dormitory room compared to others. But she was not looking forward to moving to Steward Hall University Apartments. There, a person could have as many as three roommates, which was why not many people opted to live there, even though they were apartments. Those who did choose Steward either hand picked their roommates or prayed they would get lucky and have none. But Steward was known for its influx of students due to roommate fallouts, so anyone who hoped for the latter was either crazy or clueless.

Monday morning, Tamika went to the Residential Life Office to return her old keys and pick up her new ones before classes, which she decided to attend before her grades actually did suffer, as Makisha had warned. Tamika definitely was not thrilled about going to her classes, but she was less thrilled about the repercussions of not attending, especially going back home to her mother, who would give her a headache about it for the rest of her life. If only she were able to make it as a singer, she at least would have her own home.

Tamika groaned, adjusting the strap to her book bag on her shoulder. She walked up the steps of the Humanities building one by one, listening to the pounding of her shoes falling on each step, in no hurry to be on time, wondering why she had selected Religion 150 as her first class. She was not in the mood to face Dr. Sanders, who was probably thinking she was a lot different than he had expected. He had been her favorite teacher, but she was skeptical as to how long that would last. After the guilty charge, she was certain their relationship would change, and he would treat her differently, especially since he felt that she was guilty of physical assault, guilty enough to pose such a great danger that she should move out of her room—immediately.

She paused outside the classroom door before entering. Dr. Sanders sat at the desk in front of the class as usual, reviewing the notes to his class, which would begin in less than ten minutes. His graying hair on his head seemed to shine under the fluorescent lights, and his unshaved beard appeared as a gray shadow upon his cheeks. His dark brown face was intense, as it normally was before a lesson. Tamika had come to admire that expression, one that was so calm, yet serious, one that had developed from nearly sixty years of life experiences, which had molded and matured him, until he had become her professor, her wise professor. She often wondered what stories he had to tell, what energies he had once had, what fights he had won and lost, and what battles he no longer fought. She often thought it would be interesting to sit down and hear him talk about his life, and she would just listen and listen until she could listen no more. She wondered what lessons she would learn, what energies it would evoke in her, what incentives it would give her, and what battles it would cause her to abandon.

Tamika walked swiftly by his desk without looking at him and took a seat in a chair that was a safe distance from him. She feared it was too drastic to sit in the back. She had never done that before, and such an action would likely not only cause him to raise an eyebrow but other students too.

"Good morning, Tamika," Dr. Sanders greeted her, no trace of the conduct hearing in his voice.

"Good morning," she replied, feigning interest in searching for something in her bag, avoiding his gaze, papers rustling.

"Can I talk to you for a moment?"

Her heart raced. Talk to her for a moment? Why? He was not allowed to talk about the case, was he? "Uh, sure." She stood and walked to his desk, acting as if everything was cool. "Yes?"

He placed his reading glasses on the edge of his nose, peering through them as he flipped through a notebook. "Did you ever give me your topic?"

Oh. "My, um, paper topic?" Inside, she was relieved. "Uh, no, I uh, haven't really decided yet."

"Miss Douglass, this is a major assignment, and you'll need ample time to complete it. The other students are already working on their research, and I don't want you to fall behind."

"Yes, I know." She could not look at him.

"Now," he reasoned, "I can give you until Wednesday, because Friday your first set of note cards are due."

She nodded.

"If I don't have it by Wednesday, then I'll have to assign you a topic."

She did not want him to do that, or else she was sure to be researching something boring. Every religion under the sun was fascinating to him.

"Now, you're aware that your presentation is scheduled for the first week in April?"

Yes, on a Monday, she knew, the timing having disappointed her, because the Friday before that was the Streamsdale Spring Formal. She did not want to be thinking about a presentation and paper that weekend, when students normally spent Friday night at the formal and the rest of the weekend partying. After the formal, students would book hotels for the night, and Saturday night was always the casual post-formal, where everyone wore street clothes. The previous year she had gone, and she ended up having the best time she thought she would ever have in college, if not in her life. And given that this school year was more stressful than the year before, she really needed that break and had been looking forward to it for quite some time. But it was February. She had enough time to prepare a twenty-page paper and presentation by then—if she could only nail down a topic.

"Yes," she told him.

He frowned. "Well, please have a topic by Wednesday, because I'll still need you to turn in your note cards Friday, although I know they will be rushed."

She nodded.

He paused then inquired. "Are you feeling okay?"

"I'm fine," she assured him, avoiding his concerned gaze.

He nodded, unconvinced. What else could he do? He was worried about Tamika, but he did not know how he could help. "Well, then, I'll talk to you Wednesday."

"Mm, hm," she agreed, then retuned to her seat and resumed searching mindlessly through her bag, uncertain what she had been looking for in the first place.

From his desk, Dr. Sanders could see Tamika take her seat, her face concentrating on whatever it was she was trying to find, but he could tell she had a lot on her mind, because she was not her normal, talkative, friendly self. Already, he missed her laugh, the laugh that so often reminded him of his daughter when she was Tamika's age. Both had a sparkle in their eye and a beautiful smile that lit their faces and the hearts of those around them. And there was something distinct about Tamika that made her stand out amidst others her age. Dr. Sanders had noticed when he first met her. He had sensed sincerity and purity that made her particularly different, as if she did not belong to the liberal, carefree student body of which she was a part. There was a peaceful composure about her, and it was one with which violence was mutually exclusive, as if her calm nature made her incapable of cruelty.

When Dr. Sanders had received the Conduct Board slip informing him of a hearing, he had thought little of it. It was normal to have to attend a hearing all of a sudden. But usually, the name of the accused was unfamiliar and the charge that of illegal alcohol consumption, given that it was commonplace for students to drink on campus. When he had skimmed the sheet of paper, he was shocked that "Tamika Douglass," the name of one of his favorite students, was printed at the top of the paper as the accused. And the accusation had surprised him even more. "Physical Assault." Momentarily, he had hoped that it was a different Tamika Douglass, but when she walked in the hearing room that day, his heart sank, feeling pitifully sorry for her. Whatever it was that had happened, he was certain that it could not have been as it was described on the paper. He knew Tamika better than that.

After hearing all of the witnesses testify against her, he momentarily entertained the possibility that perhaps she had assaulted the student. But after hearing her side of the story, he better understood the altercation and saw it as nothing more than an argument that had gotten out of hand. The other board members saw it differently though, unanimously agreeing to the guilty charge. He knew the 6 to 1 vote was not going to give Tamika a possible way out of being found guilty, but during sentencing, he planned to ease her punishment as much as he was able.

"But she busted Jennifer's head, Dr. Sanders," Sarah, the Student Head of the Conduct Board had reminded him after the hearing, as they discussed sanctioning. "Now, I know I'm not a voting member, but I do believe that someone that violent and dangerous should not only be heavily fined but should also be expelled from school immediately."

"I have to agree with Sarah," Jonathan, one of the student members, stated. "I mean, Tamika Douglass has been found guilty of physical assault, and that's serious."

Dr. Sanders had smiled knowingly. As the only African-American on the board, he knew he was standing alone on this one. The others were filled with stereotypes and prejudices, which he felt drove them to imagine an exaggeration of what had actually occurred. He knew them to be biased, because other accused students had been found guilty of crimes like possession of illegal drugs, destruction of school property, and theft, yet none of them had suggested expulsion. When a student had thrown a chair from the fifth floor window—closed window—of his dorm room and set various trash cans on fire because the school's football team had won Homecoming, the board had thought it was funny, "excessive school spirit," as one member asserted. But Dr. Sanders felt it was reckless and inexcusable, especially since he could have hurt someone, and he was not even drunk, at least not this time. This particular student, Robert Samuels (Dr. Sanders remembered his name quite well since the student's name had come across his desk several times), had appeared before the board so many times for the last couple of years that he wore a smirk on his face each time he was faced with another charge, which was most often alcohol possession and consumption. And the board had given him a warning!

"None of us are disputing that Miss Douglass pushed Miss Mayer," he calmly told them, still smiling, blinking. "We've already determined that, and even Miss Douglass herself said that she pushed her roommate. And although I disagree with the guilty charge—I cannot argue against that, and understandably so—but I do want to remind you that this was quite likely a *fight*, not an assault. And according to Miss Douglass, Miss Mayer also assaulted her, if you will."

"But Jennifer was not charged with anything," Diane, another member interjected. "So we can't consider that."

"No," Dr. Sanders interrupted, disagreeing. "We *can* consider that in *this* phase of the hearing. We could not consider that in deciding guilt or innocence because there was no charge against Miss Mayer, but certainly, before we issue a punishment of expulsion, we should consider everything, and as we learned before joining the board, expulsion should be a last resort and only issued in extreme cases in which there is a clear and present danger to the student body or school."

"There is a clear and present danger to the student body," Jonathan asserted.

Dr. Sanders chuckled at the ridiculousness of the assertion. "Even if we were to assume that this was not a fight," he began, "we cannot even begin to argue that Miss Douglass is a 'clear and present danger to the student body.'" He shook his head at the irrationality. "How many of us have gotten into fights in our lives?"

No one responded.

"And were those fights personal ones, incited by the circumstances, or were they ones in which you wished to vent your anger on the world and hurt everyone?" He chuckled. "The strains of living in a small room with a stranger are great," he reminded them, "and it's natural, although not commendable, for the roommates to fight."

"But she busted this student's head!" Jonathan exclaimed.

"She did not *bust* her head," Dr. Sanders corrected, becoming irritated with Jonathan's overuse of the exaggerated description. "Miss Mayer hit her head, which resulted in a small injury, which by the way, required nothing more than hydrogen peroxide and light pressure to the scalp."

"But she could have caused more damage," Sarah put in.

"She could have slipped on the floor and caused more damage," Dr. Sanders retorted, chuckling. "We're not here to deal with could haves, we're dealing with what is. And if we wish to deal with what ifs, why not consider the possibility that Miss Mayer may be just as guilty as Miss Douglass in this assault case?"

Jonathan groaned and rolled his eyes. "Well," he suggested, frustrated. "I motion that Tamika Douglass is expelled."

"I second it," Diane said.

"Well," Dr. Sanders offered, "I certainly don't second that, but I do motion that Miss Douglass is simply moved to another room, seeing as though that would remove any clear and present danger, at least to the party concerned, if we wish to look at it like that."

The room was silent for some time.

"I think Dr. Sanders has a point," Michael, a normally quiet member interjected, breaking the strained silence. "Now, I don't disagree with the guilty charge," he conceded, "but I do think it's fair to say that this is a roommate issue and not a general student body issue. Tamika Douglass has never appeared before us prior to this, and it may be a bit hurried to issue the sanction of expulsion."

"That's what I was thinking," another member stated.

"So, I second Dr. Sanders motion to move her from the room," Michael concluded.

"I do too," the other member agreed.

"That's three to two," Sarah tallied. "Either both of you agree to the same sanction," she told the other members who had not yet spoken, "or else we will have to meet again with Dean Floyd to decide. We cannot issue any verdict if the motion is four to three," she reminded them.

The two students looked at each other and shrugged. One spoke, "Well, then I guess I'll have to agree with Michael and Dr. Sanders, because this doesn't seem to be a case of a student who is posing a danger to anyone except her roommate."

The other student considered it for a moment then sighed. "I don't know, but I guess I can't feel comfortable expelling her either, and as long as she's not allowed to live with Jennifer, then I suppose that's fine with me."

"But I do think she should have to move right away," Michael stated.

"I agree," the other student added.

Presently, Dr. Sanders stood, preparing to begin today's lesson. He could only pray that Tamika was doing okay. The outcome of the hearing seemed to be weighing heavily on her, and he feared that her stress over the guilty verdict would affect her schoolwork. He hoped he was wrong.

That evening, Tamika strolled across the college campus as the sun set in the distance, its fluorescent orange glowing from behind the trees and buildings, which sat like silhouettes in a painting. An occasional breeze blew her hair in front of her eyes and caused her skirt to cling to her legs. She gently tucked her hair behind an ear, pushed her free hand into her jacket pocket, and adjusted her bag with the other as the air became chilly. The day had been nice for February, the winter months having brought only light snow, which melted before the new year and never returned. Having been accustomed to extremely cold weather and lots of snow back home, she was still adjusting to Georgia weather, one day being hot and the next cold, especially during February. She should have been grateful that she did not have to wear a winter coat for so long, but she was beginning to miss home.

As she approached the University Apartments, Tamika sighed and paused briefly at the entrance and removed from her bag the keys and the slip that the residential office had given her. She read the room number assignment again to make sure she had remembered it correctly. 212. Good, she did not have to take the elevator everyday. She was on the second floor of the fourteen story high-rise.

At the entrance, she tried each of the two keys until one slipped in the main door. She pulled the door open, letting out a deep breath. She had no idea towards what or to whom she was heading. She could only pray that everything would work out for the best and that her current roommate situation would turn out better than her former.

Tamika had visited the apartments on several occasions before, since many of her friends lived there, so she was familiar with its set-up. But now, she paid close attention to its appearance, taking notice of every imperfection, such as paint chipping and writing on the walls, that she normally would have overlooked, given that none of it was noticeable to a person simply passing through. The building smelled peculiar, but she had come to learn that this was normal for any college dormitory, where people from various backgrounds and walks of life lived together in one place.

She climbed the stairs two at a time until she reached the plain white door with a large black "2" spray-painted on it, reminding her of an old factory building. She pulled the heavy door open and let it slam behind her as she made her way down the hall to apartment 212.

Some doors bore the names of its residents, while others were either decorated or plain, with no indication of who resided within. "Christina, Natasha, Samantha and Megan," she read on door 210, reciting the names in her head. She would likely need to know them later, she reflected, since they were her new neighbors. It was too bad no last names were on any of the doors. She would have liked to know the full names of her neighbors, because full names gave her a better indication of who the students might be.

There it was—212. There was nothing on the door except a small dry erase board, which had become a popular door hanging for students living on campus. And just her luck, there were not even any messages scribbled on it to give her any clue as to whom she would be living with. So Tamika accepted that she would simply have to find out about her roommates the old fashioned way.

She unlocked and opened the door, the sweet smell of potpourri immediately filling her nostrils, pleasing her and reminding her of home. She closed the door, locked it, and glanced around the apartment approvingly. The apartment was attractively set up with mostly black furniture. A dark gray couch with a black floral design sat near the blinds that covered the patio. In front of it sat a shiny black coffee table with a glass top, a few books and magazines neatly stacked on it. In one corner was a tall black vase with gold trim at the mouth, adorning the large peacock feathers that it held. Black and gray pillows aligned the wall in a cozy design, and various poetry and quotations hung on the walls, each in a gold-trimmed frame, written in gold letters on a black background. Across from the couch were several 3-unit black shelves filled with books. Tamika was impressed, the only eyesore being her boxes and bags that were stacked in a corner near the front door. She hoped that her roommates had not been bothered by the clutter.

Tamika heard a shower being turned on somewhere in the apartment. Someone was home. She had not heard anything when she had come in. Perhaps, they had been in the bathroom. She walked around the apartment to pass time as she waited for the person to finish. She peered into the kitchen, which was tidier than her clean-up job would have been. And the bedroom was just as clean, with four beds, two of which were lofts and the other two beds under each one. Each was neatly made up in black comforters and gray pillows. She glanced about the room for any clue about her roommates. But there were no photographs hanging, although there was a small, framed picture atop the only desk in the room. But the picture was of several people, having been taken the year before at the formal, indicated not only by the elegant dresses and tuxedos that the students wore in the photograph but by the small inscription at the bottom. Tamika leaned forward to see if she recognized anyone and saw three people who she either had met or seen around campus.

"You must be Tamika."

Startled, Tamika jerked around to find a tall, slender young woman standing at the doorway, dressed in a large black bathrobe with a matching towel wrapped around her head, accenting her attractive face. Her hands were tucked comfortably in the oversized pockets, reminding Tamika of a scene from a movie. The student smiled, revealing her dimples, and immediately Tamika recognized her.

"Are you Dee?" Tamika had seen her photograph several times in the school's paper. The student had won several academic awards, not to mention almost every beauty contest she had entered. The combination of a lovely singing voice and a beautiful face almost guaranteed her taking home the first prize. Tamika had gone to one of the school's talent shows and had never forgotten Dee, mesmerized by her powerful voice and breathtaking beauty. Tamika had introduced herself to Dee once, but she doubted that Dee remembered her. It was customary for Dee to be swarmed by strangers after a show, people who would eagerly introduce themselves while complimenting and congratulating her.

The young woman laughed, nodding, having become accustomed to everyone knowing who she was. "Yes."

Tamika could not keep from smiling. She could not have been matched with a better person! Perhaps, Dee, although still an amateur herself, could give her tips on her own singing career.

"What level are you?" Dee inquired, sliding the closet door open and removing some clothes and placing them on a bed.

"Sophomore. You?" Tamika asked more out of politeness than curiosity. She was already aware that Dee was a junior; every photograph caption stated that information.

"Junior."

She nodded.

"Where are you from?"

"Milwaukee."

"Wow. That's kind of far," Dee commented. It was uncommon to find students from farther than Tennessee.

"I know," Tamika replied, smiling self-consciously. "That's what everybody says."

"Hear it's cold up there."

"It is sometimes," she admitted. "Where are you from?"

"Atlanta." Dee laughed. "Practically down the street."

Tamika was familiar with the city, which was forty minutes away, because it was where she and Makisha normally went whenever they wanted to go to a party on the weekend. "You grew up there?"

Dee nodded, removing the towel from her head. "Yeah, I was born here, but my family's from Cuba."

Tamika wrinkled her forehead in confusion. "You're Hispanic?"

Dee laughed, nodding. "Yes, why?"

"I thought you were—"

"Indian?"

"Yeah or mixed with it."

She shook her head. "No, but that's what everyone says." She shrugged. "I don't know why."

They were silent for sometime, and Tamika stared at her, trying to see her as Hispanic. "You speak Spanish?"

Dee nodded. "Yes, I do, at home mostly, but a lot of times, we just speak English."

Tamika was still in shock. Dee did not even have the slightest trace of an accent.

"What's your major?" Dee inquired a moment later.

Tamika chuckled uncomfortably and shrugged. "Still undecided, but I was thinking about religion."

Dee raised her eyebrows in surprise, brushing her long, dark, wavy hair while looking at her reflection in the full-length mirror that was on the closet door. She nodded approvingly. "That's good." She laughed. "Then I guess you've come to the right place."

Puzzled, Tamika inquired, "What do you mean?"

Dee glanced at her and grinned, then turned back to her reflection. "Wait till you meet Aminah."

"Aminah?"

"Your other roommate."

Oh. "It's just you two?" Tamika hoped there were no more.

Dee nodded. "Now," she added emphatically, shaking her head, smiling. "There were two other girls here at the beginning of the year, but I think they had enough of Aminah and called it quits."

Oh no. Tamika's heart sank. "What's wrong with Aminah?"

Dee laughed. "Nothing." She paused. "She's just Muslim. A strict Muslim," she added for effect.

"Muslim?" Tamika repeated, astounded. Perhaps, her new living arrangement *was* going to be stressful after all.

Dee nodded, laughing. "But you'll probably get along fine with her," she assured Tamika, "being a religion major."

Tamika wrinkled her nose. "I don't think so," she disagreed. She had heard a lot about Muslims and how strict they were, and she was not sure she would get along with Aminah at all, religion major or not.

"Why do you say that?" Dee chuckled.

"I don't know," Tamika shrugged, face still contorted. "How can *you* stand it?"

Dee laughed. "'Cause Aminah and I are good friends."

"You are?" Tamika was taken aback. "Why?" she asked, almost disgusted.

"We grew up together."

"You did?" She was surprised.

Dee nodded, now adjusting the blow dryer comb, snapping it to the nozzle, her long, thin fingers cradling it. "Our families are real close."

"And you get along?" Tamika asked in disbelief, wrinkling her nose.

Dee laughed. "Not all the time," she admitted, "but we're so used to each other, you know."

"And it doesn't bother you that she's Muslim?"

Dee glanced sideways at Tamika again, raising a dark, arched eyebrow, a half smile developing on her face. "If Aminah was here, she'd lecture me if she heard you ask that."

"Why?"

"Because I'm Muslim too."

Tamika's eyes grew wide, and her jaw dropped. She was floored. Dee? Muslim? Impossible. "You are?" she asked carefully, almost apologetically, realizing her prior comments may have been offensive.

Dee shrugged. "I'm supposed to be anyhow. I go back and forth."

"You don't like it?"

She sighed thoughtfully, considering the question as she removed the towel from her shoulder and set it on the bed. "I wouldn't say that," she stated honestly. "But I guess I consider myself lazy."

"So you do like it?"

She shrugged her shoulders again. "I know it's the right thing," she offered as a satisfactory answer.

Tamika was at a loss for words. The sound of the blow dryer filled the room as Dee combed through her hair. Dee? Muslim? This bit of information would take some getting used to.

Tamika had not even realized it, but she was staring at Dee, studying the young woman who was only a few feet from her, the same student whom she admired, the same one she had read and heard about throughout her freshmen year. During that time, Dee had merely been a name and picture on a page, unreachable, much like famous people were, but now Dee was before her, in person. It was interesting, Tamika noted, how with some prominent personalities who were known for their beauty, their attractiveness lessened when seeing them up close, their appeal more a camera or make-up trick than reality. But with Dee, it was the opposite. As intriguing and complimentary Dee's photographs were, none did her justice. She was flawless, Tamika could not help but think, studying Dee's smooth complexion, unpolished by make-up or photo adjustments. Most people's appearance would have suffered without the adornment of lipstick or foundation, but not Dee's.

But Muslim? Tamika could not see it. The words *Dee* and *Muslim* did not seem to belong in the same sentence.

After about ten minutes, the sound of the blow dryer ceased, and the room grew awkwardly silent, the only sound being Dee removing the comb from the dryer and placing it in a desk drawer.

"You have any brothers or sisters?" Dee inquired, breaking the silence.

"I have an older sister and brother."

"How old are they?"

"They're nineteen."

"They're twins?"

"Yeah." Tamika paused then asked, "You?"

Dee nodded. "It's seven of us."

"Seven?" Tamika was surprised at the large number.

"Yeah, four girls, three boys."

"You the oldest?"

"Yeah."

Tamika nodded, taking in the information. "How old is the youngest?"

"Three." A pause. "How old are you?"

"Me?"

"Yeah."

"Eighteen. You?"

"Nineteen, but Aminah's eighteen too."

Oh great, something in common—who cared? "What level is she?" Tamika was not interested in this "Aminah," but she should be polite, especially if she was to be living with her.

"Junior."

"And she's eighteen?"

"Just turned it too."

"She did?"

"She's a brain," Dee joked about her friend. "Like her brother."

"Her brother?"

"Yeah, Sulayman Ali."

"Sulayman Ali!" Tamika repeated in surprise. "The one who does the editorial column in the paper?"

"Yeah, that's him," Dee stated, grinning and shaking her head, her thick hair bouncing, as she thought of the powerful words he used in his "controversial" articles, which were no more than him expressing the strong moral views that he had as a Muslim.

Tamika was smiling and nodding admirably, but inside she was groaning. If Sulayman was Aminah's brother, Tamika knew she was in for a rocky road. Sulayman was unapologetic in his articles in which he lashed out at students for their "loose behavior" of drinking and fornicating. He was so judgmental,

Tamika had observed her freshman year—before she had stopped reading his offensive articles because they made her so upset.

"Guess he tells it like it is, huh?"

"Yeah, he does," she agreed, still smiling. How could Dee be friends with his sister? It made no sense.

"*As-salaamu-alaikum[1]!*" someone called from the living room, and Tamika heard the front door shut, although she had not heard anyone come in.

Dee smiled, leaving the room.

"*Wa-'alaikum-as-salaam,*" she replied cheerfully. The Arabic sounded strange to Tamika's ears, especially coming from the mouth of Dee.

"She get here yet?" the voice asked.

"She's right here," Dee pointed to Tamika, who emerged from the room a second later.

"Oh, hi," the young woman greeted, walking toward Tamika, her hand outstretched. Tamika accepted it, shaking her hand lightly and smiling with forced cordialness. "You must be, uh," the young woman tried to remember her name.

"Tamika," Dee reminded.

"Tamika," the young woman repeated.

Tamika nodded. "And you're, uh, Aminah?" she inquired, observing the woman's Arab dress. A large blue cloth sat on her head and around her shoulders and was pinned under her chin, falling down at an angle near her waist. Her thin pale face looked awkwardly small behind it. And her large, loose black dress appeared much too big for her and only exaggerated her tiny stature.

Aminah laughed, her green eyes sparkling. "I guess Durrah must've told you all about me, my claws and all."

"Durrah?" Tamika repeated, glancing at Dee, confused, too distracted to notice Aminah's friendly joke.

Dee laughed. "That's my Muslim name."

Oh. She had a Muslim name too? This was becoming too much—too strange. Tamika wondered how many other people knew Dee was Muslim. She imagined Makisha would get a kick out of that news.

"Shame on you, Durrah," Aminah teased her friend, pointing at her, scolding her playfully.

Dee laughed. "You know me."

"Yeah," Aminah agreed, smiling and shaking her head at how predictable her friend was. "Unfortunately, too well."

"Where are you from?" Tamika inquired politely.

---

[1] "Peace be upon you," the standard Muslim greeting

"Here."

Oh, she had forgotten. Atlanta. Dee and Aminah had grown up together. "And your family?"

"Here too."

Tamika was confused, and it showed on her face.

Dee laughed, which she did often, Tamika began to notice, her bubbly personality nothing like the "conceited snob" Makisha had described once. "Now, *she's* black."

"What!"

Aminah nodded, smiling. "Yes, I am."

Tamika had thought she was Arab, and if not Arab, she could see white, but not black.

"My dad's half black, and my mom's white."

"Oh, I see," she replied, now understanding, but still in shock. She had never imagined that an American would dress in that manner—by choice.

Aminah removed the pin from under her chin, and tossed one part of the cloth over her shoulder.

"She won't uncover her hair till she trusts you," Dee whispered to Tamika, smirking.

"I heard you," Aminah told her friend as she made her way to the bathroom.

Dee laughed. "You hear everything!"

"Not everything, just mostly everything," she corrected, kidding. Aminah usually dealt with Durrah casually, not wanting to come down on her too hard, especially since they were peers, Durrah actually being a little older. But sometimes Durrah's behavior irritated her until she lost her patience, after which she would rebuke her best friend about her lifestyle. Although Aminah brushed it off most times, she hated the way Durrah told others about Islam, as if it were a joke. This was most likely due to the fact that Durrah did not take Islam seriously herself, at least not anymore, which, in turn caused her to take serious matters of the religion lightly. Aminah often had to remind Durrah that mocking any part of Islam was disbelief and took a person outside the fold of Islam. But sometimes, she questioned whether Durrah was in it in the first place.

She had come to dislike living with Durrah and would have opted to live in a single if their mothers had not insisted that they live together. But fortunately, this year had been a bit easier for Aminah since they had an apartment—at least it was easier after their old roommates moved out. But their first two years had been rocky. Aminah was often tempted to call Durrah's mother to ask her to do something about her daughter. But she would decide against it, fearing it would cause Durrah more harm than help to have her mother involved. Durrah's mother knew her daughter did not cover in Islamic attire and that she participated in fashion shows and the like, this being hard to conceal since Durrah's face was on the front page of practically every local and school newspaper whenever she won a contest. But her mother did not know about the parties and the bad company Durrah kept, not to mention her lax attitude about praying. Durrah was even "friends" with several young men, and she knew better than that. Her mother thought that her daughter's only weaknesses were uncovering, singing in talent shows, and an occasional desire to listen to music, which was, in reality, more an obsession than an inclination.

After performing ablution in the bathroom for prayer, Aminah returned her *khimaar*[2] to her head and again pinned it under her chin to keep the covering in place. She tugged at her sleeves to pull them down, and she buttoned them at the cuffs.

"Durrah!" she called, emerging from the bathroom and walking into the living room.

"Go ahead," Dee told her from the bedroom, where she and Tamika were talking.

"Durrah," Aminah warned in frustration. "Just go make *wudhu*," she told her, referring to the ablution.

Dee groaned irritably. "Just go ahead, Aminah."

Aminah walked over to the doorway and placed her hands on her hips. "Durrah, just come on."

Dee rolled her eyes, giving in. "Alright already."

After Dee came out of the bathroom, she dressed herself in a large *khimaar* and long skirt. She looked so different that it was difficult for Tamika to believe the young woman dressed in the Arab garb was actually Dee.

Tamika watched as the two friends stood shoulder to shoulder and foot to foot facing the corner of the living room where her boxes were stacked. While Aminah was in the bathroom, Dee had informed her that Aminah was preparing to pray in a few minutes and that she should not play music or talk too loudly during that time. Tamika had asked if she could watch, having never before seen a Muslim pray, and Dee had told her she thought that was fine. But Tamika had not expected Dee to pray with her, and apparently, Dee had not expected to either.

Aminah raised her hands just above her shoulders, as if she was surrendering, Tamika observed. She then said something that Tamika could not understand, and Dee did the same. Tamika walked over to the couch and

---

[2] A *khimaar* is a head covering worn by a Muslim woman that covers her entire head and neck and is drawn over her bosom area, exposing only her face.

sat down, watching intently, wondering what they were saying, unconsciously admiring how spiritual they appeared. As Aminah's voice filled the room, Tamika was awestruck by the words that Aminah recited in a manner that reminded Tamika of singing, but she knew it was not. She could not understand what Aminah was saying, but she sensed it was something special, powerful.

As they continued, Tamika found the most interesting position of their prayer the one in which their heads touched the carpet in humble prostration, and she could not help admiring that they were actually praying, praying like she would have never imagined people did, at least not people who lived during modern times, and definitely not students at the university. She felt as if she were watching a special on television about the religious societies of past generations, except it was real, up-close, and unfolding before her eyes.

When Aminah's voice shook and she began to cry during the recital of the strange words, Tamika was moved, and she found herself empathizing with whatever Aminah was feeling at that moment, sensing tears forming in her own eyes. As they prayed, the room was filled with a calm, peaceful atmosphere that Tamika had never experienced, and she could only imagine what the prayer meant to the friends. She would not have expected that college students even prayed, aside from on a Sunday or when they wanted something badly enough. But Dee and Aminah were actually praying, side by side. Really praying.

Chapter Three

Tamika tapped lightly on Dr. Sanders' office door before she heard him say come in. She glanced in before actually entering, unsure if she had disturbed him. "Did I interrupt you?"

His face brightened at the sight of her, and he smiled, his eyes peering over the rims of reading glasses, as he placed the book he had been reading on his desk. "No, no, please come in," he welcomed her, gesturing her to sit down, removing his glasses.

Tamika would have waited until Wednesday's class to inform him of her research topic, but she did not want to risk anyone else overhearing. It was likely not a big deal, she knew, but she disliked her classmates knowing more than what she wanted to share, even if they would find out later, at least by the time she did her presentation. She was not thrilled about speaking with Dr. Sanders either, but she figured he would be his normal self, and she hoped that he and she could simply move on and forget about what happened. Besides, she could not go on avoiding him, especially if she wanted a good grade in his class.

"How are things going?" he inquired as she sat down.

"Pretty good," she replied. "I can't complain."

"Everything working out okay?"

She knew what he meant. "Yeah, my new roommates are pretty nice."

"Who are they?"

"Dee Gonzalez and Aminah Ali."

He raised his eyebrows, impressed. "Good combination."

"You know them?"

He chuckled, nodding. "Well, everyone knows Miss Gonzalez, but she and Miss Ali were students of mine their first year here. Both of them are very intelligent young women." He added, "I'm sure they will do well after college, especially Miss Gonzalez."

"You know her well?" Tamika could not help wondering if he knew she was Muslim.

"As a student."

Perhaps, he was unaware of her religious affiliation, but she was too ashamed to ask. The inquiry would appear out of place, awkward.

"But Miss Ali, she's a really special person."

Tamika listened, surprising herself by her interest in what he had to say about Aminah.

"Don't find many people like her anymore." He paused then added, "Or her brother."

"You like him?" She had not intended to ask the question, especially not in the shocked manner in which she had, the inquiry having passed her lips before she could withhold it.

He laughed, scratching the unshaved gray fuzz on one side of his face. "Yes, I do, actually. You know, I'm from the old school," he explained, smiling. "Our parents were sort of like him, take no stuff, you know."

Tamika nodded, forcing a smile. Interesting. But she could not say that she shared his sentiments.

"Why, you know him?"

She shrugged. "I know of him."

He laughed. "I suppose he's not everyone's favorite columnist."

She did not respond. "Actually," she began, changing the subject, not wishing to spend her time participating in a discussion about someone she disliked, "I wanted to tell you my topic."

"Oh," he raised his eyebrows. "So you decided?" He returned his reading spectacles to the end of his nose, opened a notebook and picked up a pen, waiting.

"I guess I'll just do it on Islam," she informed him nonchalantly, avoiding his gaze, not wanting to reveal her sudden interest in finding out about the religion.

After watching Dee and Aminah pray the night before, Tamika had a million questions, but she had withheld, not wanting to appear nosy or irritating. Most people hated lots of inquiries regarding personal matters. But while they prayed once more before going to bed, she listened to Aminah recite the strange words again, and she could not shake the desire to understand what it was they were saying, what they believed, and what made them so content and spiritually connected, if not genuinely righteous. What they had seemed so pure.

Although she was a Christian and believed strongly in her religion, she had never realized there were others (aside from Buddhists) who had any real spiritual inclination. She did not know much about Muslims aside from what the media portrayed of angry black nationalists, religious fundamentalist men, and oppressed women—nothing like Aminah appeared, and definitely nothing like Dee. Aside from what she had heard, she honestly had no idea what they believed, except that they did not believe Jesus was God but a prophet.

"Okay," he agreed, no signs of surprise on his face as he jotted down the information. "Just make sure you have your note cards by Friday."

She nodded.

"And if you need anything, just let me know. As you can see," he told her, gesturing his head and hand toward his bookshelves, "I have plenty of books."

"On Islam?"

"On everything."

Oh, of course. He had a doctorate in religion. "Thanks," she replied eyeing his library of books.

"No problem."

There was a long pause as Tamika's eyes grazed the shelves, her mind less on the books than on the question she wanted to ask, her curiosity now burning inside. She searched her thoughts for any idea as to how she could inquire while appearing insouciant.

"So you studied Islam too?" she asked finally, hoping her voice sounded as disinterested as possible.

"Sure I have," he replied, no signs of suspicion in his voice, Tamika taking this as an indication that she should delve further.

"What do you know about it?" That was a general question, she decided—she hoped.

He chuckled. "Well, lots."

She waited, hoping he would continue. Her ears waited intently while her eyes still skimmed the shelves, refusing to meet his.

"It's a pretty vast religion, I must say."

"Really?" She now turned to him, glancing at him then to her skirt, dusting something from it, something she did not see, utilizing the gesture to conceal her curiosity. "What do you think of it?"

He chuckled again, but more thoughtfully this time. "I actually admire it a great deal."

"You do?" she hoped she did not sound as astounded as she really was.

"Yes, I do actually," he replied honestly, eyes sincere, deep in thought. He forced laughter. "Considered joining it for a second."

Taken aback by the confession, Tamika's eyes widened, unable to keep from looking at him, but he did not meet her gaze.

"But I, uh," he explained, toying with his gray fuzz of a beard then scratching it, "just grew out of it I suppose."

"Why?" She was shocked, but she did not quite understand why she felt this way.

He forced laughter again, now leaning back in his chair ponderingly. "I guess I just started to appreciate the good in all religions."

"Were you ever Christian?"

Dr. Sanders' eyebrows rose. The question surprised him, but his affable expression did not leave his face. "Born and raised," he replied as if she should have known.

"You don't believe it anymore?" Tamika inquired in disappointment, suddenly feeling both hurt and defensive.

He sighed, considering the inquiry, then nodded. "I suppose you can say that." He paused then continued, "I was very serious at first." He chuckled, shaking his head as he recalled. "'Was in the junior ministry and was actually planning to become a full-fledged minister."

"Really?" Tamika would have never guessed. "What happened?" She could not imagine a person turning away from the religion after treading such a worthwhile path.

"Read a bit," he told her with a half smile. "Had a lot of questions, and," he breathed broodingly, "I suppose you can say I didn't feel comfortable teaching something I didn't understand myself."

She was silent, in her heart relating—empathizing, but not wanting to.

"Then I started reading about other religions, and it really opened my eyes."

Tamika nodded, listening, the intensity of the implications sinking in. "How so?" She no longer cared if her keen interest was apparent. She was drawn in.

"Well, for one," he replied in a matter-of-fact manner, "it made me realize there was something else out there." He forced laughter. "As a teenager, I never knew that others even had any real beliefs. I had thought of the people of the world as belonging to either one of two groups." He smiled, shaking his head as he remembered his ignorance. "The Christians and the heathens." He chuckled. "I wanted to bring the lost and the blind back to God's path."

She swallowed, their similarities scaring her.

"But I mean," he said, shaking his head reflectively, "you read a bit and realize that's just not how it is."

"So, uh," she began, clearing her throat, hesitant to ask about that which she did not want to hear, but she needed some answers, "what do you think now?"

"You mean religiously?"

"Yeah."

He chuckled self-consciously. "I'm not sure if I have a religion really," he told her honestly. "But I believe in God and just kind of take the good from all religions, you know, like I was saying earlier."

"So you don't believe Jesus is God?" Tamika inquired, stunned, too engulfed in her own shock to realize that the question may have been too personal.

He forced a smile and replied almost apologetically, "No, not anymore."

Tamika left Dr. Sanders' office in a daze, pondering what her professor had said. She was not well-read on any religion, not even her own, but she could not help but agree that there had to be some explanation for the presence of other religions, especially if hers was in fact true, as she had been taught and believed. At times, she had been curious and wondered what other religions believed, but her mother had warned her against studying them, saying they would "lead her astray." But Dr. Sanders' words pricked at her conscience, uncovering buried questions that had been left unanswered within her for years. What he had stated made sense, and she could actually relate. However, she was skeptical about his "taking the good of every religion."

Since she was a child, Tamika believed in God, and when she would hear the stories of the prophets of God in the Bible, she was always attentive, a sharp contrast to others her age. The narrations were intriguing—captivating to her, and as she listened, she would imagine the enormity, the power of God's message, a message entrusted to a few divinely chosen men. She never doubted that the message that God sent was for her, as for all people. Thus, she was never able to accept the idea that the truth, the divine message, was scattered about in various religions, bits and pieces here and there, no faith encompassing it totally, each person left to sift through falsehood and find truth buried under it—somewhere—and forced to put together an impossible puzzle, the completion of which would render different results for each person. That made no sense to her and seemed contradictory to the way of God. Tamika did not think of God as one to play games, one to scatter truth. Even when such was done by a human, this was unacceptable, if not unethical, to people. And if the "scattered truth" theory were correct, it would mean that there were no divinely revealed scriptures, and each book would necessarily have come from other than God. For a book from God had to not only be flawless, but be found in one place and as the basis of one faith, the foundation of a religion—the true religion. Or, if they believed in divine revelation, the holders of the "scattered truth" theory had to believe that God had revealed books and intentionally tricked His creatures by placing only part of the truth in each of them and the other parts elsewhere. And Tamika could not—would not—accept that God would ever do such a thing.

"Hey, Tamika!"

Tamika, who had had left Dr. Sanders office a few minutes before and was walking across campus on her way to lunch, turned and found Makisha walking swiftly to catch up with her.

"What's up?"

"Nothing much, you?"

"Nothin' much," Makisha shrugged. "You eat?"

"I'm about to now."

"Oh, good, me too." She paused, walking next to Tamika now. "You move in okay?"

Tamika nodded. "Yeah, but I still have to unpack a lot of stuff."

"You like your new roommate?"

Oh, Tamika had forgotten to tell Makisha. "They're okay."

"They?"

"I live in Steward, remember?"

Makisha wrinkled her nose. "Oh yeah. That's messed up." She paused. "Anyone I know?"

"Yeah."

"Who?"

"Dee Gonzalez."

"Dee!" she repeated in disgust. "How did *that* happen?"

Tamika shrugged, ignoring her friend. She was actually beginning to like Dee, having admired her for some time anyway. "She's actually cool."

Makisha stared at Tamika in amazement. "Girl, you crazy."

Tamika could see right through her best friend. Makisha was steaming with envy of Dee, who likely did not even know Makisha, let alone have time to give her a reason to dislike her. "But I don't know if you know the other girl."

"Who?"

"Aminah Ali."

"Sulayman's sister?"

"Yeah."

Makisha contorted her face. "I know her."

"You do?" Tamika had never heard Makisha mention her before.

"Yeah," Makisha told her, waving her hand to underscore the insignificance of the knowledge. "She was in the Chemistry Club for a second."

"She's majoring in chemistry too?"

"Heck if I know," she replied, rolling her eyes, not wanting to appear as if she paid Aminah any attention. "But I do know she ain't too different from her brother."

Judging from her response, Tamika doubted if Makisha had ever talked to Aminah before. It was not unlike Makisha to exaggerate her knowledge of a person if she did not like her.

Tamika opened the door to the cafeteria and entered, Makisha behind her, the noise level immediately rising as they entered the crowded food court.

"What're you gonna have?" Makisha inquired as they made their way to the line, each getting a dull orange plastic tray.

"A burger and fries probably."

"I think I might have chicken."

Tamika felt a hand on her shoulder, and she glanced behind her.

"Hey, Tamika!" Dee greeted, her tan face covered in a large smile, revealing her white teeth.

"Oh, hi Dee, what's up?" Tamika replied, now turning around, as did Makisha.

"Just coming to grab a bite before class. You?"

"Same here."

"And what's your name?" Dee asked politely, noticing a young woman standing next to Tamika.

"Makisha," Makisha replied, barely giving Dee a smile, abruptly turning her back and busying herself with reading the menu that hung on the wall.

Tamika smiled apologetically to Dee, who waved her hand and shook her head, letting her know she understood.

"I better hurry up and grab something," Dee said, glancing at her wristwatch. "I have class in seven minutes."

"Oh yeah," Tamika agreed. "You better hurry."

"I'll just talk to you later," Dee told her, disappearing into the crowd.

"Okay."

"She's so irritating," Makisha commented after Dee had gone.

"Makisha," Tamika interrupted her in aggravation, "chill."

"She is," Makisha insisted. "She acts so preppy," she criticized viciously. "And fake."

Tamika laughed at her friend's irrational reaction. "Makisha, some people are just nice."

Makisha rolled her eyes. "No," she disagreed with insistence, "some people are just stuck up."

Tamika shook her head, still smiling. Sometimes Makisha could be impossible.

She reached under the food lights and removed a wrapped burger and bag of fries, the heat momentarily warming her hand. "You want one?"

"Just give me the chicken. But I'll take some fries."

After serving themselves something to drink and paying for their meals at the register, they found an empty table on the far side of the cafeteria away from where the food was being served.

"You really like her?" Makisha asked curiously after they were sitting down.

"Why wouldn't I?" Tamika inquired, unwrapping her burger and taking a bite.

Makisha shrugged, sucking her teeth. "Whatever." She sipped her soda through the straw. "Just don't come cryin' to me when they drive you nuts."

"Don't worry," Tamika grinned, "I will."

Makisha laughed. "You'll just be sleeping in the hall then."

Tamika chuckled.

They ate in silence for some time, sounds of chatter and laughter of the students rising in the background.

"You know Aminah's Muslim, don't you?"

Tamika nodded, chewing her food, and pulled a fry from its bag. "Mm hm."

Makisha stared at her, warning. "Don't let her get to you."

Tamika swallowed. "What do you mean?"

Makisha sucked her teeth. "Casting doubt on what you believe," she told her matter-of-factly. "You know all of 'em do that, always trying to argue with you about something."

Tamika shrugged. "I wouldn't know."

"Well, I do," Makisha assured her. "And all I know is, like my mother told me, you just gotta be well grounded in what you believe."

"You argued with one before?" Tamika inquired, suddenly interested.

"Girl, yeah," Makisha told her emphatically. "My ex-boyfriend's sister was Muslim."

"He wasn't?"

"She converted."

"Oh."

"And she was always trying to tell me about contradictions in the Bible and this and that." She forced laughter, remembering, but she was not happy. "Had me doubtin' my religion for a while."

"She did?" Makisha had never mentioned this before.

"Girl, yeah. Please." She rolled her eyes and sucked her teeth. "'Cause a lot of what they say gets you thinking, but after talking to my preacher," she chuckled, "he set me straight."

Tamika listened nodding, pondering what Makisha was saying, slowly eating her food, eyes staring beyond Makisha, mind elsewhere.

"But when she starts comin' down on you, just remember that we ain't here to question God. We're just here to believe."

She nodded, agreeing, eyes distant. "That's true," she replied. "You're right."

That evening, when Tamika returned to the apartment, she found Aminah there studying on the couch. Aminah must not have been expecting Tamika, because she appeared startled when Tamika entered, quickly covering her hair with her head cloth, which had fallen off.

"Hey," Tamika greeted, her exhaustion apparent in her voice. At that moment she noted the marked difference between Aminah's appearance when she was wearing the head covering and when she was not, surprised that without the cloth on her head, Aminah actually looked normal, like an average person. If she had not seen her with the head covering, she would never have guessed she was Muslim.

"Hey," Aminah replied, forcing a smile, her mind on whatever she was reading.

She must have prayed already, Tamika deduced. It was almost dark outside, and Dee had told her that Aminah prayed at sunset. Slightly disappointed to have missed watching her, Tamika sighed and decided to unpack some of her boxes before studying.

For a while, the two worked in silence without a word spoken between them. Aminah studied and Tamika moved things out of the living room into the bedroom. As Tamika organized her belongings, she kept thinking about her religion paper and the note cards that were due in a couple of days. She needed a lot of information on Islam. She had to interview a Muslim, visit the place of worship, and have at least ten sources cited in her paper. She had planned to ask Dee for the information, but Dee was not there, and Tamika had planned to begin writing her note cards that night.

As she walked from the living room to the bedroom and from the bedroom to the living room, Tamika continually glanced at Aminah, searching for any indication that it was okay to interrupt her to ask her a few questions. Although Aminah was merely reading her book, showing no signs that she would be upset if interrupted, Tamika could not bring herself to strike up a conversation, the room carrying a polite but distant atmosphere. Tamika hoped Dee would return soon.

For a moment, Tamika felt herself thinking, *what the heck* and started to say something to Aminah, but she stopped herself, shying away from the opportunity. She convinced herself that she could just wait for Dee, and even if Dee did not return until late, tomorrow would be fine.

"Did you want something?" Aminah inquired, glancing up from her book.

Was it obvious? "Oh, um," she replied, unsure what to say. Should she tell her about her paper or just wait for Dee? "No, that's okay." She waved her hand. "Don't worry about it," she said, mentally kicking herself for turning down the unique opportunity.

"Are you sure?" Aminah asked, having noticed that Tamika had started to say something.

Tamika shrugged, forced a smile, and nodded. "Yeah."

"Okay," Aminah replied slowly, uncertain, sensing that Tamika was not being completely honest. A second later, she resumed reading, hoping that whatever it was, Tamika could complete it without her.

"Actually," Tamika began, deciding that now was probably the best chance she would have to tell either roommate about her project. "I just wanted to see if you knew of any books I could read or something, um—."

"On what?"

Why was Tamika nervous? This was unlike her. "On, um," she could not say it. "Your religion," she said finally.

"On Islam?" Aminah's interest was sparked, Tamika could tell, hoping that that was a good sign.

"Yeah, I mean, if you know of any."

Aminah chuckled. "I know of lots. Why, you interested in becoming Muslim?"

"No, no, no," Tamika laughed, remembering Makisha's warnings. "I just have to do a project for my religion class."

"Oh, I see." Aminah glanced around the room. "You can look on the shelves if you want," she offered, pointing across the room. She paused. "You have Dr. Sanders?"

Tamika nodded, smiling, as she made her way to the shelves, kneeling to read the titles. "Yeah."

Aminah stood and walked over to the shelves. She reached for a book. "You may want to start with this one." She handed it to Tamika, who read the title.

Fundamentals of Tawheed (Islamic Monotheism)

"You ever heard of it?" Aminah inquired.

Tamika shook her head. "Not really."

"Well, it's pretty good in giving you the basics of Islam in terms of how Muslims view God," her roommate explained. "And this one," she told her, bending down to pull another from the shelf, "it's pretty basic too."

A Brief Illustrated Guide to Understanding Islam.

"Never heard of that one either, huh?"

Tamika shook her head.

Aminah nodded, now standing, eyes skimming the shelf. "Well, feel free to read anything you want."

"Thanks."

"Even the Qur'an."

The Koran? The Muslim holy book? Should she—would she dare? No, that was unnecessary. "Thanks, but I think these are fine."

"Are you sure?" Aminah questioned, finding it difficult to see how Tamika could efficiently write a paper on a religion if she had never even opened its holy book, the foundation of the entire faith.

"Yeah."

"Well," she said slowly, not wanting to offer her suggestions but also not wanting Tamika to report on the religion incorrectly, "if you change your mind, it's right over there."

Tamika's gaze followed the direction of Aminah's finger, which pointed to the large green book that Aminah had been reading on the couch.

"I usually keep it on this little stand," Aminah told her, referring to a wooden book holder, which was shaped like an X. "Feel free to read it, because I think it'll give you a better understanding for your report."

Tamika nodded, eyes now fixed on the books she held, the immensity of the waiting knowledge weighing on her.

"And feel free to ask me anything if you have any questions," Aminah offered. "And don't worry," she assured her, chuckling, "I love questions, so don't hold back."

Really? Tamika was pleased. Aminah was likely to be a big help for her project. But she tried to conceal her pleasure, merely nodding mechanically. "Okay, thanks."

Aminah returned to the couch and sat down, opening the Qur'an and continuing her reading where she left off. Tamika again began organizing her belongings, having set the two books on top of a shelf, planning to read them later. As she unloaded her boxes, she found herself inadvertently glancing up at Aminah, studying her intent expression, curious as to the subject she was reading at the moment. Tamika had never even seen a Koran before, and, of course, she had never seen a person reading one. She had heard about the book from her mother and preacher once or twice, but they had never said much about it except that Christians did not need it since they had the Bible.

But what was it that it said? Why should she stay away from it, as others suggested? Why not read it, even if just to learn? The questions hung in her mind like a rain cloud hovering. Perhaps, she should read it. What could it hurt? Wasn't she doing a report on the religion anyway? She would not be reading it for herself, she reasoned, but for her paper.

That night she could not sleep, her curiosity tormenting her. Her mind's eye still held the image of the thick book as it sat opened, its green ribbon marker hanging from the place at which Aminah had stopped, the wooden stand that cradled it inviting her. She could hear the rhythmic breathing of her roommates in the dark room, sleeping soundly. Tamika tossed, pulled the covers over her head, shut her eyes and tried to relax herself, her mind. She adjusted herself again, now lying on her left side, unable to get comfortable on her right. She situated the covers again, but still she could not relax.

"Feel free to read it," Aminah had told her, the voice still echoing in Tamika's head.

Frustrated, Tamika sat up and climbed out of bed. She needed to go to the restroom.

After finishing, Tamika stood at the sink washing her hands, staring at her reflection in the mirror. The weary eyes stared back at her, and her skin appeared somewhat pale. Her hair was slightly disheveled as it hung just below her shoulders. She needed sleep. She sighed, turned off the bathroom light, and went into the living room, where she turned on the light and sat down on the couch, calmly lifting the heavy book from its stand and placing it on her lap.

The night was unusually quiet, no sounds of students' voices or footsteps in the hall, the cold wind blowing outside the only sound she heard at the moment.

Tamika opened to the beginning of the book and began reading.

"In the name of God, Most Gracious, Most Merciful. Praise be to God, the Cherisher and Sustainer of the Worlds. Most Gracious, Most Merciful, Master of the Day of Judgment. You do we worship, and Your aid we seek. Show us the straight way, the way of those on whom You have bestowed Your Grace, Those whose (portion) is not wrath and who go not astray."

What was so bad about that, she wondered, turning the page, continuing to read.

"*Alif Lam Mim.* This is the Book, in it is guidance, sure without doubt, to those who fear God, who believe in the Unseen, are steadfast in prayer and spend out of what We have provided for them."

Curious, she then opened the book to where Aminah had been reading,

"Behold! The angels said, 'O Mary! God has chosen you and purified you—chosen you above women of all nations.

"...Behold! The angels said, 'O Mary! God gives you glad tidings of a Word from Him: his name will be Christ Jesus, the son of Mary, held in honor in this world and in the Hereafter and of (the company of) of those nearest to God.

"He shall speak to the people in childhood and maturity. And he shall be (of the company of) the righteous.

"She said, O my Lord! How shall I have a son when no man has touched me?' He said, 'Even so, God creates what He wills. When He has decreed a plan, He but says to it, 'Be' and it is!

"And God will teach him the Book and the Wisdom, the Law and the Gospel, and (appoint him as) a messenger to the Children of Israel (with this message), 'I have come to you with a Sign from your Lord, in that I make for you out of clay, as it were, the figure of a bird, and breathe into it, and it becomes a bird by God's Leave. And I heal those born blind, and the lepers, and I quicken the dead, by God's Leave, and I declare to you what you eat, and what you store in your houses. Surely therein is a sign for you if you did believe.

"'(I have come to you), to attest the Law which was before me, and to make lawful to you part of what was (before) forbidden to you. I have come to you with a sign from your Lord. So fear God and obey me. It is God who is my Lord, then worship Him. This is a way that is straight."

Drawn in, Tamika read on. She had not even realized Jesus' name was mentioned in the Koran. "The similitude of Jesus before God is as that of Adam. He created him from dust then said to him, 'Be' and he was. The truth comes from your Lord alone, so be not of those who doubt"[3].

"So be not of those who doubt," the words lingered in her mind, nagging her, tugging at her conscience. What was wrong with her? She mentally scolded herself. Didn't she believe as she was taught, that this book was not true? That what she was reading was false? But she could not shake the reality of the parallels—the virgin birth, the teaching of the Gospel, the miracles of Jesus. Then what was it that made this religion so different from Christianity? Why did people say Muslims did not believe in Jesus as God's son when in their book it talked about Jesus having no father? Was it that they did not believe Jesus was actually God, a belief that had led Christians, like Tamika, to believe Muslims would go to Hell?

---

[3] *Ali Imraan*, 3:42-60

The night drew on and the questions kept coming, her mind overflowing with curiosity and puzzlement, the desire to know burning at the depths of her mind. Then who was Muhammad? And what was Islam truly?

She flipped through the book again.

> "...A Book revealed unto you. So let your heart be oppressed no more by any difficulty on that account—that with it, you might warn (the erring) and teach the Believers.
>
> "Follow (O men!) the revelation given unto you from your Lord, and follow not, as friends or protectors, other than Him. Little it is you remember of admonition."[4]

Tamika felt her heart begin to pound in her chest. What was she reading? And why couldn't she put it down? And it all seemed so—no, it could not be. But it must be if—no, no, she should know better.

But she wanted to know more, needed to know more.

Instinctively, she turned to the index, searching for the name again. She needed to read more on him, the man whom they believed to be a prophet, the man whom she believed—or at least was taught to believe— *no*, she fought her subconscious (what was she thinking?)—who she *knew* was not only God, but His son, the Father, what everyone must believe to go to Heaven. But what if...

There it was, "Jesus." She turned to one of the referenced sections.

"O People of the Book (Jews and Christians)!"

Was this addressing her?

"Commit no excesses in your religion; nor say of God aught but the truth. Christ Jesus the son of Mary was (no more than) a Messenger of God, and His Word, which He bestowed on Mary, and a Spirit proceeding from Him. So believe in God and His Messengers. Say not 'Trinity:' desist. It will be better for you. For God is One God. Glory be to Him. (Far Exalted is He) above having a son."

Wait, no son? But she had thought... what about the virgin birth?

"To Him belong all things in the heavens and the earth. And enough is God as a Disposer of affairs."[5]

Enough is God... Enough is God. He did not need anyone, Jesus or otherwise. It made sense, but still, religion wasn't about sense. Wasn't she just supposed to believe, not question? But it made sense! *No, no,* she fought

---

[4] *Al-Araaf,* 7:2-3
[5] *An-Nisaa,* 4:171

herself. What was she thinking? Didn't she want to go to Heaven? Makisha was right, but still, this book...

Another reference.

"In blasphemy indeed are those who say that God is Christ the son of Mary."

Tamika's heart pounded fiercely, the night suffocating her, blaming her. There was no way to deny it. *She was guilty!* This book! What was it saying to her? About her?

"Say, 'Who then hath the least power against God, if His Will were to destroy Christ the son of Mary, his mother and all—everyone that is on the earth?"

Her hands shook holding the book as the question engulfed her. Who *would* have power against God if He did that? But wait, what was she thinking? Jesus *was* God, wasn't he? But then, didn't God create Jesus? And certainly, anything He created He could destroy? *But then—no, but well, yes—no!* But...

"For to God belongs the dominion of the heavens and the earth, and all that is between. He creates what He pleases. For God has power of all things"[6].

He has power of all things. Yes, this was true. This was true. She could not deny it.

"(Both) the Jews and the Christians say, 'We are sons of God, and His beloved.'"

Yes, this was true. Children of God. It was in the Bible...

"Say, 'Why then doth He punish you for your sins?"

Why? She did not know. But Jesus died for her sins! ...Or did he?

"Nay, ye are but men—of the men He hath created."

Was Tamika not merely a human, a creation of God? Couldn't He punish her if He wished? And she had done a lot to deserve punishment, the alcohol, the boyfriends, but that was all over now. She had left all of that...after being born again. Saved. But still, she had done it, guilt still haunting her... What was she saying? Jesus died for her! She was forgiven for everything! Saved! *...Or was she?*

"He forgives whom He pleases and He punishes whom He pleases."

That included her! Suddenly, she felt weak, helpless.

"And to God belongs the dominion of the heavens and the earth and all that is between. And unto Him is the final goal (of all)" [7].

---

[6] *Al-Maa'idah*, 5:17
[7] ibid, 5:18

48

Unto Him is the final goal. Final. The word was so...final. What if she *were* wrong? What if everything she had been told *was* a mistake? A lie? *A lie!* Not possible.

Final.

But if it was wrong? Then, when she died it would be over for her.

Final.

No turning back.

Final.

No asking for another turn!

Final.

No saying she didn't know.

Final.

Because she did...*now!*

Final.

But no, no, why? Why! It couldn't be. Not this religion of oppressed women!

Final.

Not the religion her preacher mocked.

Final.

Not the religion her mother laughed at.

Final.

Not the religion Makisha warned her about!

Final.

But what if...?

No!

But *what* if...?

It couldn't be! Not possible!

But what if she was wrong? Dead wrong? What would she do when she died?

Final.

O Lord! She felt her body shaking. Trembling. She could barely lift the book to return it to its place. The holy book. The true book. No! The book, that book. She needed to rest, clear her head. She was tired, delirious. *Makisha! Mom!*

What time was it?

An alarm sounded.

Alarm? But it couldn't be morning! Had she been here that long?

The sound of movement in the bedroom. The alarm ceased.

She tried to quickly return the Qur'an to its place.

But it was too late.

"What are you doing up?" the sleepy voice asked her, eyes blinking, struggling to wake. Her roommate had been about to go to the bathroom. Why did she have to glance in the living room?

Oh. The light.

"Uh," Tamika stuttered a reply to Aminah, whose hair was uncovered and disheveled, her gaze falling to the book in Tamika's hands.

Tamika was guilty.

Her roommate smiled.

A groan. She had not wanted anyone to see her.

Aminah walked over to her, pleased. "So you read it?"

Tamika forced a smile. She was not in the mood for friendly conversation. She shrugged. "A little."

"That's good." Aminah, now standing over Tamika, stole a glance at the page, nodding approvingly. "You understand everything?"

Understand? She was overwhelmed. She could not even think straight. "Pretty much." She paused, avoiding Aminah's gaze. "I mean, I have a few questions, but it was pretty, uh, clear."

A nod. "That's good." She started to walk away.

Good. Relief.

"Feel free to ask," she told Tamika before disappearing into the bathroom and closing the door. Tamika could have kicked herself. How could she be so careless? Stupid? She should have waited until she was home alone. But the curiosity. Why couldn't she have been patient?

Water was running in the bathroom.

She should leave the living room while she still had the chance. Quickly, she put the Koran back in its place on the stand and stood.

Then it hit her. She had not slept. How could she go to classes today! What was wrong with her! Perhaps, she would sleep. *Perhaps?* She *had* to sleep. She had no choice. She hated to miss classes again, but she was not one to push herself beyond her limits. She had never even pulled an all-nighter for a test!

But she had while reading the Koran.

But why? How? Why had she been drawn to the book so? And why hadn't she noticed the time? What time was it when she had gotten up in the first place? She had no idea.

She yawned, growing tired all of a sudden. She was too exhausted to think about anything else. Her mind needed rest. She needed rest. Stretching, she dragged herself to her room and climbed in bed.

Chapter Four

"I guess my first question is what exactly is Islam and how is it different from Christianity?" Tamika inquired that evening, seated on the couch a few feet from Aminah. Dee stood leaning lazily against one side of the kitchen doorway, listening and eating from a bag of chips. Aminah and Dee had finished praying a few minutes before, which sparked Tamika's curiosity again, reminding her of the religion paper and note cards she needed to do. After missing her classes that day, Tamika was inspired to do well in her courses, fearing that her absences would greatly affect her grade. When Dr. Sanders had called early that afternoon while she was sleeping, inquiring if everything was okay, she was mortified, and felt even worse. But now she was determined to do better.

"Well," Aminah replied, considering the question. She no longer covered her hair in her room, Tamika had noticed, most likely because Tamika had accidentally seen her hair uncovered on several occasions, and she was now accustomed to Aminah's appearance without the head covering. "Islam literally means submission or surrender," she explained, "but in the religious sense its complete, voluntary submission to God alone. It's different from Christianity mainly in its concept of God. In Islam God, or Allah in Arabic, is the Creator, and everything else is creation. And these two, Creator and creation, are separate and never overlap, in that the Creator is not creation, half-man, half-God, or anything like that, nor does the creation share any attributes of the Creator. In other words, there is the Creator and the created, period.

"But," Aminah continued, her soft voice rising, showing a command of the subject, "in Christianity, God is viewed as Creator and created at the same time. So the notion of half-man, half-God is a possibility for Christians, in that a person who is created can also be the Creator. Of course the best example of this is of the prophet Jesus, peace be upon him, whom the Christians look at as God and the son of God, while still accepting that he's man." She raised her eyebrows and shook her head as if it made no sense to her. "But anyway, in Islam, we don't believe creation procreates with God."

"Christians don't believe creation procreates with God," Tamika interjected defensively, momentarily forgetting that this was an interview for her research paper.

"But," Aminah blinked, green eyes on Tamika, "don't you believe Jesus is God's son?"

"Yes, but not like *that,*" Tamika retorted defensively. Her face contorted in abhorrence of Aminah's implying that Christians believed in God procreating.

"Then what makes him God's son?"

"He didn't have a *father,*" she emphasized.

"But think about it," Dee interrupted, crunching on her chips, walking into the living room, inviting herself into the conversation. "You say God does not procreate," she gestured with her hand, a chip waving in the air between her fingers, "but then you say he has a son." She shook her head, forcing a chuckle. "Then how does he have a son?"

Tamika felt suffocated by the roommates. She was outnumbered. She groaned and rolled her eyes. "It's not that kind of son."

"Then what kind of son is it?" Dee inquired, appearing to be taking pleasure in Tamika's frustration.

Before Tamika could respond, Aminah cut in, "Anyway," her voice was calm and diplomatic, apparently sensing what was about to happen. "God says in the Qur'an that the similitude of Jesus before God is that of Adam, who He created from dust and said 'Be' and he was. So that shows us that even if a person has no father, this does not make him God or the son of God, because then that would make Adam the son of God too, and, anyway, Muslims believe God does whatever He wants and says, 'Be' and it happens."

Just then Tamika remembered reading about that. Hm. That was something to think about. Then how was it that Jesus was God's son? "It's just in the spiritual sense, not literal," she explained more for her benefit than her roommates'.

"But then that makes us all God's children, wouldn't it?" Dee argued, still smiling, irritating Tamika, who wished she would just leave it alone. "I mean, if it's not literal and you don't mean God procreated with anyone, *God forbid,* then what makes Jesus so special?"

Tamika started to say something.

"But another major difference between the two religions is that Muslims believe in God's last prophet and messenger, Muhammad (s)[8]," Aminah interrupted, intentionally redirecting the conversation back to Tamika's paper.

Tamika was grateful, inside, sighing relief. "So Muhammad is like your savior?"

"No, no, no," Aminah replied, shaking her head emphatically, chuckling and gesturing with her hand. "Prophet Muhammad (s), prayers and peace be upon him, was simply a man, a prophet and messenger, with no power to save

---

[8] The symbol (s) is an abbreviation of the Arabic statement that translates to mean, "Prayers and peace be upon him," which a Muslim says at each mention of the Prophet's name out of respect for him.

anyone. He was here to convey to humans the Qur'an, God's last book, and to show us how to live by that book, and we call his example the *Sunnah*."

Tamika nodded. "I see," she said, jotting down notes in her notebook, comfortable that the tension was now gone. "So you don't believe he died for your sins like Christians view Jesus?"

"No, not at all. And," she added, "we actually don't even believe Jesus died."

She jerked her head up in surprise, staring at her roommate. "You don't?"

"We believe that he was not crucified and that God raised him up, body and all, and he will return as a sign of the Day of Judgment."

"You don't believe he was crucified?"

Aminah smiled and calmly shook her head. "God made it appear like that to the people though."

Tamika was still staring, confused. "But you do believe he's returning."

"Yes, at the end of time, and he will rule by Islamic law."

"He will?" What was Tamika saying? She knew that she should not pay any attention to this information.

"Yes, he will."

Really? She sat thinking about it for a moment. "So, he's still alive then?"

"Yes, he is."

"Where?"

Aminah shrugged. "We don't know where he is exactly," she told her. "We just know God raised him up and that he has not yet died."

"Oh." Tamika was amazed, having never heard this information before. "So it just looked like he was crucified?"

Aminah nodded. "Yes."

They were silent momentarily.

"Did you have any other questions?"

"But how can you think *that?*" Tamika asked, realizing something suddenly. "He had to be crucified, because he died for us, and that's why he came."

Aminah smiled, still calm, confident. She shook her head gently, as if correcting a child. "We don't believe that's why he came."

"You *don't?*"

"No, we don't."

"But he died for our sins so we can go to Heaven," Tamika told her. "Because he said none can get to the father but through him."

"So," Dee interrupted again, asking incredulously, paraphrasing for Tamika, grinning and disbelieving that Tamika actually believed all of this, "you're saying the entire purpose of Jesus coming was to die for our sins and be our Lord and Savior?"

"Yes," Tamika replied emphatically.

"Okay," Aminah interrupted, raising her hand to Dee, letting her know she would handle this one. "Do you believe in the prophets like Noah, Abraham, and Moses and that they were sent by God to their people?"

"Of course," Tamika responded. "That's in the Bible."

"And what's the purpose of a prophet?"

"To deliver God's message to their people," she replied simply.

"Then what do you believe was the message of those prophets to their people?"

Tamika wrinkled her forehead, not understanding the relevance of the question. "What do you mean?"

"What I'm saying is," Aminah began, "you say you believe in the other prophets and that they were sent by God to their people with a message, and of course, we all can agree that their message was one that was necessary to share with the people so their people could go to Heaven, right?"

"Of course," Tamika replied, blinking, trying to figure out where Aminah was heading.

"But if the only way to Heaven is through Jesus," Aminah reasoned, "then what was the message of the other prophets who came *before* Jesus— the message that God told them to tell their people so they could go to Heaven?"

Oh. Now Tamika understood Aminah's point. She waved her hand as if it did not matter. "Anyway, they're not responsible for accepting Jesus because they never knew of him."

"But still," Dee insisted. She chuckled, shook her head, and stared at Tamika, creasing her forehead in apparent dissatisfaction with her response. "God sent the prophets with a message, and, certainly, *He* told the prophets everything their people needed to know to get to Heaven. So what was it that He told them if Jesus is, in fact, the only way to Heaven?"

"Jesus was not there yet, though," Tamika insisted.

"But the way to Heaven was," Dee replied. "I mean," she said, grinning, "what was that way to Heaven before Jesus?"

Tamika did not know how to respond.

"Okay, think about it like this," Aminah offered. "If you say Jesus said that none shall get to God—we don't call Him Father—but through him, as a Muslim, I can accept that in principle," she leveled, "in that the people during the time of Jesus could not get to God but through him because the only way to Heaven was through following what God revealed to him. So none of the people of Israel could make up their own religion or turn away from Jesus and think they could go to Heaven. They had to go through Jesus, by worshipping and obeying God as Jesus showed them."

It made sense, Tamika could not deny it, but still... But still what? What could she say? "But that's not what the Bible says." That was a satisfactory response, wasn't it?

"Actually that *is* what the Bible says," Aminah corrected

"Where?" Tamika asked challengingly. She had never heard of such a passage.

"In John 6:29," Aminah replied matter-of-factly, shocking Tamika with her knowledge, "where a person is reported as asking Jesus what the work of God requires, and Jesus is reported to have said, 'The work of God is this, to believe in the one he has sent.'" She casually added, "You can also read Exodus 20 verses three and four and Exodus 34 verse fourteen, where it proves Jesus can't be God."

Aminah went on, "So that shows that the way to Heaven has always been to believe in God's prophets. And, by following them—or *through them*, if you wish to call it that, you go to Heaven."

Speechless, Tamika said nothing. She did not even recall reading the passages. But if they were actually in the Bible, then that was definitely something to think about. But she would have to check later to make sure they were actually there, because she could not just go on what Aminah was saying.

"But anyway, the point is that in Islam, the message of God does not change. We don't believe that originally the way to Heaven was to worship the Creator and follow His messengers and now the way to Heaven is to worship His creation, whereas that was the way to Hell before." Aminah shook her head at the confusion.

"In Islam, it's simple," she told Tamika. "The way to Heaven is, as it has always been since the time of Adam, to worship God alone and follow His prophets, and most specifically the one He sent to you, as even the Bible tells you," she added. "The people to whom Noah was sent will be held accountable for obeying his message, and, likewise, for the people of Moses' or Jesus' time. For us, our prophet is Muhammad, may prayers and peace be upon them all."

Tamika was silent, almost dumbfounded. She sat blinking, trying to think of a rebuttal, but she could not. It all made sense. What could she say? Even if she did not believe it, there was nothing that she could say against it. "Well," she heard herself saying before even thinking about it, "we don't question God and try to make sense of it, we just believe."

"Believe what though?" Dee challenged, mouth full of chips, some of its salty dust falling from her mouth, she catching it instinctually.

"Believe in what God says," Tamika replied matter-of-factly.

"But," Aminah interjected in her soft voice, "you should actually know what God says, and *then* believe. We certainly shouldn't question God, but we should question others to make sure what they're saying is from God."

"That's why we have the Bible."

"But the Bible's not from God," Dee told her, staring at her as if she were crazy. "Only some of it is true, because humans wrote that book."

"They were inspired by God though," Tamika told them.

"How do you know that?" Dee challenged.

How *did* she know? She shrugged, frustrated. "You just believe."

Dee laughed. It was a chuckle at first, but then it developed into steady laughter, culminating in hysteria. She laughed so hard her abdomen hurt. She had not intended to laugh, but she had nonetheless.

Aminah glared at her. Dee cupped her hand over her mouth in embarrassment and apologized profusely with her eyes. She should not have had such an outburst, even if by accident. It was extremely rude.

Tamika's cheeks grew hot, and she felt herself becoming angry, fed up.

"In Islam," Aminah said sighing, upset with Dee, "we have what's called our *fitrah.*"

"Your what?" Tamika asked, trying to force herself to ignore Dee.

"*Fitrah,* our nature. It's an Arabic word," Aminah told her.

"Oh," Tamika said slowly, now listening, looking at Aminah.

"In the Qur'an, God tells us about the covenant He took with Adam and all of Adam's descendants before they were born, and we all testified that God was our Lord. And God told us that this testimony was just in case we came on the Day of Judgment and pleaded ignorance, blaming our parents and others for our sin of not worshipping Him properly." She put in, "I'm paraphrasing, and I apologize, but you can read it in the English translation of the Qur'an if you like. But, anyway, we forgot about this testimony, although we all did it."

"You mean even you and me?" She decided against inquiring about Dee.

"Yes," Aminah nodded. "Even you and I testified, but we forgot about it, as everyone did, but that testimony is still with us, and our *fitrah,* our nature, recognizes it. So what this means," she explained, "is that we won't be guessing as to what is the right religion or what to believe. This *fitrah* within us guarantees that we will know the truth when it reaches us."

Tamika wrinkled her forehead. "So you're saying, deep inside, we all know the truth?"

"Innately, yes," Aminah told her. "But you're only held accountable for that knowledge if you heard the truth while you were alive."

"And the truth is?" Tamika asked, her question dangling.

"Islam."

"Islam?"

"Yes," Aminah told her flatly, politely, as if hinting at something else, but Tamika did not want to know about that something else. "So whenever a person hears of Islam, they recognize it, but—."

"Then why are there different religions?"

"That's what I was about to say," she chuckled. "Everyone who hears of Islam clearly and properly recognizes it as true, but many people don't actually submit because of various reasons, like pride, fear, or weakness, because they don't want to be ostracized by family and friends, etcetera. But for many others, they just want to hold on to the religion of their parents. God even talks about that in the Qur'an when He says that when you ask them to come to what God revealed and come to the Messenger, they will say, 'We will follow the ways of our fathers,' and then God says what is translated as, 'What? Even though their fathers were void of knowledge and wisdom?'" She sighed, as if to express how sad it was. "But that's why many people turn away from truth and follow different religions."

Tamika was speechless, dazed. The information took hold of her and disrupted her peace. She could ask Aminah no more questions for the interview, even if she wanted to, at least not then. Her mind was clouded and confused. She was unable to see clearly, think clearly.

Her body felt heavy all of a sudden, as if something enormously powerful was weighing her down. Everything around her was surreal, as the world, although the same, became strangely different. It was terrifying, the feeling that engulfed her at the moment, as if all of her comfort and security—her internal peace— had been snatched away from her. She was aching with sorrow and wanted to fret, to vent, but she did not know why, could not admit why. She felt herself become frustrated and angry, thoughts of her mother flashing through her mind.

Had Tamika been lied to? Was that it?

No, that was not possible. Not Ma, not her. She would never.

Or maybe... Maybe she never knew, but—what was Tamika saying? What was she thinking!

The *fitrah,* Tamika had one, did she not?

But how could that be right? It could not be right because it was not fair! Or was it?

At that moment, Tamika's mind drifted, and she could almost feel the warm sweat from the firm grasp of her mother's large hand as she pulled Tamika to her side while ascending the church steps when Tamika was merely a child. The smell of the cotton dress that her mother wore every Sunday had given Tamika a sense of tranquility and protection. Whenever her mother ironed that dress, that same dress every Sunday, Tamika would lean in the doorway. The room had captured the warmth from the iron's steam, and the aroma of perfume and cheap laundry soap filled the room with each press against the dress, which lay neatly on the ironing board.

"It's the Lord's day," her mother would fuss. Tamika knew her mother was complaining about her brother and sister sleeping. "No time to rest this day. The Lord gives us life and what do we do?" Tamika's mother shook her head, her hair moving, its curling-ironed ends brushing the collar of her shirt.

"Don't just stand there looking stupid," her mother would glare at her all of a sudden. "Go wake up Latonya and Philip."

Tamika, already dressed in the maroon velveteen dress with the ribbons dangling from the front, white dress socks pulled up to her knees and shiny patent leather shoes that made a click-click noise when she walked, would saunter down the hallway, half-smiling, half-pouting as she went to wake her sister and brother. She was always the first one ready, even before her mother, who would make sure Tamika was dressed before she ironed her cotton Sunday dress.

"Girl," her mother would say when she combed Tamika's hair, the comb yanking her head abruptly with every stroke, "I can tell you gonna be something special one day. I knew it the day you were born." Her mother's strong, rough fingers would gently grasp Tamika's chin and turn it towards her slightly. "You know the Lord gives you signs, huh?"

A nod.

"And those signs are small miracles, pointing to something higher, and when you were born, I got one, not like with your brother and sister. It wasn't nothin' but a feeling, but I knew that when you came out, *child,* I knew the Lord was giving me a gift." She frowned, letting go of Tamika's chin too quickly, then resumed her combing. A moment later, she began parting and pulling at Tamika's hair to start a small braid that would become one of many "corn rows."

Tamika remained dutifully still despite the burning sensation on her scalp as her mother braided, not wanting to disappoint her mother, who called her "my strong one." Occasionally, she would blink to both fight back tears due to the pain and to make sure the braids were not too tight.

"But it wasn't nothin' like that with my others." Her mother shook her head. "Knew they'd be trouble.

"You see that book over there?" Her mother's large finger suddenly pointed toward the worn bible on top of a stack of books. "That's what it's all about. And with that book, child, nothin' else matters.

"So don't let no boy sweet talk you," her mother would say abruptly, although Tamika was only seven years old. "Got them sweet words and sharp fangs and then they gone."

At the time, Tamika had no idea what her mother was talking about. It was not until years later that she had a clue, when her mother said that

Latonya and Philip didn't know no better, getting fooled by the "sweet talking," when both Latonya and Philip started to "go out."

"You have anymore questions?" Aminah's voice startled her back to reality.

"Huh?"

"Anymore questions."

"Oh," she replied, suddenly self-conscious, wondering how she must have appeared sitting on the couch reacting so dramatically to a simple question. "No."

Tamika stood, placed her purse strap on her shoulder, and started for the door. "But thanks." Where was she going? She opened the front closet, removed her coat, and slipped on her shoes.

"Is everything okay?" Aminah inquired with concern.

"Yeah," Tamika replied, forcing a smile. "I just, uh, forgot to do something."

"Oh," Aminah nodded, unconvinced, but she accepted the excuse nonetheless. "Well, be careful."

Be careful? Why? Oh, it was late. "Okay," again, forcing a smile. "Thanks." Had she said that already? She opened the door, put on her coat, and waved to the roommates, still clueless as to what she was doing, but inside knowing that whatever it was, she needed to do it—immediately, before it was too late.

She closed the door and locked it, and walked swiftly down the hall. The neutral hallway gave her a chance to breathe and get her needed space. She opened the exit door and made her way down the steps to the side door.

The cold night air sent a sudden chill through Tamika's body as she left the building. Other students were outside talking and smoking. The odor offended her nostrils, causing her to wave her hand in front of her face as she walked by them. Too focused on where she needed to go, she did not notice their rolling of the eyes and harsh whispers directed at her.

She walked faster, pulling her coat tightly around her as the wind blew, pushing against her face and body. She quickened her pace to a jog through the grass, opting to avoid the walkways, which took longer. Finally, after almost ten minutes, she was there. Sighing relief and struggling to catch her breath, she opened the main door to the building. She hoped Makisha was in her room.

"I don't care what you were trying to do, Durrah, it was rude," Aminah blurted in frustration, her pale face now pink with anger. "You may have scared her away." She rolled her eyes and shook her head at Durrah, who stood in the living room several feet from her in front of the couch. "What were you *thinking*?"

"I know," Dee smiled from embarrassment, waving her hand at Aminah. "I just thought it was funny." She laughed forcefully. "I mean, she just kept saying you just gotta believe, you just gotta believe."

Aminah groaned. "But that's not the point, Durrah," she told her friend angrily. "When you're talking about religion, you gotta be sensitive."

Dee's expression became serious, and regret was apparent on her face. "I know," she brooded.

"You don't know what's going on in Tamika's head now. She probably doesn't want anything to do with us anymore."

Biting her lower lip in deep thought, Dee frowned as she pondered the likelihood of what Aminah was saying.

"You better apologize to her," Aminah suggested reprovingly. She shook her head. "And," she started to say, but stopped, throwing her hands up in frustration. "Whatever," she said finally, then walked out of the living room into the bedroom.

Dee dragged herself to the couch and collapsed on it, filled with shameful regret. What if Tamika *had* gotten a bad impression of the religion because of what she had done? She wiped her hands over her face and groaned. Her guilt taunted her, pulled at her, reminding her how she, of all people, had no right to make another person feel bad for her religion.

It was strange how quickly she talked about the senselessness of another person's religion but barely practiced hers herself. She knew Islam was right, but she felt herself becoming lazy, praying sometimes, fasting only some days during Ramadan, and eating like a pig on others. Even on the days she actually fasted, she had to force herself not to break the fast before sunset. Before going to college she had covered completely, showing only her face and hands, always wearing a large *khimaar* on her head and a large dress to cover her body as Aminah now did, and she had even considered covering her face at one point. But what happened? Dee herself had no idea, as she had gradually stopped covering toward the end of her senior year. And after being showered with compliments on her appearance, Dee began to enjoy the attention, never before realizing that she was even partially attractive. But she had not entered any beauty contests until she was a freshman in college. She won the first pageant she entered, having sung a song she had known before she had stopped listening to music—and before she started listening to it again.

Of course, when Dee's mother heard of the contest, she was livid. She lectured Dee day after day on how wrong it was, and although Dee knew her mother was right, Dee had already tasted the sweetness of popularity and was drawn in. Dee would listen to her mother without a word, shamefully replying with, "I don't know" to every question of why, an answer she knew was unacceptable to her mother but was strangely true. At such times, Dee would feel regret for her actions. But when she returned to school, she was thirsty for the attention again, curious if there was actually something special about her and if she had genuine talent. She would find herself pondering if she was really beautiful or if she had won the contest on luck. When she won yet another contest, this one held at a local mall, she was ecstatic. This time she had won a thousand dollars, money that was all hers. Although thrilled at the thought of having so much money to herself, she was in no need of it, since her father was doing quite well financially from the shoe store he owned.

Dee's father was disappointed with her, Dee knew, but he did not say much. Dee was unsure if his silence was due to too much anger or too much sadness. But either way, it tore her apart. She often wished he would yell at her, scold her, just say something. But whenever her mother lectured her, he would just stare at her with a disappointed expression on his face, remaining silent. It was as if he were trying to gather his thoughts, pull himself together, and come to terms with the fact that this was actually happening. He, like her mother, was a strong Muslim, dedicated to the religion, having accepted it while Dee was a young child. They had not been married then, but after becoming Muslim, they married and raised Dee and their other children in the religion.

Although only four then, Dee remembered the wedding—quiet, simple, nothing like she had seen on television. But she was dressed in her favorite dress at the time, and it made her feel special, as if everyone was admiring her. After the wedding, her parents came and talked to Dee, then their only child, explaining everything to her at home that night.

Still dressed in the formal attire, her mother held Dee on her lap while her father sat next to them, holding his wife's hand.

"We're Muslim now," Dee's mother told her. Dee batted her innocent bashful eyes with her thumb in her mouth, as was customary whenever she sat on her mother's lap. "Do you know what that means?"

Dee shook her head, her eyes now admiring the pretty shoes that adorned her small feet.

"It means we're going to start praying," Dee's mother explained.

"And it means we're going to go to Heaven," her father added.

"Do you know what Heaven is?" her mother asked, her voice rising in its soft, child-friendly tone, as it normally did when she talked to Dee.

Dee shook her head and leaned against her mother's chest, enjoying the comfort more than the conversation. Her small world precluded any real comprehension of things that did not interest her.

"It's the place where people who worship God go," her mother told her, her soft voice now above Dee's head, which brushed her mother's chin.

"But only if you're Muslim," her father added almost sternly, but in a child-friendly tone.

"Are you gonna be a good Muslim?" her mother asked, now gently pulling Dee from her chest and establishing eye contact.

A nod.

"Good."

Dee again leaned on her mother's chest, the sweet smell of perfume relaxing her as she nestled against the warm body.

"And we thought of a special name for you," her father told her, excited.

From her mother's lap where she relaxed, she stared at him blankly, confused. She already had a name.

"And it means pearl," her mother told her.

"Pearl?" Dee repeated in her small voice, wrinkling her nose, thumb still in her mouth, somewhat muffling her voice. "What's that?"

"It's a clean white piece of jewelry."

"Like in your secret treasure box?" she asked, anticipating.

"Yes," her mother told her, referring to her jewelry case, "like in my secret treasure box."

Dee's eyes widened with hope, and she sat up, her childish eyes staring at her mother as her thumb fell from her mouth. "I get to go in the secret treasure box?"

"If you're a good girl, you can one day, but right now you can have a secret treasure name."

"I can?"

"Yes."

"Will I be a princess?"

They laughed.

"You'll be better than a princess if you're good," her mother promised.

"I will?"

"Of course."

"With a big, big castle, like this much tall?" she asked, her hands opening wider and wider, signifying her castle.

"Even bigger," her dad told her, amused.

"And we can call you Princess Durrah."

"You will?" she asked full of hope and excitement.

"Yes, because that's your name now."

"Princess Durrah?"

"Our princess Durrah," her Dad chimed.

He tickled her, and she giggled. "The princess Durrah!" he called out, suddenly lifting her from her mother's lap as he stood, now swinging her around. "The best princess of them all!" he announced as her giggling filled the room. "The princess of the Gonzalez Castle!"

Her mother laughed from the couch, amused by her husband and child.

"Princess of the secret treasure box!" Dee's tiny voice squealed, begging.

"Princess of the secret treasure box!" his voice deepened, announcing. "But," he stopped, holding her in the air, her small head almost grazing the ceiling, bony legs dangling awkwardly, "only if Princess Durrah is good!"

"I'm good, Daddy! I'm the bestest princess of them all!"

"The bestest bestest?" he frowned playfully, staring at her, waiting for her to agree.

"The bestest, bestest, bestest!" she shrilled, giggling as he swung her around again.

"Okay, the bestest bestest bestest Princess Durrah!" he agreed, letting her down to the floor, both of them falling playfully on the carpet, exhausted.

He sat up suddenly, eyes narrowing waggishly. "But only if you be a good princess and pray and fast so you can get the bestest bestest bestest castle in the next world."

"The next world?" she sat up, eyes wide in anticipation.

"The next world for the princesses and princes who get their castles because they were good girls and boys in this world."

"There's another whole big world, Daddy?"

"Yep! And if we're *really* good, Mommy, Daddy, and Princess Durrah will have a castle!"

"We will!"

"Yes, we will!"

"And I get to be the princess of the treasure box!"

"You'll be the princess of a lot of treasure boxes!" he promised.

"All for Princess Durrah?" she hoped.

"All for Princess Durrah," he assured her. "But," he raised a finger, "only if Princess Durrah is good."

Presently, Dee sighed and a lump developed in her throat. There were so many things she was struggling with. How could she find time to make someone else's life difficult? How could she blame Tamika for her confusion? Dee herself was confused, and she had little reason to be. It was not truth that confused her but her failure to live according to it despite her belief in it. It was understandable that Tamika thought she just had to believe and everything would be okay. She had not known anything else. It was completely logical for people to believe wholeheartedly in what they had been taught, even if others misunderstood the conviction. Perhaps, it had been so humorous to Dee because she had taken for granted the fact that, although correct belief in God was a prerequisite for Paradise, certainly there was more to religion and going to Heaven than merely believing.

Dee had been taught since childhood that even after a person took the first step in giving herself a chance to enter Paradise by believing in and worshipping God correctly, the road was just beginning. There were minimal requirements that had to be fulfilled in order for the correct belief to not only benefit the person but to even be classified as correct belief. Her parents had taught her that it was incorrect for a person to simply profess correct belief, hold it in her heart, but live as she wanted to live, content with being "saved." Each day was a struggle to stay on the right path, because there were obstacles constantly being placed in a person's path. The temptations of the world were numerous, many of which were difficult to turn down. Sins like avarice, arrogance, and illegal sexual relations were among the most profligate. But the most serious sin was that of associating partners with God. Although Dee understood the difficulty of avoiding the former three, she could never imagine doing the latter. How could a person either deny God's existence or worship creation along with or instead of Him? It made no sense to her.

As a young adult, Dee was constantly asking her parents about Christianity, a religion that had always confused her. She had a difficult time understanding how Christians could possibly view God's prophet as God and His son. Didn't they know that worshipping God's creation was the gravest of sins, she would wonder? Didn't they know that the committing of that sin forbade a person entry into Heaven—eternally? But what had confused her most was that the Christians she knew thought *she* was going to Hell for *not* worshipping God's prophet Jesus. Furthermore, the Christians, although they worshipped Jesus, thought that pagans were wrong for worshipping idols and stone. In her mind, she thought, *what's the difference?* If worshipping a man was okay, why not stone? Neither had any power except through God's permission. Wasn't the very definition of paganism the worship of creation? And certainly humans were creation, Jesus among them.

She became perturbed whenever she argued with Christians. Sometimes she would come home in a daze, dumbfounded that they actually thought *she* was wrong. When she would ask her parents why that was so, they would most often explain that people generally followed the religion of their family, friends, or society. But why, Dee wanted to know? Why, when their souls were at stake? Why the blind following? Why the conviction? Did they study other religions? Did they ever think that perhaps the Bible was not God's revelation?

No matter how much Dee argued with Christians, she could never get over their blind conviction to the concept of the trinity, of which Dee never got a satisfactory explanation. And being "saved" was a concept that made no sense to her either, in that the entire purpose of living each day was removed. And a man as God? That was mind-boggling. How could a man, as helpless and in need of God as she, be her creator and savior? It would have even made more sense to Dee if they had believed that God was a man and nothing else, at least that was consistent. But the half-man, half-God, yet fully man and fully God concept blew her mind. They actually believed it, that she could never quite get over. Their most popular explanation was the metaphor of an egg. *An egg!* The trinity, they would confidently explain, was like an egg, three separate parts but all one—one egg. But she was too ashamed to tell them that such an analogy was actually proof *against* the trinity.

Many times she left them alone, amazed and astounded that they were serious. An egg? The senselessness of it tormented her. Such an analogy could be used to argue that *everyone* was god, all different people but making up one human race—"one god." But still, an egg? How? An egg was a thing with three parts that were inexorably separate, termed an egg for terminological simplicity, not to point to their three parts being the same. Unlike the parts of the trinity, if the egg yolk was removed, the whites and shell remained. But, in Christianity, if you removed one part, the Father, son, or the Holy Ghost, all were supposed to be gone, because they were all the same.

Once Dee had asked a Christian classmate in high school why he thought Muslims were going to Hell, and he told her because they didn't worship Jesus. When she told him they worshipped God, he had told her that was not good enough.

"Then you *don't* believe Jesus is God then?" she asked him.

"Of course I do."

"Then why would I be going to Hell for worshipping God?"

"Because you don't accept Jesus."

"I accept Jesus as the prophet he was."

"But you have to accept him as your Lord, as God."

"But I accept God as God."

"Not if you don't accept Jesus."

She chuckled, shaking her head, confused. "Wait a minute," she stopped him. "Define God."

"Define God?" he repeated, the request baffling him.

"Yes, define what you mean when you say God."

He did not respond for some time but said finally, "He's Jesus, who shed his blood—."

"No," she interrupted him, "what I'm saying is, before we can discuss who is and who is not God, shouldn't we first know what we mean by the word 'God?'"

He stared at her blankly.

"You see," she said to him, smiling, "Muslims believe that God has attributes, certain characteristics that make Him God."

"We do too," he interjected.

"But Muslims believe God is All-Hearing, All-Seeing, All-Knowing and—."

"We believe that."

"Then you don't believe Jesus is God?" she asked, feigning ignorance.

"Of course we do."

"But doesn't your Bible quote Jesus as saying he does not know when the Hour is, that only the Father knows?"

"That was him talking about himself as the son."

She laughed. "So when he doesn't know something, he changes into the son, when he's supposed to be God?"

"God can do anything."

"Yes," she agreed, clarifying, "God can do anything that's consistent with Him being God."

He was becoming frustrated. "What's that supposed to mean?"

"It means that God is All-Powerful, yes, and He can do whatever He wants, but He does nothing that is inconsistent with His Majesty or Power.

"Think about it," she had told him, reasoning. "I say I'm a strong person, but if I tell you I'm so strong I can drink till I'm drunk, what would you say?"

"I'd call that stupid," he told her emphatically.

"That's my point," she told him. "My strength is not demonstrated by doing whatever I want, like getting drunk, because this does not show any strength on my part, even though it took energy to do it. But my strength, although it *is* shown sometimes by being able to *do* certain things, it is also shown sometimes by *not* doing certain things, if those things contradict my strength, like getting senselessly angry, or getting drunk, or whatever. Similarly, you can't point to a weakness, like lack of knowledge, and then attribute this to God's Power, saying He can do whatever He wants. Because the fact that someone does not know something, especially if he's supposedly all-knowing, demonstrates his *limits*, *not* his strength, power, or capabilities. And thus, it demonstrates his *lack of* divinity.

"So," she continued authoritatively, "we can't argue that God can do whatever He wants to justify the argument that He is a man and God at the same time, because being a man in flesh, as Jesus was, having to walk here and there, or having to eat, to pray, to have limited knowledge on things, all of these things are *weaknesses*, inconsistent with and contradictory to Godhood. And, certainly, experiencing pain and chastisement, as you believe Jesus experienced on the cross, is unbecoming of God, where you say he cried out helplessly, 'My God, my God, why has Thou forsaken me?' Killed, *killed,*" she underscored, "at the hands of the humans he supposedly created and over whom He has power? Was that God, the All-Powerful, the One capable of doing anything, talking then? And if it was, who was He talking to?"

Until they graduated from high school, that student never spoke to Dee again, constantly avoiding her, although they had many classes together. She knew he was avoiding her on purpose, unable to give any intelligent answers to her questions, although he was constantly carrying a Bible, which was tucked under his arm, and inviting people to "the Lord" so they could be "saved."

Dee had felt sorry for him, awfully sorry for him. His uncertainty and ignorance was apparent on his face. He had no idea why he was calling people to "the Lord" in the manner he did or why he believed Muslims or anyone else who did not worship Jesus was going to Hell. He had no idea. For, although he "called people to God" everyday, he clearly exhibited that he did not even know what he meant when he said "God."

Chapter Five

The night grew cold and dark in Makisha's room, and although Makisha had spread out several blankets and sheets for her, Tamika was unable to get comfortable on the uncarpeted, cold tile floor. The sound of Makisha's rhythmic breathing filled the room, her silhouette but shadowy curves created by her comforter, which rose and fell with each breath.

"You better sleep here," Makisha had advised Tamika after she told her about how the two roommates ganged up on her, Dee laughing and Aminah asking questions to intentionally mislead her.

"I told you," Makisha had reminded her, shaking her head knowingly. "You need to talk to the residential office about moving out of that place before they drive you nuts. You can file a conduct suit, if you want," she casually suggested with a shrug. "And you can call it harassment. They like that word."

Tamika had shrugged. Although upset with her roommates, she was unmoved to take such a drastic measure, certain the problem would pass. "It was just a misunderstanding," she concluded after calming down.

"Girl, that wasn't no misunderstanding!" Makisha told her, staring at her as if she was crazy. "They tryin' to convert you."

Yeah, maybe, Tamika considered. But she didn't care. If they thought what they were saying was true, why wouldn't they try to convert her? Hadn't her mother told her to convert people to Christianity for the sake of their souls? Why then should she view it as an insult if Aminah and Dee were doing the same? Wasn't it a person's love for you that moved her to want you to have what she thought was best?

"They have some good points, though," she had said reflectively, her eyes distant, arms hugging her knees as she sat on the floor facing her friend, who sat on the bed.

"Naw, naw," Makisha stopped her, waving her hand in the air, her thick braids moving as she shook her head. "Don't go there, girl," she cautioned Tamika "That's all they want you to do."

"But what was it that the other prophets taught, Makisha?" Tamika asked, her question seriously intent, her voice far away, as were her thoughts.

"Who cares?" her friend retorted. "They're dead."

Tamika groaned and sucked her teeth. "But it's in the Bible, Makisha, we can't just say that."

"Well, if it's there, it's there, so what? I gotta go with what I know. I ain't nobody's preacher."

"You think the preachers know?" Tamika asked hopefully, her tired voice becoming slightly more alive.

"Of course," Makisha replied simply. "They studied all that stuff."

"Isn't one of your uncles the reverend of his church?"

"Yeah," she said slowly, unsure where Tamika was heading.

"Why don't you ask *him?*" Tamika sounded like a helpless child, aching for any answer someone could give. She did not care what it was, anything, so long as it satiated her appetite for peace of mind.

"Girl, he lives in North Carolina!" Makisha reminded her, staring at her friend as if she had lost her mind.

"You know his number, don't you?"

"His number?" she asked incredulously. "I ain't calling him long distance to ask him that."

"Why not?" Tamika begged her. "It'll be real quick. I'll pay you back."

Makisha was silent, touched. She suddenly felt sorry for Tamika. She realized then that her friend was a mess, hungry for answers, as she had once been. When Makisha had gone through her confusion, her mother had come to her rescue, gently giving her the answers, each one with a reminder that we weren't to question God. We were only here to believe, and although the responses were simple, they changed Makisha's life and increased her faith. Since then, she had never questioned again. She was ever so grateful to her mother for being patient with her during those fragile moments.

"Okay," Makisha agreed finally. "But you better pay me back, girl!"

"I will," Tamika promised, forcing a smile on her stressed, contorted face.

After finding the number in her phone book, Makisha called her uncle. They exchanged small talk, and she told her uncle about Tamika, after which he eagerly agreed to talk to her, especially after Makisha mentioned that it was Muslims who were bothering her.

Makisha handed the phone to Tamika, whose heart was pounding wildly.

"H-h-ello?" she stuttered, barely able to speak, her hands trembling from nervousness.

"Yes, Tamika," his deep, comforting voice replied. "My niece tells me you have some questions."

She chuckled self-consciously. "Yeah, I, uh, do, just a few."

"Anything."

Her first question was about the message of the other prophets to their people.

He cleared his throat, "Well, uh, they just told their people to do good and worship God."

"Jesus?"

"Well, uh." There was a long pause—too long for Tamika's comfort and waning hope. "We can't quite say that. But they worshipped God as best they could."

"So they didn't worship Jesus?" Her heart sank. She did not want to hear that.

"Well, he hadn't come yet, so, uh—"

He was making excuses. She could see right through it, the way he fumbled for answers, just like she had.

Just then, Tamika felt as if the world was caving in on her. She wanted to cry.

"So then is Jesus God?" Certainly, he could answer that for her.

"Yes and no."

Yes and no! She wanted the throw the phone against the wall. "E-e-excuse me?"

"Yes, in the sense we must worship him to get to Heaven, but no, in the sense he was also a man in flesh until he died."

"So God died?"

He chuckled. "No, no, dear, the son died, and God left the flesh then."

"So when we say he's the son, the Father, and the Spirit, is that at the same time or is it like the father went into the flesh of the son until the son died?"

"You can say that."

She could say that! She was asking him!

Tamika had hung up the phone more puzzled than when she had picked it up, frustrated with Makisha's uncle and everyone else.

Her mother, the idea had suddenly come to her.

After again promising to pay Makisha back, she called her mother (to whom she lied about her reason, claiming that she was just reading the Bible and wanted to know).

But her mother only confounded her more. Her explanation was different than the reverend's! Her mother explained the trinity as the three existing all at once, and she had claimed that when Jesus was crucified, it was not the son but the Lord, which was why he shed his blood for them and died for everyone's sins, because only the Lord could die for their sins, although he was the son too.

That night Tamika was fuming, feeling as if her entire upbringing, her life, had been a lie. No one seemed to have any idea upon what the religion was truly founded, each having his or her own explanation for Jesus' divinity, everyone's view drastically different from the other's. It was crazy. How was she supposed to reconcile all of that and "just believe"? In what! How was she supposed to accept the religion for herself if she did not understand it clearly, let alone try to convert people to it? What was she supposed to say to potential Christians when explaining what they should believe? Was she to make up an explanation, and so long as it made sense to her, tell them it, although it could likely contradict with another Christian's? Although she wanted to believe it, *tried* to believe, convinced herself she had to believe it, she could not. She simply could not. Inside, she knew better.

...Was it her *fitrah* that prevented her from accepting it?

Tamika wrestled with her thoughts for a couple of days, sleeping in Makisha's room until Thursday night. They spent the evenings discussing Christianity, and Tamika would express her frustration, asking question after question, while Makisha downplayed all of Tamika's concerns. She told Tamika not to question God, to just believe, and she warned that questioning could cause her to "turn her back on Christ." But Tamika wanted to know how Makisha was sure that Christianity was the religion of God, the one in which she should "just believe" and not question. Tamika told Makisha she had no problem "just believing" and not questioning, so long as she was sure that what she was believing was in fact from God. So she would insist on knowing how Makisha was sure—absolutely positive—that Christianity was *the* truth, from God, and not any other religion. Once she had that answer, Tamika told her, she would have no problem "just believing." Makisha had no answer except that it was what the Bible taught, and that the Bible was the word of God. But why the Bible and not the Qur'an, Tamika wanted to know? How was Makisha so sure, so content that she was right?

Although Makisha thought Tamika was trying to be difficult, "brainwashed" by her roommates, Tamika seriously wanted to know how Makisha was able to be so comfortable and strong in her beliefs, as this was something Tamika wanted, envied. She wanted to be at peace, sure she was doing the right thing, but she simply could not achieve that by "just believing." Why couldn't Makisha understand that? Why didn't she get it?

"Just believe" what? That was the question that remained in Tamika's mind. She had no problem "just believing," she kept telling herself, but only *after* she was sure that what she had was truth! But how could she be sure? How? *How!*

After analyzing her own situation, Tamika had come to the conclusion that she had believed in Christianity only because it was all she had been taught. And if that was a sufficient reason to "just believe," then how could Tamika believe her religion was right and others wrong, given that everyone was taught something, and, for many, it was not Christianity? So should they too "just believe" because it had been taught to them by their parents and community? It made no sense. Certainly, there had to be more to truth than "just believing" without questioning, especially when it was not even clear what the authenticity of the source of "truth" was.

Was it possible that this *fitrah* Aminah was talking about was actually real? Was it possible that deep inside she knew what was true?

It sounded too easy, too good to be true.

But what if it were true? What if God *had* taken a covenant from all humans before putting them on earth? And what if Tamika was one of them?

Friday afternoon, after her classes, Tamika returned to her apartment, having almost forgotten that she had been upset with her roommates. Her heart and mind were filled with a determination that eclipsed anything she may have felt about the past occurrence. She wanted to know the answers to her questions about religion and Christianity.

She was relieved that no one was home when she arrived at the apartment, because the first thing she wanted to do was to browse through some of the books on the bookshelves. Although she had written about Islam on her note cards based on what she had learned from the interview with Aminah and turned them in, she was not satisfied with her knowledge thus far, her mind filled with questions and curiosity about Islam, pushing her to learn more.

After selecting several books from the shelves, including the two Aminah had shown her, Tamika sat on the couch and eagerly began to read. The first book from which she read was *The Fundamentals of Tawheed (Islamic Monotheism)*. She glanced at the author's name before reading: Dr. Abu Ameenah Bilal Philips. *Bilal Philips?* He must have converted, she concluded judging from his last name, unable to help wondering what it was that made him choose Islam. But she had never heard of him.

She skimmed through the book, and the words "...Covenant With Aadam" caught her eye. She flipped through the chapter, and, sure enough, there it was, a section entitled "The Fitrah." Unexpectedly, her heart raced as she began reading the chapter. She was hopeful and scared as she read, hopeful because she was going to have some answers, but scared because it possibly meant that what she feared for the last few days was true.

"Allaah's Covenant With Aadam." Tamika already knew that Allah or "Allaah," as this author spelled it, was the Arabic word for God, as had been explained to her earlier.

As she read, she came across a reference to the verse to which Aminah had referred regarding the covenant:

> "When your Lord drew forth from the loins of the children of Aadam, their descendants and made them testify concerning themselves. (Saying): 'Am I not your Lord?' They said, 'Yes, we testify it.' (This) in case you say on the Day of Judgment, 'We were unaware of this.' Or in case

74

you say, 'It was our ancestors who made partners (with Allaah) and we are only their descendants. Will you then destroy us for what those liars did?'"[9]

The author went on to explain:

> "The verse and prophetic explanation confirm the fact that everyone is responsible for belief in God and on the Day of Judgment excuses will not be accepted. Every human being has the belief in God imprinted on his soul and Allaah shows every idolater during the course of his life, signs that his idol is not God. Hence, every sane human being is required to believe in God beyond His creation and not manifest in it."[10]

Tamika felt herself becoming nervous. What he said made sense. It made sense that God would have some indicator for people to know what was true and what was not, aside from what they were told by parents and others, because this inevitably varied from person to person.

Drawn in, she continued reading until she came upon, "The Prophet (s) also said, 'Each child is born in a state of *Fitrah,* but his parents make him a Jew or a Christian.'" Heart racing, she read on,

> "So, just as a child's body submits to the physical laws which Allaah has put in nature, its soul also submits naturally to the fact that Allaah is its Lord and Creator. But its parents try to make it follow their own way and the child is not strong enough in the early stages of its life to resist or oppose its parents. The religion which the child follows at this stage is one of custom and upbringing and Allaah does not hold it to account or punish it for its religion. When the child matures in youth and clear proofs of the falsehood of its religion are brought to it, the adult must follow the religion of knowledge and reason."[11]

The adult must follow the religion of knowledge and reason. The words hung in her mind, and she asked herself, although she did not want to, *Am I*

---

[9] Al-A'raaf, 7:172-3

[10] Philips, p. 46

[11] *Al-Aqeedah at Tahaaweeyah,* (5th ed. 1972), p.273, cited in *Fundamentals of Tawheed;* p.49.

following the religion of knowledge and reason? Or am I following my parents? As she reflected on what she had read, she could not deny that, inside, she knew the author was right. She did not want him to be, because his being wrong would make her life a lot simpler. But she could not deny that he presented something that was most likely correct, especially when compared to the other alternative, which was to "just believe"—in whatever—without questioning.

And then, she wondered, confirming what she feared, how could it be that the only "true religion" was confusing, wherein everyone was forced to rationalize, create analogies, justify his beliefs, and, consequently, end up with a different religion than the next person because within that "true religion," everyone's concept of God was different? No, it was not possible that God would put humans on earth and fill the true religion with confusion and contradictory concepts, making its very foundation unclear, while maintaining that it was the only path to Heaven. Where was the justice in that, the sense? Tamika could not, *would not*, no matter how she tried to rationalize it, accept that God would do such a thing. How could He truly be "Just" if He did not make truth clear from falsehood? And then, as Aminah had asked her, if Christianity was in fact the path to Heaven, how could she explain the sudden change in the message of the prophets? Yes, Tamika even remembered reading in the Bible that people should not worship other gods besides God and that they should make no images of Him, and that God was neither a man nor the son of man. But Jesus was both man *and* the son of man, not to mention the fact that other prophets did not worship him—and that necessarily meant he fell under the category of "another" god, which, of course, she was not supposed to worship.

Then why was it that Christians believed that the only way to Heaven was through worshipping Jesus, a man, the son of a human being? And why was it that they believed that worshipping God alone was a path to Hell, when in the Old Testament it was the path to Heaven? Would God burn His servants in Hell because they worshipped Him alone, and would He put others in Paradise because they worshipped a man, a part of His creation, Jesus?

Even as an adolescent, when Tamika had become very much involved in the church's youth group and choir, she had questions about what she was supposed to believe, namely the trinity and God dying. Although the spearhead of many evangelical activities, she did not understand what she was teaching. Oftentimes, she would ask her mother or other family members about the trinity, but no one answered her question directly, continually telling her that she had to "believe." Over time, she had come to leave the issue alone, and although never coming to terms with what was actually true, she accepted that she should just believe and not question God. But it had never occurred to her that what she was being taught was possibly not from God.

…Until now.

The sound of keys in the door interrupted her thoughts, but she resumed reading, now not caring if anyone saw her. She had a major paper and presentation to do for her religion class, and her roommates would most likely attribute her avid reading to her trying to complete the assignment.

"Oh, hi!"

Tamika looked up and forced a smile in response to Dee, the memory of Dee laughing at her suddenly returning to her. She resumed reading, unsure what else to do.

"We were so worried about you." Dee's voice filled the room, again interrupting Tamika.

Worried? Oh, she had forgotten. She had not come home the other night. She forced a smile, glancing at Dee then back to the book. "I was with a friend."

"Yeah, I figured that may have been it," Dee replied, concerned. "But we had *no* idea."

"Sorry," Tamika mumbled, hoping that Dee would leave her alone.

And she did. A moment later, Dee was in the bedroom.

Having completed the section on the *fitrah,* Tamika picked up the next book, *A Brief Illustrated Guide to Understanding Islam.* As she read, she learned that there were various references in the Qur'an to scientific subjects that had only recently been discovered, like details on how a fetus formed, the formation of mountains, the origin of the universe, how the cerebrum functioned, the barrier between fresh and salt water, deep seas and their internal waves, and clouds. Concerning these scientific miracles in the Qur'an, a Dr. T. V. N. Persaud had stated:

> "It seems to me that Muhammad was a very ordinary man. He could not read or write. In fact, he was illiterate. We are talking about fourteen hundred years ago. You have someone who was illiterate making profound pronouncements and statements and that are amazingly scientifically accurate about scientific nature. I personally cannot see how this could be a mere chance. There are too many accuracies and, like Dr. Moore, I have no difficulty in my mind concerning that this is a divine inspiration or revelation which led him to these statements."[12]

And the book contained many more similar quotes from experts in science. And although Tamika was in no way a scientist, she too found it

---

[12] *Darussalam* Publishers, p.27

hard to believe that such a man could have known all of those things at that time. Even for a literate man, this would be amazing, even if that man lived later than the time that the prophet Muhammad lived. But given that he was not only illiterate but lived a long time ago, there was no way he could have know all of that. ...Unless God had revealed it to him.

"Tamika?"

Startled, Tamika glanced up to find Dee standing a few feet from her, arms folded, biting her lower lip, eyes gazing sadly at her as if something had been troubling her for some time.

"Yes?" Tamika replied, forehead creased in confusion, wondering if she had done something wrong.

Dee sighed, dragged herself to the couch and sat a comfortable distance from Tamika. She frowned and leaned forward, resting her lower arms on her thighs. "I was just thinking about when you were asking Aminah about Islam."

Oh, that.

"And," she breathed, unable to explain herself clearly. "I just wanted to, uh." She let her gaze fall to her fingers, with which she played, face full of shame. "I just wanted to apologize if I offended you, you know, for, uh," she paused, "laughing and stuff."

Tamika was quiet.

"I mean, I was just thinking about it, and, gosh, you know, I feel so bad."

Tamika felt sorry for Dee all of a sudden as she watched her carry on. Tamika could tell that this had been really bothering her roommate.

"I don't know," Dee sighed, "but I just wanted to apologize."

Tamika forced smiled slightly and shrugged. "Don't worry about it," she told her sincerely. "I mean, it's confusing, I know."

"Religion, you mean?"

She nodded, surprising herself by her confession. "I still haven't figured it all out myself."

Dee was silent, hesitating before asking, "You ever think about becoming a Muslim?"

The inquiry startled Tamika. She was not prepared for such a question. But she calmed herself. "Not really."

There was silence again, and the two did not speak for some time.

"You ever think about becoming Christian?" Tamika did not know why she asked it, except it was a logical response to Dee's question.

Dee chuckled and shook her head. "Never."

Inside, Tamika grew curious, defensive. "Why not?" she asked nonchalantly, concealing her kindling interest.

"I read a lot about it," Dee shared, "you know, because most of my family is Christian, but it never made sense to me, any of it."

Tamika was silent, relating, but not wanting to.

"I mean," Dee went on, "I don't mean it offensively when I say it doesn't make sense."

Tamika nodded, understanding.

"But for me, it's unclear what they believe. Some believe Jesus is God, some just that he's the son of God and some that he's both."

"There are a lot of different sects."

"Yeah, but still."

"Don't they have a lot of sects of Muslims?" Tamika asked.

"Yeah, I guess you can say that, but we're not supposed to."

"You mean that there's only one sect that's correct?"

Dee shrugged. "I suppose you can say it like that, but I guess I'd explain that there is only one Islam."

"But don't all the sects say that?"

She smiled. "I suppose they may, but the difference is that in Islam, you still have the Qur'an and the authentic statements of the Prophet (s), so there's not too much room for arguing." She added, "Although people do."

Tamika paused before inquiring, "So what kind of Muslims are the black Muslims?"

Dee glanced sideways at Tamika, eyebrows raised. "Black Muslims?"

"Yeah, like the ones who sell newspapers and stuff."

"Oh," she laughed, "you mean the Nation of Islam?"

"Yeah."

"Those aren't Muslims," she replied simply.

"They aren't?" Tamika was confused.

"They're not even considered a sect of Islam."

"Really? But they say they're Muslim."

"But they believe that God came in the person of Fard Muhammad and that Elijah Muhammad is the messenger of God."

"They do?"

"Yeah, and that the white people are devils and black people are gods."

Tamika had heard bits and pieces about them, but she did not know what they truly believed.

"They have absolutely nothing to do with Islam at all," Dee stated emphatically. "Their beliefs are more like reverse Christianity than Islam."

"Reverse Christianity?"

"Yeah, because they believe a man is god and that he's black instead of white, like most paintings portray Jesus as being."

"But we don't look at him as having a color."

"I'm just saying how they portray him."

"Oh."

"But, in any case," Dee continued, "Jesus was a man, so he necessarily was of some race, whatever race it was, only God knows."

"But it doesn't matter."

"I agree," she told her, "but only when we look at him as a prophet, as prophets were various races, but when people look at him as God, then," she nodded her head, "that's when it begins to matter."

"How so?" Tamika had never heard that assertion before.

"Well, for one, it can be used to further racism if God is this color and not that color."

She nodded, understanding. "But God isn't really any race anyway."

"I know," Dee told her. "That's what Muslims believe, that God is not a man, and thus not any race or culture. In fact, we believe He's nothing like His creation at all."

"So you don't believe we were created in God's image?"

She shook her head emphatically. "Not at all, because creation and God are entirely separate. Nothing can compare to God."

Tamika nodded. That made sense.

Dee stood, noticing the time and also not wanting to argue. "I didn't mean to divert you from studying, but I did want to apologize."

"That's okay," Tamika assured her, not caring anymore.

Dee walked over to a shelf and removed a pamphlet. "Here," she said, handing the papers to Tamika, who read the title.

What Is Islam and Why You Should be a Muslim

Dee shrugged. "Just something to look over when you have time." She added, "Aminah thinks you might like it."

Tamika nodded, but she was not offended by the gesture. She knew the roommates were only trying to be friendly.

"What are you doing tonight?" Dee inquired, changing the subject on purpose.

"Tonight?"

"Yeah."

"Uh," Tamika had nothing planned, having told Makisha she was not going out tonight. "Nothing really."

"You wanna go shopping?"

"Shopping?"

"Yeah," Dee replied, excited.

Tamika smiled and shook her head. "I don't have any money."

"Don't worry," Dee told her, waving her hand. "It'll be fun."

"I hate going shopping without money," she told her, chuckling. "What are you trying to buy?"

"A dress."

"A dress?" Tamika was suddenly interested. "For what?"

"The formal."

Oh yeah, Tamika had wanted to buy a dress, but she could not afford to.

"Wanna help me pick one?"

Actually, Tamika liked that idea. She shrugged, smiling. "Why not?"

Chapter Six

The drive to Atlanta was usually a long one for Tamika, but Friday evening had passed quickly. The ride was filled with laughter and friendly conversation with Dee, whom Tamika learned shared a lot of her interests. Tamika enjoyed the cozy atmosphere of Dee's warm car, which smelled of artificial strawberries, a pleasing scent coming from the small car freshener that was clipped to the soft gray of the passenger side sun visor, the atmosphere a comfortable contrast to the cold weather of the darkening evening.

"I always wanted to write songs," Dee told Tamika, sucking her teeth, eyes on the road. "But I could never think up anything." Her hands were covered by leather gloves, which gently gripped the steering wheel, her neck covered by the large collar of her thick coat.

"I guess I never really thought about it," Tamika confessed, shrugging. "I've been writing them since I was little."

"Songs?" Dee raised her eyebrows, glancing sideways at Tamika, impressed.

Tamika chuckled. "Well, they started off as poems, but I would always end up singing them," she shared, "and I guess that's when they became songs."

"Sing one."

She shot a disbelieving glance at Dee, an uncertain expression developing on her face. "What?" she asked, almost laughing.

Dee laughed, nodding, looking at Tamika and back at the road. "Sing one," she told her again, laughter in her voice, but her seriousness was evident.

Tamika chuckled uncomfortably. "You're playing, right?"

"No!" Dee exclaimed playfully. "I'm for real. Go ahead."

"You're crazy," Tamika told her jokingly.

Dee considered the comment then nodded. "That's true," she stated finally, still grinning. She widened her eyes and looked at Tamika expectantly. "I'm waiting," she announced, almost singing the words, which made Tamika laugh more.

"You really want me to sing."

"Of course."

"Then you have to too," Tamika offered, making a deal.

"Fine."

Ugh! Tamika thought good-naturedly. Why did she say that? Of course Dee would not mind singing, having been accustomed to singing in public, whereas Tamika had only sang in front of others at home and church. "Okay," she agreed, her kind displeasure apparent in her voice. "But," she said, making a condition, raising her index finger, "you can't laugh."

Dee closed her lips, exaggerating the gesture, then motioned her gloved fingers across her lips as if she was zipping them close, but Tamika could see she was about to laugh.

"Girl, you betta not laugh at me!"

Dee burst out laughing. After she calmed herself, she stated accusingly, still chuckling, "You're making me laugh."

"I'm not!" Tamika protested, laughing herself.

"Just sing," Dee told her sternly, tinted by an increasingly jocular tone.

"You're gonna laugh."

"No, I'm not," she said, eyes widening innocently, as if to say, "Who *me?*"

"You will."

"If you don't sing," Dee warned her playfully, "I'm gonna pull over to the shoulder of the road, and we won't go anywhere until you do."

Tamika laughed. "Yeah, right," she said, waving her hand, knowing Dee was only bluffing.

"You think I'm joking?" Dee asked, biting her lip, eyebrows raised as if welcoming the dare.

"I *know* you're joking."

"Sing."

Tamika shook her head while looking out the window, grinning, enjoying the moment.

"Sing," Dee dared, glancing to her blind spot on the right, then going to the interstate's right lane, slowing the car.

Tamika chuckled, still shaking her head, knowing that the slowing of the car was only a deception.

"You betta sing." The car slowed.

She laughed, refusing. "No, 'cause you're gonna laugh."

A moment later, Dee was on the shoulder slowing. Then she stopped.

Tamika stared at her in disbelief, jaw dropped and eyes wide as Dee turned on the emergency lights. They could hear the sound of speeding cars passing. Dee turned off the engine.

"Sing," Dee demanded, trying to keep a serious face but failing.

"You're crazy," Tamika commented, shaking her head, giggling, covering her mouth at the crazy scene.

"I'm not going anywhere till you do."

She paused and glanced at Dee, whose expression was unchanging. Dee was actually not going anywhere until Tamika sang. Tamika laughed, amused by her roommate's sense of humor.

"I'm waiting," Dee announced, a grin still on her face, as she tapped her fingers on the steering wheel.

"Fine, fine," Tamika gave in, realizing there was no winning with Dee. "But you first."

"Me?" Dee asked, surprised.

"Yeah, why not?"

"Okay, okay," Dee agreed, her expression playful, bold, as if she were saying, "I'm not scared." "What do you want me to sing?"

"Anything."

"Okay, um—." Just then it came to her, and she began singing, "You are my sunshine..."

Tamika listened, and although she knew Dee was not doing her best, she was amazed at how beautifully she was able to sing, especially with such a simple song.

As Dee finished, she glanced at Tamika, turning slightly to face her, folding her arms in the small space between the wheel and the back of her seat. "Now, sing."

Tamika frowned good-naturedly, sucking her teeth, then laughing at how ridiculous they must seem, parked on the shoulder of the interstate, emergency lights flashings, singing songs. "I guess I have to then, huh?"

"Thaaat's right," Dee nodded, smirking.

"Fine." Tamika sighed, searching her mind for what she would sing.

"And it has to be one *you* wrote," Dee reminded.

"Uh," Tamika thought aloud, the car growing quiet as she tried to choose. Then it came to her. "Okay," she said finally. "But you can't laugh, because I made this up when I was thirteen."

Dee tucked in her lips and nodded.

"It's, um," Tamika chuckled uncomfortably. "It's not much, 'cause I just made it up real quick one day, but it was my favorite." She chuckled self-consciously again, never having sung this song for anyone, not even her family. She cleared her throat, more for procrastination than necessity. She forced a cough, hoping she could get out of it, but the waiting silence told her she could not. She took in a deep breath and began.

"I don't know how," she sang, as Dee calmly listened, "and Lord knows I don't know why," Tamika's powerful voice rose, singing in a spiritual tune, and though shaking nervously, its strength and beauty surprised even herself. "But I can't stop thinking if I'll ever have a chance not to cry.

"...Each day I wake, and it's the same as before

> *And I can't help wondering, if there is any more*
> *Is there anything else after this, I want to know*
> *Because if it is, Lord, I want to go*
> *So many love life, but I can't say the same*
> *Because it hurts too much, oh the pain*
> *The questions I have no one can tell me for sure*
> *So I can't help wondering if there's any more*
> *Any more to life than this, the questions, the tears*
> *So please, I want something else, no more fears*
> *There must be something else, I need to know*
> *Because if it is, Lord, please, please, I want to go"*

Tamika's voice stopped with the words, and the car grew uncomfortably silent. Tamika did not know if Dee was looking at her, too shy to glance up. She gazed out the window as the memory of the reason behind those words came back to her, a lump developing in her throat.

The car started, its gentle engine jerking them a bit. Then its speed picked up and the car zoomed, suddenly falling in line with the other speeding cars.

"It's beautiful," Dee commented sincerely a few minutes later, still reflecting on what its words meant to her. "What's it about?"

"My father," Tamika told her, immediately regretting the confession.

"Your father?" Dee repeated, forehead creasing. "How's that?"

"I never knew him." Tamika had already said it. It was too late to take it back. She had not planned to discuss her father. He was a subject that she had never even discussed with Makisha. It hurt too much. She had always imagined how he must have looked, often remembering one of her mother's old friends commenting on how she was a "spitting image of Craig." And Tamika knew who Craig was. She used to ask her mother about him, but her mother never told her much, not wanting to discuss him. But one of her aunts on her mother's side told her about him one day, angry with Tamika's mother for not being open with her children.

"I don't care what Thelma thinks," Tamika's aunt had said that day, angrily grasping Tamika's hand so tightly that it hurt, pulling her along the hallway and down the steps. "Always fretting about her problems, paying no attention to what her kids need." Aunt Jackie had taken Tamika to the front steps of her apartment building that day when Tamika and her family had come to visit. Her mother was still upstairs arguing with one of Tamika's uncles about something.

"Now, what I'm gonna tell you child, you don't tell nobody."

Tamika, ten years old then, listened.

"'Cause if your momma finds out, she won't ever speak to me again."

Aunt Jackie leaned back on the cement steps and took in a deep breath. She lit a cigarette, brought it slowly to her lips, and puffed as she spoke. "His name was Craig," she began, Tamika knowing immediately whom her aunt was speaking about. "Nice man, too, real tall, healthy, you know."

Tamika nodded dumbly, listening like she had never listened before.

"Thelma wanted to marry him," her aunt remembered, eyes staring off into the distance, gently blowing the cigarette smoke from her mouth. "And he always said he wanted to marry her." Jackie shook her head sadly. "But one day he just left."

Tamika swallowed, scared to ask, but she did, "Wh-why?"

"Who knows?" Jackie shrugged. "But you were only a little baby then. 'Couldn't been more than two months old." She sucked her teeth. "I think he and Thelma had a big fight, and who knows what got into him, but he just up and left."

Silence.

"Never came back again."

That was it? Tamika could not believe it, did not want to believe it. It was too simple, too cold, to be true. There was more to it, there had to be. Had she been too much trouble? The questions remained in her mind for years, and she cried many nights, wanting to know but no one helping her. Her aunt Jackie could not help her, for she only knew what she had shared. And her mother, whatever she knew, she was not telling. The emptiness it brought to Tamika's life was immeasurable. She often stared at other families, wondering, why not she? Why didn't she have a father?

The pain it must have caused her mother, Tamika could only guess, because her mother held it all in, trying to be strong, always giving advice after advice, as if she knew all the right things to do to make the world tilt in your favor. One thing she constantly advised was to never marry.

"You take care of yourself, child," she would tell Tamika, "not no man." She would shake her head. "And if you ever do let one 'em sweet talk you, you betta have all them degrees behind your name and a good job."

The words stuck with Tamika, who took them to heart, determined to establish herself and not wait for a man, except her definition of "establishing herself" was different than her mother's. Tamika wanted to be a singer, and her mother wanted her to go to college.

"You 'ain't gonna be nothin' but a statistic, girl, if you tryin' to make it out there," she told Tamika, referring to the music industry. "They don't care nothin' about no child like you. You got a good voice, yeah, but that ain't what it's about. They'll snatch away your innocence before you can blink." She would eye Tamika intently, pointing at her, almost threateningly. "And that's what 'dat business is all about."

"I'm sorry," Dee's voice interrupted her thoughts, suddenly reminding Tamika where she was. Dee did not know what else to say. She wanted to relate, but she could not, having grown up with both of her parents.

"It's okay," Tamika comforted. "You didn't do anything."

"But what happened?" Dee asked, eyes sympathetic. "I mean, if you don't mind me asking."

Tamika sighed. "Nothing really, I guess, except—." She took in a deep breath and heard her voice confessing everything before she agreed to share it. She went on and on, starting with how her mother never told her anything and the conversation with her aunt. She went on to explain her own frustration with her mother demanding so much from her.

"So she doesn't want you to sing, huh?"

She frowned, sighed, and shook her head. "Not as a career."

Dee was silent. She could relate to that. "My parents don't want me to either."

"Why not?" Tamika almost mumbled, staring out the window at the passing lights.

"I mean, I, uh," Dee tried to explain, searching for words. "You see, they're Muslim."

"Muslims aren't allowed to sing?" Tamika shot a disbelieving glance at Dee.

Dee forced a chuckle. "Well, uh, not, well," she began, fumbling for a good answer, searching for one that was the truth and protected her own faults at the same time. "They can sing, I suppose, but I guess the point is that, um, that women aren't supposed to sing in front of men."

"Really?" Tamika had never heard that before.

"You can ask Aminah," Dee suggested, not wanting to discuss it too much. It was too personal. "She can probably explain it better."

"What if a person sings, though? Are they still Muslim?"

"Yeah, yeah," Dee nodded emphatically. "They're still Muslim, but it's just not good to do, um, in public," she added.

"But what about you?"

She sighed sadly. What about her? She usually avoided that subject. "It's what I want to do," she confessed.

"What do your parents say?"

"They don't really know how much I like it, and they don't know that I," she paused, hesitating then decided there was no harm, "that I want to do it professionally."

"You do?" Tamika asked, suddenly interested.

"Yeah," Dee replied slowly, sadly.

Tamika nodded sympathetically. "You ever tell them?"

Dee forced laughter. "No," she replied. She sucked her teeth. "They won't agree, so it doesn't matter."

The car grew silent, and Dee exited the interstate and started down the street toward the mall. "But I'll have to talk to them," she continued in deep thought. "Soon," she added thoughtfully, seemingly more for herself than for Tamika.

"Why soon?"

Dee tucked her lips for a moment, not wanting to say too much, but a second later she did not care, wanting to talk to someone, anyone who could give her a sympathetic ear. Aminah would not want to hear it. "'Cause, um," she began, smiling self-consciously, nervous about the whole thing. "'Cause, um, there's kinda a chance, a good chance," she stated honestly, "that I could be going professional."

"You are!" Tamika stared at her in amazement.

"But don't say anything," Dee begged her.

"I won't," Tamika promised, still grinning with disbelief at Dee, who would not meet her stare.

"That's kinda why I'm tryin' to pick out this dress today."

"But I thought it was for the formal."

"It is."

Huh? Tamika did not understand.

"The producer—."

"The producer!" she repeated in excitement.

Dee laughed. "Listen."

"Oh, oh, okay," Tamika calmed herself, anticipating the explanation.

"He's coming to the formal."

"He is?"

"Yeah."

"Why?"

"I'm gonna do some songs there."

"Really?" Tamika was impressed, envious, wishing it were she. "How'd that happen?"

Dee laughed forcefully. "It's a long story, but, anyway, some people at the school knew some producers in the area and they mentioned me, and, so," she breathed, smiling, "they wanna hear me live."

"Wow ," Tamika was amazed. She could only dream of getting that far.

"They heard some of my tapes, but—."

"You have tapes!"

Oh no, what had she done? Dee had not meant to say that. "Oh, yeah, just a few," she told her quickly, downplaying it. "I did the recording at a friend's house."

"Wow," Tamika admired in a loud whisper, staring at Dee, amazed. If only she was so lucky.

"So, anyway," Dee continued, redirecting the conversation, "the producer is coming to the formal. His wife is the cousin of one of the staff there."

"At Streamsdale?"

"Yeah."

"Wow," Tamika kept saying, making Dee laugh uncomfortably.

"But they're coming to the formal, and that's where they say he's gonna decide."

She sucked her teeth, shaking her head. "You're so lucky."

Dee nodded smiling, unsure if it were actually luck or a huge test from God, the latter of which she feared she would fail.

"What are you gonna sing?"

"I don't know yet," she admitted, her immense concern traceable in her voice. "I'm still tryin' to decide."

Tamika nodded, taking it all in, still envious but happy for Dee.

"Hey," Dee said, as an idea came to her suddenly. "Why don't you write a few songs for me?"

"Me?" Tamika was stunned. Dee could not be serious.

"Yeah," Dee replied, the idea becoming more real by the moment. "Why not?"

"Well, I, uh," Tamika stuttered, wanting to jump up and scream "Yes!" at the top of her lungs but keeping her composure, however difficult it was. "Okay, I mean, if you think you'll like them."

"Of course I will," Dee told her. "And anyway, I do a lot of ad-lib as it is."

Tamika nodded slowly, heart racing, the reality of what Dee was saying building up in her mind, her heart. Was this really happening, she wondered? *This could be her foot in the door!*

"But I'll need it within a month or so, so I can practice."

"That's fine," Tamika agreed, her voice exhibiting a calm she did not recognize at the moment.

"Maybe I can see what you have already too."

"Okay," Tamika agreed, still trying to play it cool, as if this all were no big deal, though she detected a slight quiver in her voice.

"Oh yeah!" Dee said, smacking one hand against the steering wheel, as another idea came to her as she turned into the mall's parking lot. "Why don't you do a song with me?"

"A song *with* you?" Tamika repeated, hoping that Dee was asking what she thought she was hearing. She breathed slowly, carefully, and her heart began to pound wildly. *O God, was this really happening?*

"Yeah, at the formal."

"A-a-at the formal?" she stuttered dumbly, immediately feeling ashamed for her stupor. But Dee did not seem to notice.

"Yeah, why not?" Dee casually suggested.

"Me?" Tamika smiled nervously, glancing at Dee to make sure she was serious.

"Yeah," Dee replied excitedly. "It'll be fun!"

"*Me?*"

"Yes, stupid!" she teased, as she put the car in park. "Who else!"

"You serious?"

"Yeah, girl, you have a good voice."

"Well, okay," Tamika agreed cautiously, hoping Dee had heard. "If you want."

"Then the producer can hear you too."

"Okay." She swallowed. Inside, Tamika was ecstatic.

"Don't worry," Dee told her, turning off the engine. "It'll just be one song. Everyone'll just think that's how the song was supposed to go," she reassured.

"Okay," Tamika nodded, excitement filling her, unable to keep from grinning.

"And just for helping me out," Dee added with a smirk, "I'll have to pay you back." She winked playfully.

"Pay me back?" Tamika repeated in confusion, sensing Dee was up to something, a cautious grin forming on her face.

"Yeah, by buying you a dress for the formal."

Her eyes widened. Dee could not be serious. "How?" Tamika asked with concern, aware of how expensive formal dresses were, especially at malls.

Dee waved her hand at her, unlocking the doors with the press of a button. "I have enough money, don't worry."

"Do you know how much those types of dresses cost?"

She laughed. "Yes, I've only bought them, what, a zillion times?"

Oh yeah, the pageants. "Well, I mean, you don't have to—."

"I insist!" Dee chimed as they both got out of the car.

"Okay," Tamika said slowly, unsure if she should accept all of the offers but too excited to turn them down.

Dee laughed. "Come on!" she encouraged, putting an arm around Tamika playfully. "Let's go pick out the best dresses this mall has!"

Chapter Seven

The weekend went by too quickly for Tamika. She and Dee had spent it selecting songs from Tamika's collection. After Tamika sang several to Dee, Dee selected a couple of them for herself to sing at the formal, but she requested that Tamika write one especially for their duet, a task to which Tamika eagerly agreed. They had laughed and joked singing the songs, pushing and nudging each other if either one was off-key. Then they had sung popular songs, saying, "Do you remember this one?" each person singing her favorite.

Aminah had gone home for the weekend, so they had the apartment to themselves. But when she returned Sunday evening, their fun came to a sudden stop, Dee having warned Tamika not to tell Aminah of their plans.

"She'll kill me," Dee told her, half-joking, half-serious. "If Aminah finds out, she'll probably tell my parents." She added more seriously, more thoughtfully, evoking sympathy from Tamika, "And I want to tell them myself." She sighed. "I just can't figure out what to say."

Tamika wished she could help Dee, almost wanting to tell Dee's parents herself. She wanted to yell at them, tell them they were being selfish by imposing such strictness upon their daughter. Why did parents have to live through their children, Tamika wondered? Why couldn't people have their own lives, doing what they wanted to do? It was not fair, simply not fair.

"As-salaamu-'alaikum!" Aminah chimed Sunday evening, closing the front door behind her, disgusting Tamika by her gleeful smile. Dee and Tamika were sitting on the couch reviewing the lyrics to some of Tamika's songs when Aminah had come in. *Why did Aminah have to live with them?* It would have been perfect if she and Dee had the apartment to themselves.

"How's it going?" Aminah asked in a polite, routine manner, removing her coat.

"Pretty good," Dee replied, nodding. "You?"

"Alhamdulillaah[13]," Aminah responded, smiling, her cheerful mood apparent to both of her roommates.

"So I guess your weekend went okay?" Dee asked politely.

"Yeah," Aminah replied honestly, "real good."

"What'd you do?"

"Nothing really," she responded. "But your parents came over."

"They did?" Dee asked, smiling and feigning pleasure, suddenly self-conscious at the mention of them.

---

[13] "All praises are due to God alone."

"Yeah, and," Aminah shook her head, smiling reflectively, "it was just nice hearing them talk."

"About what?" Dee inquired, hoping her disinterest was not apparent in her voice.

"Just their life and everything."

Oh. About how Islam had changed them, Dee immediately knew. She did not want to hear anymore.

"But *mashaAllaah*[14]," Aminah remarked, hanging her coat in the closet and removing her large over garment, under which she was wearing a big shirt and pants. "It was nice."

Aminah paused then inquired, "How's your research going?"

"Mine?" Tamika asked, looking up from the paper that she was mindlessly skimming.

"Yeah, for your religion class." Aminah slipped her hands into her pant pockets walking over to the couch and standing there.

"It's going good," Tamika told her, uncomfortable with Aminah in such close proximity. "I turned in my note cards on Friday," she said, inconspicuously folding the paper she held so that Aminah could not see the songs.

"So the books were helpful?"

"Yeah, a lot. Thanks." She hoped Aminah would go away.

"It's no problem," Aminah assured her with a wave of her hand and a kind smile. "You have any questions on anything?"

"Uuum," Tamika said slowly, thinking about it, the gesture more out of politeness than serious thought. "A few."

"Well, anytime," Aminah offered, smiling, now heading to the bathroom.

"Thanks."

Dee and Tamika were quiet for some time until Dee stood, glancing at her watch. "Oh," she said, sucking her teeth and groaning as she realized something. "I'm supposed to be meeting with this girl in a few minutes."

"Really?"

"Yeah," she laughed. "I totally forgot."

"You betta go then."

She sighed. "Oh well, I guess I'll be a few minutes late."

"You betta hurry."

"It's nothing anyway," she assured Tamika. "It's just a study group."

"You have a test?"

"Yeah," Dee replied nonchalantly.

---

[14] A common Arabic termed used by Muslims in response to hearing some news; the term literally means, "It was God's will."

"Tomorrow?" Tamika stared at her incredulously.

Dee forced a chuckle. "Yeah, but it's not a big deal."

"Girl, you should've told me!"

"No, no, no," she insisted. "It's fine."

"In what class?"

"Bio."

"Biology!" Tamika could not believe what she was hearing.

"It's gonna be easy, anyway."

She stared at Dee. "But you didn't crack a book!"

"I looked over it Friday."

Tamika still stared at her in disbelief.

Dee laughed again. "Don't worry. I do this all the time."

Oh, Tamika remembered. She had heard that Dee was smart. "Okay," she said finally, still unsure, but giving in.

Dee started for the door. "Just pray for me," she grinned, grabbing her coat.

"Whatever." Tamika forced a smile, still amazed at Dee's ability to do well without studying hard.

A moment later the living room grew quiet as the door closed and Dee disappeared into the hallway. Not knowing what else to do, Tamika picked up the paper Dee had given her Friday and that she left on the table next to the couch. It had been on her mind for quite some time. The sound of water running in the bathroom was all Tamika could hear amidst the silence of the apartment building since most students had not yet returned from their weekend activities.

Tamika sighed, now holding the pamphlet, and she began reading as she relaxed on the couch. One section in particular jolted her curiosity: "Why Are There Different Religions?"

Yes, why were there? Tamika wanted to know, the bold question on the page the same one that resonated in her mind.

> "There are different religions practiced today, namely that of Judaism, Christianity and Islam due to certain historical factors that caused the evolution of what is commonly referred to as 'the three Abrahamic faiths.' Judaism came about after Prophet Jesus came to call the people of Israel to submit to God and to accept him (Jesus) as their messenger. However, some people, although professed followers of Prophet Moses, refused to accept the message of Prophet Jesus, thereby becoming disbelievers and forming what is today called 'Judaism,' whose people

still await the Messiah, although he has already come in the form of the prophet Christ Jesus.

"Christianity began when..."

Tamika felt her heart pounding nervously. Was it possible that she would now find out?

"...Prophet Jesus was sent to the people of Israel, and his followers accepted his message and worshipped God alone, as Prophet Jesus did and instructed them to do. However, after Prophet Jesus was raised up to his Lord after his mission was complete, the idea of the trinity was introduced, in which Jesus was said to be one of three in the Godhead. Paul, who never met Jesus or saw him alive, was the primary teacher of this concept, and in time, it was officially embraced by the Christian church. However, during that time, there existed monotheistic Christians who opposed the innovation in the religion, and they opposed the new teachings of Jesus' divinity, while upholding his teaching that he was a prophet. Long after Jesus was gone, the compilation of the Bible began, and the book underwent numerous changes, resulting in several versions still used today, none of which contain a completely accurate description of Jesus' message. The Bible is currently used to propagate the divinity of Jesus, although Jesus never witnessed or oversaw any of its compilation, nor was he on earth when his divinity was being taught, and he himself never claimed divinity."

It made sense, this Tamika could not deny. She had heard bits of information about how much Paul had influenced the religion of Christianity, and she also knew, as most Christians did, that the Bible had gone through several changes. But whenever asked about them, she, like most others, always responded that the changes were "inspired by God." Tamika had never given the response much thought, but she now questioned the validity of the claim. If the book were actually from God, why did "corrections" have to take place at all? How could God "inspire" a book that was wrong to begin with? Did He later *discover* He was wrong, then "inspire" the corrections? Or worse, he needed humans to proofread and correct His revelation? This tormented Tamika's better senses. She had never thought much about these inconsistencies before, having taken the advice of her preacher and mother, to "not question God."

She continued reading:

> "When Prophet Muhammad (s), the last messenger and prophet sent by God to humankind, came to call people to the religion taught by Noah, Abraham, Moses, and Jesus, people of all nationalities, races, cultures, and religions, including Christianity and Judaism, accepted his message, and Islam became the fastest growing religion on earth and remains so today. However, like some Jews during the time of Jesus, people rejected God's messenger and continued to teach and live what is now common day Christianity, and thus became disbelievers by rejecting a messenger of God."

As Tamika reviewed the brochure, the possible veracity of Islam gnawed at her conscience and rekindled the same questions of faith that had plagued her since the beginning of her investigation. She swallowed, suddenly feeling ashamed. Was she a *disbeliever*? A rejecter of God's messenger? The question taunted her, the answer haranguing her. But she did not want to acknowledge it, mentally swatting it away like a nagging fly buzzing around her head.

"Oh," Aminah commented with pleasure, her sudden presence startling Tamika, who had not even heard her come out of the bathroom. "So Durrah gave it to you?"

Tamika forced a smile, her mind still storming with doubts and confusion, realizing that Aminah was referring to the packet. "Yeah."

"Well, let me know if you have any questions," Aminah offered smiling, now walking into the kitchen. "I'll be in the room studying."

"Thanks."

"No problem."

"The Amazing Claim of Modern Day Christianity," the title seemed to jump out to her. She knew better than to read on, but inside, she knew she had to. Too drawn in to put it down, she began reading,

> "Given that God's message is and always has been to worship God alone, it is indeed amazing that most sects of Christianity claim the exact opposite. The prophets Noah, Abraham, Moses, and others came with the message to worship God alone as the only path to Heaven, whereas modern day Christians claim that the only path to Heaven is to worship God as part of a trinity—the Father, son, and the holy spirit—a requirement that they attribute to Prophet Jesus, who was gone long before the concept was even

introduced to the Christian church. The worshipping of created gods is the gravest of all sins, so much so that the caution against it is mentioned in two of the Ten Commandments and can still be found throughout today's version of the Bible.

"Modern day Christians go on to say that those who worship God alone and associate no partners with Him, namely the Muslims, will burn eternally in Hell for the grave "sin" of not worshipping Prophet Jesus as their Lord and Savior. They further claim that the Prophet Jesus, a messenger of God, called people to worship him along with God, although not a single verse or quote from Jesus exists in the Bible to substantiate such a claim (rather, this inference is drawn based on human interpretation of ambiguous texts). They also teach that this is the entire purpose of Prophet Jesus coming to earth, yet no such claims come from Jesus himself."

As Tamika read, she was dumbfounded, fumbling for an intelligent rebuttal, finding none. What could she say?

"Some substantiate this claim of Jesus' divinity by referring to the miracles that he performed. However, every messenger of God performed miracles with the permission of God for the purpose of making it undeniably clear that the message with which they were sent was true and that they were not false messengers. The proof of this fact can still be found in the Bible, which quotes Jesus as saying, 'Unless you people see miraculous signs and wonders, you will never believe.'[15]

"God confirms in the Qur'an that the miracles are merely signs from God when He quotes Jesus as saying what can be translated to mean, 'I have come to you with a Sign from your Lord, in that I make for you out of clay, as it were, the figure of a bird, and breathe into it, and it becomes a bird by God's leave: And I heal those born blind, and the lepers, and I quicken the dead, by God's leave; and I declare to you what you eat, and what you store in your houses. Surely, therein is a Sign for you if you did believe.'[16]"

---

[15] John, 4:48
[16] *Ali Imran*, 3:49

She held the pamphlet, almost trembling at what was before her. Her heart sank and began to race, pounding uncomfortably in her chest, and she could almost feel it in her throat. She read on, reading passage after passage from the Bible itself, where it was reporting statements from Jesus himself that proved his lack of divinity:

> "'My teaching is not my own. It comes from him who sent me. If anyone chooses to do God's will, he will find out whether my teaching comes from God or whether I speak on my own.'[17] 'I have not come on my own, but he sent me. Why is not my language clear to you?'[18] 'By myself I can do nothing.'[19]"

The section ended, leaving Tamika feeling shamefully bare, stripped of her beliefs—of her self, the page saying what her heart had cried for years but what her mind had been unable to admit:

> "Would it not be an amazing, misleading thing for God to do, Who is High above such misleading, to first tell humans through Noah, Abraham, Moses, and others to worship Him alone as the only path to Heaven, then change His mind entirely when He sends His prophet Jesus, by calling people to worship a man along with Him as the only path to Heaven, rendering the earlier message of the prophets the path to Hell? Perhaps, those who believe such an enormity, which accuses God of both lying and changing His "mind," should refer to the Bible, which still contains the following passage: 'God is not a man, that he should not lie, nor is he the son of man, that he should change his mind.'[20]"

The words stung, penetrating Tamika's heart and mind, and internally, she submitted to the truth. She was too weak to fight it anymore. It was futile to deny or oppose it any longer. She had been wrong. Islam was true after all. Tamika did not need anymore convincing, but she read on anyway:

---

[17] John 7:16
[18] ibid, 8:42-43
[19] ibid, 5:30
[20] Numbers, 23:19

> "In summarizing this section on Christianity, it is best
> to end it as God has stated in His final revealed book, the
> Qur'an, the translation of which is as follows, 'The truth
> (comes) from your Lord alone, So be not of those who
> doubt.'[21] "

Doubt. No, she no longer had that. She knew. She was certain. It was staring her in the face. And although her heart and mind already submitted, she was not ready to face the truth, not yet. That would mean too many things, far too many things that she did not want to acknowledge. Maybe later, but not then. She only wanted to know, what next for her?

"Why You Should Be a Muslim," the title of the section stood out, inviting. Should she read it? Could she handle a final blow, a knockout, one that could possibly drain the very life from her?

It did not matter then, she realized. She had read too much already. What would more do other than confirm what she now already knew?

"Islam, without a doubt, is not in need of people," she read. "Rather, people are in need of Islam." She sighed, feeling weak, knowing God was watching her, waiting to see what she would do...

> "...By becoming Muslim, each person returns to the religion
> that God intended for every human being, and the person
> returns to the religion practiced by Noah, Abraham, Moses,
> Jesus, Muhammad, and all of the other prophets and
> messengers. Furthermore, by becoming a Muslim, a person
> enters into the only form of worship that God will accept.
> A translation of what God says in the Qur'an is as follows,
> 'If anyone desires a religion other than Islam, it will never
> be accepted of him, and in the Hereafter, he will be in the
> ranks of those who lost (all spiritual good).'[22]"

Lost? Tamika did not want to lose everything she had dreamed about and hoped for. She had always felt an eagerness for something more, this life having brought with it too much pain...

> "Thus the reason why each person should become a
> Muslim becomes clear. Islam is the only path through
> which a person can avoid the ultimate loss in the Hereafter,
> which is eternal Hell Fire. When one accepts Islam and

---

[21] *Ali Imran,* 3:60
[22] ibid, 3:85

dies a Muslim, he is guaranteed Heaven. Whereas if a person dies a non-Muslim, he is guaranteed an eternal abode in Hell Fire, if he had heard of Islam while alive..."

...She had certainly heard. There was no chance for her except to submit...

"...A Muslim who dies a sinner may enter Hell Fire for purification if God chooses to place him there, but he will not remain there forever, on account of having fulfilled the minimal requirement that God has mandated for the human being to enter Heaven, which is dying a Muslim. On the contrary, no matter how much good a non-Muslim does, no matter how much a non-Muslim claims to love God, he will never enter Heaven, because a mere acceptance of God's existence and a claimed love of Him is not enough to earn God's mercy, as God says in the Qur'an, 'Say, (O Muhammad, to the people), 'If you love God, follow me. God will love you and forgive you your sins. For God is Oft-Forgiving, Most Merciful,'[23] and 'As for those who disbelieve and die as disbelievers, never will be accepted from any (of them) such as much gold as the earth contains, though they should offer it for ransom. For such is (in store) a penalty grievous, and they will have no helpers.'[24] God also says, 'Those who disbelieve, hinder men from the path of God, and resist the Messenger after guidance has been clearly shown to them will not injure God in the least, but He will make their deeds of no effect'[25]..."

O Lord! Tamika's heart cried, terrified. She did not want to be of those people!

"...Obedience to God's Messenger is the only form of love that God accepts from His creatures, and this is fulfilled only through becoming Muslim, a person who not only claims to believe in and love God but who illustrates that love by submitting completely to and worshipping Him as God wishes, not as the person chooses for himself."

---

[23] ibid, 3:31
[24] ibid, 3:91
[25] *Ash-Shoora*, 42:32

Tamika began to ponder how she had come to learn all of this. How was it that she had come to live with Dee and Aminah? Luck? Coincidence? She doubted it, having always believed that everything happened for a reason, a predefined reason, planned by none other than God. Then why was she handed this pamphlet? After being kicked out of her room, she had thought matters could get no worse. But they had. She was now at risk of losing her soul...to Hell. Eternally.

"How To Become a Muslim," the next section was titled. She wanted to put down the pamphlet, but she could not. God would not accept this, she knew. It was too late, the answer now literally in her hands:

"A person becomes Muslim by testifying, *Laa ilaaha illa Allah Muhammadun Rasoolu Allaah,*" or what can be translated as, 'None has the right to be worshipped except God alone, (and) Muhammad is the Messenger of God.' Once a person is certain that Islam is true, he or she should not delay this testimony..."

...O Lord!

"...This testimony of faith does not need to be done in public; nor does it need to be done in Arabic, although this is preferable. One may say it in his or her own native language whenever he or she can, but it should be done at the person's first opportunity (although it will still be valid later), even if it is said aloud in the privacy of one's own room..."

Tamika glanced up, looking around the room. Aminah was now in the bedroom, and Tamika could hear her moving about. Should she go ahead and say it? Her hands trembled. She was scared, uncertain, but she knew she should. She opened her mouth to start to say it, but she stopped herself. *I can't,* she weakened. *I'm not ready.* There were so many questions she still had, about covering, singing, women and men's relationship, marriage, and many other things. She was not ready to give up everything. She did not doubt it was right—and worth it (for what were those things compared to one's soul?)—but not just yet, she told herself, not now. Besides, she reasoned, she knew nothing of how to pray or anything.

"...Furthermore, a person does not have to know how to pray..."

What was she reading!

> " ...or perform any other required act of the Muslim before
> making the testimony, and a person should <u>not</u> wait to
> become Muslim in order to learn these requirements. The
> only requirement for reciting these words is that a person
> knows, accepts, and sincerely believes that God alone
> deserves to be worshipped and that His last Messenger is
> Prophet Muhammad (s), meanwhile understanding and
> accepting that he or she must obey God and His Messenger
> after the testimony, which is an agreement between a person
> and his or her Lord. However, after the testimony, the
> person is required to do his or her best to learn what is
> required so that the person may fulfill the requirements to
> the best of his or her ability..."

Tamika fit those requirements, did she not? Something egged her on, pushing her to say it, but something else pulled at her telling her no, she was not ready. After wrestling with herself for a few minutes, she submitted to the latter. What would she say to her mother, her family? To Makisha? They would think she had gone nuts. They would never understand. No, she was not ready. She would have to wait until she had enough courage to tell them...

"...For no one knows when he or she will die...," the words warned her... "and delaying the testimony can be detrimental to one's very soul..." She did not want *that*.

> " ...because if someone dies after hearing of Islam but never
> accepting it, he or she will never enter Paradise (Heaven)
> and rather, the person will abide in Hell Fire forever for
> neglecting the most basic requirement of human existence
> on this earth, which is the complete submission to the will
> of God, which is only achieved through Islam."

Chapter Eight

"It makes sense and all," Tamika admitted to Aminah that night during an interview session for her paper, sparked mostly by what she had read earlier. "I just don't know about some things."

Aminah, who had inquired about Tamika's opinion on what she had read, nodded, listening, as Tamika's concerns were common for those studying about Islam. "Like what things?"

Tamika contorted her face and replied, "Like dressing up in all those clothes and wearing a sheet on my head."

Aminah smiled complacently, unstirred by the comment, having grown accustomed to non-Muslims' displeasure with Muslim dress. "In Islam," she explained, "the Muslim woman's body is private, her personal business, a beauty enjoyed by her husband."

"But why can't she wear what she wants?"

"She wears what God wants," Aminah replied simply. "Like the owner of any entity decides what its workers wear, God decides what His creatures wear." She paused. "You actually *can* wear what you want," she clarified so as to not be misunderstood, "so long as it fits God's conditions." She compared, "Just like any institution, like school, stipulates conditions for dress, and so long as your choice does not violate the basic code, you're fine."

Tamika understood, but she did not want to, frantically searching her mind for any excuse for it to be wrong.

Aminah continued, "Anyway, the Muslim woman views her body somewhat like you may view your money. If you had lots of money, would you pin it allover your clothes or put it in a transparent bag and walk down the street?"

"No," Tamika replied, chuckling.

"Why? Because it's valuable to you," Aminah answered her own question. "And it's not that you think that everyone is a criminal that makes you tuck your money away," she pointed out. "It's just in case someone is, it's protected. Or," she added, "it may be in case the sight of the money may tempt a person to take it, even if he is not a criminal. Similarly," she compared, "our body is valuable to us, and we don't flaunt our body, just like you don't flaunt your money. Like your money, our body is ours, used and enjoyed only by those who are supposed to enjoy it. We don't desire to flaunt our body anymore than you desire to flaunt your wealth." She paused then added, "Because *we,*" she said, distinguishing the Muslim women from others, "value our body."

Tamika nodded, understanding. "But can't you just dress modestly then?"

"Who defines what's modest?"

She shrugged her shoulders. "Just whatever society you live in or your culture."

"And if I live in a nudist colony?"

She laughed. "That's extreme."

"Not for those who live there," Aminah pointed out. "It's the custom there to be nude." she argued, "So does that make putting on a string bikini modest?"

"No," Tamika replied emphatically, chuckling at the ridiculousness of the example.

"But says who?"

She shrugged again. "It's obvious."

"To whom?"

She gave up, not knowing what to say.

"The point is that there has be a line drawn somewhere," Aminah stated finally. "And who has a better right to draw that line than the One who created us?"

Tamika was silent.

"Anyway," Aminah continued, "The dress of Muslim women should not be strange to people, especially Christians." She explained, "This has always been the dress of religious women," she pointed out. "Even during prophet Moses' and Jesus' time and before that."

"How do we know that though?" Tamika asked with skepticism.

"Well," Aminah replied calmly, smiling, "we know because Islam has been the religion of humans since the time of Adam. But even Christians acknowledge that women covered similar to how Muslims do."

"Christians don't believe that," Tamika contended.

"Well, look at the nuns."

"They're not Christians. They're Catholic."

"Still," Aminah insisted, "why do they dress like that?"

Tamika shrugged, not caring. "I don't know."

"First of all," Aminah stated, "the Bible says women should cover their head." She paused, and upon noticing Tamika's disagreeable expression, suggested, "Look in II Corinthians. But anyway," she continued, "the nuns dress like that because they know that the religion commands women to cover themselves, except what's generally acceptable to uncover, like face and hands." She went on, "And it was only recently that even in America women dress like they do. There was a time, not too long ago, that a woman was considered 'fast' if she even showed her ankles."

Yeah, Tamika had read about that.

"It's the recent so called Sexual Revolution that called for the indecency of women and their sexual exploitation," Aminah explained. "And one of the things these people called for was the undressing of women." Aminah breathed, "But anyway, even when Christians paint who they think is Mary, they paint something on her head covering her hair."

"But still," Tamika contended, unsure what her argument would be. "I don't agree with all of that stuff. I mean," she admitted, "there are a lot things about Islam I understand and can deal with. But," she wrinkled her nose and shook her head with displeasure, "some of it, I just can't get with."

"Well," Aminah interjected calmly from her place near Tamika on the couch. "The way I look at it is like this," she began, eyes intent, serious. "I don't search for a religion that I agree with, or one that fits my lifestyle." She paused, letting the words sink in. "I search for what God's religion is, and then," she raised her voice slightly, underscoring her point, "and *then* I change my opinions and lifestyle to fit *that.*"

Tamika was silent, speechless.

"'Cause we're all gonna run across things in life that we don't like or agree with, but even as young as we are, we know that many of those things turned out to be true after we learned a few things about life. And what did we do? Did we stick to what we *thought*? Or did we just change our thinking to fit reality?"

She did not respond, unable to, incapable of arguing with Aminah. "But I don't know," she insisted stubbornly, not wanting to give up what she loved. "Why can't women sing?"

"Sing?" Aminah repeated, confused. "What makes you think women can't sing?"

"Dee said they can't sing in public, or something like that."

"Oh," she smiled, nodding, realizing what Tamika was saying. "It's just that in Islam, a women's beauty is not to be shared with the world. Only other women, her close male relatives, and, most specifically, her husband can see and enjoy her beauty."

"But how is singing—."

"And a woman's voice is considered part of that beauty," she answered before Tamika could ask.

"So she can't even talk in front of men!" Tamika asked in protest, thinking that to be extreme.

"No, that's not what I'm saying," Aminah clarified. "She can talk in front of other men."

"Oh," Tamika exhaled, relieved but still skeptical.

"But she can't purposely beautify her voice in front of strange men."

"But singing is not doing that," she argued.

"Singing is not only doing that," Aminah disagreed, "that's the entire definition of singing."

"But not for strange men."

She decided to tackle the issue differently. "What's the purpose of singing?"

"To just sing," Tamika responded defensively.

"To just sing?" Aminah repeated with a smirk, staring at her as if to say, *"Come on!"* But instead, she leveled, "Now, you know that's not true."

"It *is*," Tamika insisted.

"So I can just get up there and sing and I'll sell a million records."

"If you can sing," she chuckled.

"What do you mean?"

"If you sound good," Tamika concurred.

"Exactly," Aminah nodded with a smile. "So it's for the purpose of people listening to a beautiful voice, am I correct?"

Tamika shrugged. "I guess you can say that."

"So then what's the point of men listening to you?"

"What's the harm?"

"What's the good?" Aminah challenged.

"I mean," Tamika defended, "it's not like the world is full of perverts."

"That's not the point," Aminah replied. "Similar to the fact that my covering is not to say the world is full of perverts. That's irrelevant. The rule is to cut off the path to evil, not to assume anything about the people who are being cut off. Just like in Islam," she gave an analogy, "a man and a woman who are not related are not allowed to be in a room alone together."

Tamika's mother had once told her to never do that, telling her it led to "no good."

"This rule doesn't only apply to people who aren't friends or men whom you don't trust. It's a protective action, not an assumption or accusation against a particular man. The prohibition simply closes the doors to fornication or adultery even *possibly* occurring. The same goes for the rule on singing."

"But how is that the same as being alone in a room with a man?"

"It's not the same, and I'm not saying it is," Aminah told her. "But I used that example to show how God doesn't just tell us *not* to do a sin, He tells us to not even go near it."

"But if I'm singing in a studio a million miles away from a man, how is that tempting?"

"But is your voice staying in the studio, or is it being recorded to go into the homes in which men live, making that same singing present in their very home?"

Tamika did not respond.

"And anyway," Aminah added, "nowadays, singing is not just about a singer's voice, especially when the singer is a woman. She's all over T.V., in magazines, plastered on posters, and throughout newspapers. She also does enticing videos, which clearly awaken men's desires—on purpose," she added for emphasis. "She's always half naked, no," she corrected with a chuckle, "she's always ninety percent naked. And, in reality," she pointed out more seriously, "popular singers, especially the women, are more prostitutes than they are entertainers.

"And you can say what you want," Aminah continued before Tamika could respond, "but that's what it means to 'make it,'" she said, gesturing her fingers to underscore "make it." She forced laughter. "I don't even know how people convince themselves it's innocent when you can just go ask the average teenage boy, or even adult man, why he likes a particular singer." She laughed again. "And if he's *honest*," she argued, "it does *not* boil down to a good voice." She hesitated but decided it relevant to add, "It's a good something else he likes."

Tamika chuckled, unable to control it. But she did not know what to say.

"And that proves what the whole purpose of women singing in public is in the first place," Aminah argued convincingly. "And I think the concerts and lives of women singers speak for themselves."

There was a long pause.

"In any case," Aminah concluded with a sigh, "the prohibition is not against singing per se, but a woman singing in front of strange men. If a woman really just wants to sing because she enjoys singing, and her intentions are in fact pure, then what's the harm in singing only for women?"

What was the harm? Tamika did not know. Was there any? "It's just inconvenient," she blurted, the argument having come to her suddenly. "I mean, are we supposed to ask all the men to leave because I'm singing?" She chuckled at the ridiculousness of it. "Goodness!"

Aminah was silent, unmoved. She was not smiling, finding no humor in Tamika's words, but she waited for her to finish. "In Islam," she stated finally, her voice commanding respect, "we submit to *God*. And He's the One who outlined the laws of singing. And singing is not prohibited, just restricted, in that no musical instruments are used and that the men and women are not mixed. Now," she leveled with Tamika, "you can call it extreme all you want to. And, besides the fact that God knows what He's talking about and we should just submit," she began, "both you and I know what goes on at parties where music and singing is playing and where men and women are together." She paused then added, "I've seen it."

Tamika did not reply. She had seen it too, having gone to many parties with Makisha on weekends.

"And in any case, the believer does not view her time on this earth as time to fulfill her desires and be diverted by petty things like music and singing. She's too concerned about her soul, because she knows life is too short." Aminah added, "And she loves her Lord more than this world."

Tamika avoided Aminah's gaze, the memory of what she had read earlier revisiting her, that no one ever knew when she would die. And from that perspective, nothing mattered at all. Nothing. Except going to Heaven.

"The Muslim," Aminah explained, emphasizing the word, redirecting the conversation to reiterate her point, "submits to God. Once it is clear that God said it, they submit, no questions asked. This is the way of the believer, even if it does not make sense to him."

Yes, Tamika had believed that, even when devoted to Christianity. Hadn't she accepted the trinity on that premise? "But what's wrong with questioning?" she wanted to know.

"Nothing," Aminah replied, "if it's to seek understanding or to ascertain the truth. But if it's directed at the truth itself," she paused to allow the enormity of the statement to resonate in Tamika's mind, "that's where problems arise."

Tamika did not respond.

"Anyway, what would you think of a person who came here to Streamsdale and sat in your Calculus class and asked everyday really loud, 'Why is this chair here!' or 'Why did they paint the walls this color!' and they kept asking these questions until they never even heard a lesson of the class and thus failed? What do you think of her?"

She chuckled. "That's crazy."

"Why?" Aminah inquired, leading Tamika to her own answer.

"Because," Tamika replied as if that were a sufficient response.

"Because what?"

"Because," she laughed, "that's stupid. They should just do the work and not worry about that."

Aminah smiled, "And that's exactly what we should do."

Tamika wrinkled her forehead, then realized a moment later what Aminah was saying. "But—."

"But what?" Aminah challenged calmly.

Tamika groaned, frustrated. "But still," she insisted, searching for a counterattack. Then she thought of one. Before considering how it sounded, she argued, "I can't accept any religion where the men can oppress the women."

Aminah stared at her incredulously, squinting her eyes, blinking. "Excuse me?"

"Don't the Muslim men oppress their women?" Tamika now asked it carefully, as if she wanted to know, having realized how the original statement must have sounded to Aminah.

"Before I answer that, let me ask you something."

She shrugged in agreement, self-conscious all of a sudden, ashamed for having offended Aminah. "Okay."

"Do men oppress women?" Aminah inquired.

"Some do," Tamika admitted nonchalantly, shrugging.

"Do Christian men oppress women?"

"Some," she replied impatiently.

"Do Jewish men oppress women?"

She sighed. "Some."

"Do atheist men oppress women?"

"I'm sure some do."

"Now," Aminah said calmly, intently, "to answer your question." She repeated it, "Do Muslim men oppress women?" She nodded. "Yes, some do. Just like other men. *But,*" she said, emphasizing, "if your question is, does Islam tell them to? Then the answer is no. And quite the contrary."

Tamika nodded, understanding, embarrassed because she had not thought of the obvious herself, suddenly feeling like a bigot, her ignorance too apparent to hide. "But uh," she fumbled for a response, "I know of a lot of Muslims who say it's their religion," she exaggerated, having only heard others saying they knew of Muslims who said so.

"To oppress women?" Aminah speculated, finding it difficult to believe any sane Muslim would assert such a thing.

"I mean," Tamika shrugged and admitted, "not oppression, but that the woman has to listen to the man."

"If you're asking about the man being the head of the household in Islam, then yes, this is true." Aminah paused then added for effect, "Just like in Judaism and Christianity."

Tamika shook her head, intending to clarify but unsure of what she was going to say. "No, I mean, like there are some Muslim women who are treated badly and say it's their religion."

"Okay," Aminah began, "let's say this is true. In fact," she added, hypothesizing, "let's say for the sake of argument that every Muslim woman is mistreated by a Muslim man, which of course is not the case, but anyway, let's just say that."

Tamika listened.

"So what does that have to do with truth versus falsehood?" Aminah inquired, becoming silent as she waited for a response. But Tamika said nothing. "So am I going to go to Hell eternally," she challenged, "because some *people,* and Muslims *are* people," she reminded, "are doing wrong? Are you going to fail your class, on purpose, because you walk in and all the other students are playing around, and you know you need the class to graduate?" She waited. "Would you?"

"I see what you're saying," Tamika admitted in defeat, not wanting to respond directly to the inquiry.

"And the same goes for religion, at least for me," Aminah clarified. "And I know Muslims aren't perfect, but even your religion teaches you that humans aren't perfect."

Yes, Tamika could not deny that.

"But I'm not going to turn my back on truth," Aminah stated truthfully.

Tamika could sense the conviction in her words, and she was slightly envious of Aminah for her strong faith.

"Not for *any* person," Aminah stressed. "I don't care what they do or say. If I know something is essential for my soul, you betta believe I'm gonna do it," she promised. "Even if I'm the only one."

Tamika was speechless.

"And I personally have no problem having a man as the leader of my household," Aminah stated peremptorily. "I don't worry about being 'inferior,' because I'm not here for my husband. I'm here for God, and if God is pleased with me, who cares?" She continued, "I look at my role as a wife as I do with any role I fulfill, whether a student or employee or what have you. When I register for school, I accept that my teacher decides what assignments I'll have, but does that make me inferior to her?"

No response.

"Because I do some things for my boss at work, does that make me inferior to him?"

No response.

"So when I obey my husband, as every wife should, does that make me inferior?"

No response.

"Anyway," Aminah continued, "it's not like a woman has no say. A Muslim is instructed in the Qu'ran to conduct affairs by mutual consultation. Mutual consultation," she repeated, wanting to be certain that Tamika had heard. "And that includes a husband discussing key family decisions with his wife. It'd be chaos if there was no predefined leader, one who would have the final say," she argued. "And God appointed man as that person. And who am I to question God?"

Tamika said nothing.

Aminah shook her head, disappointed. "It's crazy how people get so diverted by insignificant details, but they accept those same things in other parts of their life, like at work or even as a citizen.

"Do you view yourself as inferior to the governor or the president?"

Tamika shook her head. "No."

"And don't you have a say?"

She nodded, considering it. "Yeah."

"And so does a wife. And if a man takes advantage of his role, that doesn't speak against the religion, that speaks against him. Just like if a woman takes advantage of her husband," Aminah explained. "As some do," she reminded. "And a man who mistreats his wife, like a wife who mistreats her husband, will have to answer to God for it, and he may just get punished in Hell for it while the wife goes straight to Heaven." She paused. "And who's inferior then?"

There was a brief pause.

"I don't spend my life questioning God," Aminah shared a minute later, as if giving advice. "Because as God tells us in the Qur'an, God will not be questioned about what He does, but you will be questioned about what you do."

Tamika did not want to say anything else, but she could not help but wonder, which was why she asked, "But you don't feel subjugated in a religion where the man is the leader of everything?"

Aminah was silent, a small smile developing on her face. A few moments later, she spoke. "I always wondered how Christians could ask that," she remarked thoughtfully. "I mean, here I am, a Muslim, who worships God and accepts that He placed man as the leader, at least in human affairs like government and family. But then I'm questioned about this role by a Christian, who views it as subjugation, inferiority, and whatever other demeaning term society wishes to label it." She shook her head in disbelief. "But for the Christian, the man is not only the leader," she stated, "but God himself."

Defeated, Tamika could not muster up a response. She had never heard of such an analogy, but it was true. How was it that Christians criticized Muslims for their position on the man being the leader, when they worshipped a man? Certainly, if any of the two cases pointed to the inferiority of women, it had to be the case in which the man was God. The man as the head of the household was understandable, but God?

"But to answer your question," Aminah remarked, interrupting Tamika's thoughts, "no, I don't have any problem with it."

Exhausted, Tamika did not care anymore. She had now come to terms with the fact the Christian religion was not true. Islam now nagged at her conscience, calling her to submit. Deep inside, Tamika wanted to argue, to fight the inevitable, wanting to find any excuse not to do what she knew she should. In reality, none of the Islamic mandates were truly extreme, or even unjust, in her view, not the women's dress and not even the women's role in marriage and society. Inside, it all made sense to her, and much of it she had known all her life, at least internally. She had always sensed the righteousness of a religious woman covering her body. She had always sensed the natural inclination to accept the man as leader, and she herself would hate to have a husband who was not the leader, maintainer, and protector of the family.

But submitting was another issue altogether. She was not ready—or perhaps just unwilling—to give in just yet. Yes, she was aware that life was about sacrifice, sacrifice for God. She knew that God's mercy could not be earned by merely doing what she wanted, expecting eternal bliss after she died. Although she had been taught that at church, she knew better, and she simply could no longer accept it. Guilt haunted her whenever she sinned, but she would convince herself that all she had to do was accept Jesus and it was "all good." But her conscience would tug at her, because it did not seem right to live that way. So she had left it all alone, the boyfriends and the drinking. She now lived an alcohol-free, celibate life, having recently become a "born again Christian" who was "saved." Or so she thought.

But now, even that was not enough. Her entire foundation had been wrong. She thought she had the ticket to Heaven, erroneously thinking the Muslims were on the wrong path. But it was she who was on the wrong path, astray, headed for nothing but misery—unrelenting misery—in the next world.

But now she knew.

But why her! She did not want to know the truth, not then, maybe when she was seventy years old, but not as a college student! Her life was just beginning. Couldn't she have all her fun first? Couldn't she just be a singer? That was all she ever wanted to do! *Was that too much to ask!*

"Ain't nothin' worth turnin' your back on the Lord," her mother would often tell her, her voice now echoing in Tamika's mind. "You got somethin' you ain't doin' right, you betta give it up, child, 'ain't worth it."

But she wanted to!

Logically, Tamika knew it was not worth it, but still, she loved it. *Then why not just sing for women,* she wondered? No, that was not her dream. She wanted to be an R&B singer, like the famous singers on television and on the radio, a modern day Billie Holiday.

Was it the money she wanted?

No, it couldn't be.

The fame?

No, she was not vain.

Or was she?

Then why not just sing for women? Her thoughts tugged at her.

It was no fun.

No fun? What was she saying, that she *wanted* men to hear her? But why? Perhaps, she *was* vain. Maybe she did want to be like the other singers, practically prostitutes, with her "ninety percent" naked body plastered on billboards, posters, and magazines. Maybe she *wanted* to do "enticing" videos and have men desire her...

"You have anymore questions for your paper?" Aminah inquired.

"Uh," Tamika searched her mind, glancing at the notebook in her lap, gathering her thoughts all of a sudden.

"Oh yeah," Tamika said, pulling herself together as she read her notes. "What's this jihad?" she said slowly, hoping she was pronouncing it correctly. That was a major question Tamika had had. She could understand obeying a man and covering her body, but she did not support terrorism, even if done in the name of God.

"Jihad?" Aminah repeated.

"Yeah."

"That's an Arabic word meaning a struggle, but under certain circumstances it can mean physically fighting in the battlefield."

"What?" Tamika asked incredulously. "So they *do* go out and fight people and say it's for God?"

Aminah chuckled. "No, I didn't say that."

"But aren't they fighting people?"

"Who's they?"

Who were *they*? People Tamika had seen on television? "Uh, the Muslims."

"What Muslims?" Aminah inquired.

Tamika did not respond.

"We have to be careful of stereotypes," Aminah cautioned. "Just like you wouldn't want a person to view blacks as they're portrayed on television, you shouldn't view Muslims, or any people for that matter, based on what you see, or hear, on television." She added, "Even if it's the news. I don't think I have to convince you that even that's biased."

Tamika nodded. "That's true, but I was just saying—."

"I know," Aminah cut in, "that's what most people say."

"So what is jihad then?" Tamika asked her question again, smiling self-consciously. "I guess I should just leave it like that and you can answer."

"Jihad," Aminah replied, "as I explained before, is simply a struggle, and sometimes it means physical fighting. And I guess you can look at the fight as you might look at the fights American soldiers partake in. Certainly, we don't look at them as terrorists, do we?"

"No," Tamika replied emphatically. Several of her friends and family were in the military, some having even fought before. She definitely did not view them as terrorists.

"But American soldiers fight in wars," Aminah pointed out.

"But it's to defend and help people," Tamika interjected.

"Well," Aminah replied, "in Islam, it's similar to that. Just like America does not tolerate oppression in the world and at times goes to help those who are oppressed, Muslims are not allowed to permit people to be oppressed. And when the oppression occurs, Muslims must defend and help the oppressed. These are the two types of jihad, the first being when Muslims fight to help people who are being oppressed, like America does at times, and the second being when Muslims defend themselves from attack."

"But is it like a holy war or something?"

"That's the term the media likes to use to paint an unfavorable picture of Muslims, but jihad is simply as I explained."

"So does this include attacking innocent people?"

"Of course not," Aminah replied emphatically. "In fact, killing and harming innocent people, as with any form of terrorism, is strictly prohibited in Islam. This prohibition is so strict that even when Muslims *do* fight, they aren't even allowed to harm as much as a tree."

"Really?" Tamika inquired with a chuckle.

"Yes," Aminah nodded. "Harming the innocent is not something taken lightly in our religion." She continued, "Terrorism is not allowed in Islam whatsoever, and whoever does take part in it, no matter what religion they claim to be a part of, is risking punishment in the Hereafter for that grave sin."

"But what about peace?"

"That's the goal," she affirmed. "But true peace will never come unless people are permitted to defend themselves from attack and are able to help others who are being oppressed."

Tamika nodded.

"And the Muslim does not view peace as refusing to fight when under attack or letting an oppressor continue to torture people, just as a sensible American won't view letting a serial killer go free as saving lives."

She laughed, nodding in agreement.

"The goal of the death penalty for serial killers is not to destroy life but to preserve it, and that can only be achieved by getting rid of what's destroying lives, which is the serial killer. If we let such a person live, we are, in

essence, murdering innocent people. And the same goes for letting terrorists oppress people," she compared.

Tamika paused, considering what Aminah was saying. It made sense.

She then glanced at her next question. "Oh yeah," she remembered. "What about those women who cover their faces? What type of Muslims are they?"

"They're just Muslims."

"But then why do they dress differently?"

"It's just a different way of dressing," Aminah explained. "Because in Islam, there are two different views based on proofs from the Qur'an and statements from the Prophet (s) on how a woman is required to dress. One view is that in public and in front of men that are not closely related to her, she must cover everything, even her face, uncovering it only out of necessity, like for identification purposes and so on. And the other view is that she must cover everything except her face and hands, the face veil being highly recommended, best, but not obligatory. So those who don't think it's obligatory will either not cover their face or will do so voluntarily, for extra blessings. And, of course, those who think it's obligatory will cover their faces."

Tamika had never heard that explanation, having been told that the ones who were single did not cover their faces, and the ones who were married covered theirs. "I thought it had to do with marriage."

Aminah laughed. "A lot of people say that, but I don't have a clue where that came from."

"So you don't think it's obligatory?" Tamika inquired curiously.

Aminah sighed, considering it. "I guess you can say that, but," she sucked her teeth, "I really don't know sometimes," she reflected honestly. "When I read the proofs for either side, I'm convinced. But, either way, I'd like to cover my face eventually."

"So why don't you do it then?" Tamika wanted to know.

Aminah laughed. "I ask myself that everyday."

Tamika chuckled, her face growing serious a moment later. "So you don't think that's extreme?"

"To cover your face?"

"Yeah."

"No," Aminah replied emphatically, shaking her head. "I think it's the best thing for a woman. I don't think it's extreme at all. It reduces a lot of problems."

"You think so?"

"Of course. I mean, I've even had guys come up and tell me that I'm pretty and I'd look better if I 'took off all of those big clothes.'"

"Really?"

"Yeah, and it gets me to thinking maybe I should go ahead and cover."

"Why, because of how you look?"

"No," she clarified, "for my own comfort and protection."

Tamika wrinkled her nose. "You don't mind walking around in all of those clothes?"

"No."

"Even in the summer?" She found that hard to believe.

Aminah shook her head.

"But won't you get hot?"

"Do you get hot in the summer?" she inquired.

"Yeah!" Tamika told her.

"Well, I'm sure it's not too much different," Aminah commented. "And you're wearing shorts, and you're still hot." She laughed. "If it's hot, it's hot."

"All those clothes make you hotter though," Tamika argued.

"Actually," Aminah corrected, "all those clothes make me cooler."

Tamika stared at her as if she were crazy.

"You're hotter uncovered in the sun," Aminah told her, smiling. "You don't find people in the desert protecting themselves from the heat by taking clothes off," she reminded. "You find them putting clothes on. Besides," she continued, "even in America, you see people with umbrellas to protect them from the sun, and people put on sun screen and all that stuff, don't they?"

"Yeah, that's true."

"Well," she said with satisfaction, "my clothes are my sunscreen."

Tamika nodded, indicating that she understood.

"I just had one more question though," she said, raising a finger and glancing at her notebook.

Aminah listened.

Tamika smiled self-consciously. "What about polygamy?"

"What about it?" Aminah asked casually.

Tamika chuckled. "Well, isn't it allowed in Islam for men to marry more than one woman?"

"Yes, they can marry up to four," Aminah replied matter-of-factly.

Tamika chuckled again. "So that's true?"

"Yes."

She smiled uncomfortably, having expected a more detailed explanation. Aminah had responded as if she viewed polygamy nonchalantly, but Tamika found such a sentiment hard to believe, especially coming from a woman. "And you, uh, don't have any problem with that?" she inquired, a half smile still on her face.

"No."

"But that's not fair, is it?"

"How is it not?" Aminah challenged.

Tamika forced laughter, eyes widening, "Can a woman marry more than one man?"

Aminah shook her head, chuckling. "Let me ask you something."

"Okay."

"Let's say I had two people to feed," she began. "And one was a 350 pound body builder, while the other was a ninety pound seventh grader. To be fair, should I give them the same amount of food?"

"No but—."

"But what?" she interjected challengingly. "Is it unjust if you don't give them the same amount?"

"No."

"Why?"

Tamika sighed, half-smiling, "But you can't compare—."

"Okay, then let's look at men and women. Is it unfair that women carry the children? I mean, why can't men?"

"That's how they were created," she argued.

"And who created them that way?"

"God."

"And God's also the one who made it permissible for a man to marry more than one woman."

Tamika paused, sighing. "But still, it's not fair."

Aminah forced laughter. "You can call it unfair if you want, but I don't view it like that." She paused. "In Judaism and Christianity, it's allowed too."

"But not anymore."

"It's still allowed," Aminah replied confidently. "Although modern day Christians wish to deny it. In fact," she stated, "there are Christian men who live in America who practice polygamy."

There was a long pause.

"But anyway, that's beside the point."

"So you don't mind your husband marrying more than one wife?" Tamika inquired, unwilling to believe that Aminah did not care.

"That's irrelevant," Aminah informed her with a smile. "What if I had a problem praying? Should we now remove that requirement from the religion?"

Tamika nodded. "I see what you're saying."

"The point is that God allows it, and that alone should be sufficient—if we believe in God." Aminah went on, "But yes, there are many, many benefits of its allowance, like the opportunity for more children, the protection of women's rights, in that they aren't doomed to be mistresses and the like, the man having no responsibility toward them, because in polygamy he has to support them and treat them fairly. And even within our nature, it's natural to accept it, even for women—if we're honest with ourselves. But, still, this point goes back to the classroom analogy I gave earlier about questioning why things are like they are. We're not here for that. God created us. He made the rules, and all we have to do in life is first find the correct religion of God, and after that, we submit, no questions asked. That's faith." She was silent momentarily. "You can think what you want, but that's the only way to salvation." She paused then added, "And if someone doesn't like it," she shrugged, "they can go to Hell if they want—and take their opinions with them."

Tamika grinned, amused by both Aminah's words and her personality. She would have never guessed Aminah was so outspoken and strong-minded. Aminah's appearance gave the impression that she was quiet and soft spoken.

"But," Aminah added more calmly and thoughtfully, "it's not obligatory or anything—just allowed. So if a person doesn't want to do it, they don't have to, and if a woman doesn't want to marry into it, she doesn't have to. But still, the allowance is there for those who choose it, and we should have no problem with that."

Tamika nodded as she listened.

"Islam is a comprehensive religion," Aminah explained, concluding. "But all of its laws are for the protection of a civilized, moral society and individual, the society's rights taking precedence at some points and the individual's at others, depending on whatever brings the greater good. Islam complements our natures completely. It did not come to oppose our nature but to perfect it," she told Tamika. "And that sometimes means permitting things we don't want and forbidding things we might want, because what a person desires is not always what's best or even complementary to his or her nature. In reality, in Islam there is nothing in which the benefit outweighs the harm except that Islam permits or mandates it. And likewise, in Islam there is nothing in which the harm outweighs the benefit except that Islam cautions against it or forbids it." She paused. "And if we carefully and honestly analyze each rule or allowance in Islam, even polygamy, we are forced to admit that, whatever potential harm it can cause, the benefit is so much greater."

That night, after listening to Aminah pray in the other room, Tamika lay awake in the darkness reflecting. Aminah was now in bed, and Dee still had not returned home from studying. Tamika reflected on everything Aminah had said. She was frustrated because it sounded so logical coming from Aminah, but Tamika still could not bring herself to actually become Muslim.

It seemed like too much, but she knew that it was just a matter of perspective. If she really wanted to, she could view everything as Aminah did, which would make her life a whole lot easier. But she could not—would not—as she kept thinking about her mother, her aunts, her uncles, and even Makisha. She despised even the thought of what they might say to her, how they would look at her. She shouldn't care, she knew. But she did. *But she shouldn't!* Was Tamika going to be the typical disbeliever and turn away from God because of family, friends, and society? Tamika hated herself for being so weak, but she knew the answer to that question was not a good one. Yes, she should she just become Muslim for the sake of her soul and worry about all of that later, if ever. Yes, that made sense. But right now, Tamika was not making any sense, not even to herself.

The sound of the front door opening and closing interrupted her thoughts. Dee was home.

Dee.

Couldn't she just be like Dee, Muslim, but still doing what she wanted? Dee was a singer, about to make it big, and yet she was Muslim. Couldn't Tamika just be like that?

Dee turned on the hallway light so that she could see in the room, not wanting to wake her roommates by turning on the light in the bedroom.

"Durrah?" Aminah's sleepy voice inquired.

"Yeah," Dee whispered, unaware that Tamika was not yet sleep.

"Did you pray all your prayers?" Aminah's scratchy voice asked with concern, reminding Durrah of her religious obligations, as she often found herself doing.

Dee groaned. "I've been studying half the night," she whispered, aggravation apparent in her voice.

"But you should still pray Dee," Aminah told her hoarsely as her voice cracked from sleepiness.

"Just don't worry about it," Dee replied irritably.

"Durrah," Aminah warned her, her voice now becoming clear.

"Just leave me alone, Aminah, gosh," Dee complained. "I don't need you nagging me all the time. I already have a mother." Her harsh tone shocked Tamika, it unpleasantly foreign to her ears.

"Shhh," Aminah reminded her to lower her voice because Tamika was still sleeping.

Dee sucked her teeth, but she heeded. "Worry about yourself," she retorted in an aggravated whisper.

"I am."

She changed into her nightclothes. "Then do it now."

"You should pray."

"I'm tired."

"Prayer is better than sleep," Aminah reminded, nearly singing the words from her bed. She knew she was getting on her friend's nerves, but she did not care.

"I'm not in the mood right now," Dee said as she climbed into her bed, referring more to Aminah's nagging than to prayer.

"Whatever you want," Aminah gave up. Displeased with her friend, she turned over in her bed in frustration.

"Yeah, yeah, yeah," Dee murmured from under her covers. "Whatever."

No, Tamika considered. Perhaps, she could not be like Dee.

Chapter Nine

Tamika spent the remainder of the week trying to write the song that she and Dee would sing at the formal, putting her religious struggles in the back of her mind for the time being. It was refreshing to focus on something else, as it brought her peace. She was now able to function in her classes without her mind drifting to the state of her soul. Every moment that she was not studying was now spent thinking of lyrics for the duet. It was difficult to decide what to sing about. There were so many possibilities. She did not want the typical love song. She liked originality. That a major producer would be there to hear the song made Tamika all the more nervous and determined to be unique. But she could not deny her excitement about the opportunity. She could possibly be taking the first step toward a dream she had wanted to realize since she was a child. Inside, she burned with a desire to prove everyone wrong, especially her mother and other family. She wanted to show them, yes, she could make it big without being exploited, as her mother assumed every female singer was.

If it was not for her religion presentation and paper assignment, Tamika could have put the topic of religion out of her mind completely. Although much of her research was complete since she had read several books and taken ample notes, there was still the visit to the Muslim place of worship she had to report on. This was a major part of her assignment. But she did not have to think much about that either, having already arranged the visit that week with Dee, who had told Tamika that she could take her to the Muslim mosque on Friday to witness the gathering called *Jumuah*. Dee had explained that it was similar to the Christian's weekly sermon on Sunday in that the gathering was obligatory upon the Muslims (at least the men) to attend. Tamika was grateful for the kind gesture, which alleviated a lot of stress.

Tamika now felt extremely comfortable with Dee. They had grown closer since she agreed to write the songs for the formal. Dee often practiced the songs with Tamika, and while practicing, Dee would ask Tamika if she was singing them properly. Dee also would go to a studio to rehearse Tamika's songs in order to have another person hear them and comment, a person who Dee said loved the songs very much. Often while rehearsing, Dee and Tamika would talk about other things, such as life, how it would be as a professional singer, and what their families would think after they made it. Of course, the latter was something Dee was less inclined to discuss than Tamika, but Dee began to open up somewhat as she felt more comfortable with Tamika. The two began to spend much of their free time together, if not laughing and talking, just studying in silence and enjoying each other's company.

Thursday night after Tamika finished studying, she sat on the couch writing more lyrics to the duet when Dee had come in, her face apologetic, appearing as though she had been hurrying. She immediately walked over to Tamika, whose face wore a puzzled expression.

"Is everything okay?"

"Yeah, it's fine, but," Dee replied, sighing. She sucked her teeth. "I'm sorry, but I can't take you tomorrow."

Tamika's heart sank. She needed to go to the mosque. The visit was the last major part of her paper that she had to do. And she needed to do it right away, because the due date was not too far away. March was less than a week away, and most students were almost finished with theirs. Many of them did not even have to do their presentation until late April, whereas Tamika was one of the first students to present during the month.

"You're joking," Tamika hoped, staring at Dee.

"I'm sorry," Dee apologized again, "but when I told you I'd take you I completely forgot about my lab practical tomorrow afternoon, and it won't end until like five o'clock."

"Five o'clock?" Tamika repeated in disappointment. "When do they finish at the mosque?"

"Two thirty at the latest."

She frowned, trying to figure out what to do.

"Is next week too late?"

"Um," she considered it. "Not really," she said slowly, thinking at the same time, "but I wanted to be working on my paper by then. 'Cause if I keep procrastinating, then—."

"Don't worry, then," Dee told her, waving her hand. "I asked Aminah if she could take you if you needed to go tomorrow."

Inside, Tamika groaned. She did not want to ride with Aminah.

"She goes home every weekend, and there's a mosque not too far from where she lives."

"But how will I get home?" Tamika wondered. "She usually doesn't come back until Sunday."

"I can pick you up after the practical," Dee offered.

"Then you won't be there before six," Tamika concluded, displeased.

"I know," Dee apologized. "But Aminah says you can wait at her house."

"At her house?" Tamika did not like the idea.

"Don't worry, her family's really nice."

That was beside the point. She sighed, shrugging. "Whatever."

"My family may be there too," Dee told her. "They're always at Aminah's."

What did Tamika care? She didn't know Dee's family either. "Okay," she agreed with a sigh. "That's fine."

"It won't be that bad," Dee assured her. "You can even ask them a lot of questions for your paper if you want." She added, smiling, "They love talking about Islam."

"I'll just see how it goes."

"I'm sorry," she apologized again.

"Don't worry about it. It's not a big deal," Tamika comforted but unconvinced of her own words.

"Thanks."

"No," she disagreed politely, "thank you for arranging this for me. And you can tell Aminah to just let me know when I need to be ready."

"Okay. But if you get to talk to her first, tell her, because I'm about to go study again."

"No problem."

"Thanks." A moment later, Dee was out the door, hurrying down the hall to study for her practical. The apartment grew silent, and Tamika found herself dreading tomorrow. Her mind drifted to what she would do during the long ride with Aminah. What would they talk about? Would they sit there quietly the entire time, occasionally discussing the weather? Perhaps, she considered, she had better think of some more questions for her paper to pass time, especially if she was going to be stuck at Aminah's house.

How did she get herself into such a predicament?

***

Friday morning Tamika went to her classes as usual, planning to meet Aminah at noon in the apartment, as they had agreed to do the night before. Between classes Tamika strolled through the campus, a contrast to her normal brisk walk. She wanted to take her time and enjoy the warm weather that had suddenly appeared. Just a few days before, it had been chilly outside. Georgia weather was strange like that, cold one day, hot another, but never too cold, even during the winter, unlike Wisconsin, whose frostbite winters lasted for several months into the new year.

The brightness of the sun pleased Tamika, and she smiled, its rays warming her neck and arms, over which her jacket lay after she had taken it off. Maybe today would not be so bad after all, Tamika pondered, as she was customarily in good spirits if the weather was nice. Even if she and Aminah found nothing to discuss, Tamika was certain that she would be content with merely staring out the window at the passing trees and grass.

After her classes were finished, which was just before noon (she had no lab that day, which usually extended well into the evening most times), she walked quickly across the campus. She was now unable to enjoy the weather, hoping that she would not make Aminah late. Tamika hated when she was doing someone a favor and the person disrupted her schedule in the process. It was one of her pet peeves. She had always felt that the person for whom the favor was being done had the responsibility to ascertain that she caused the other person no difficulties, even if she herself had to change her plans to meet the person's needs.

She glanced at her wristwatch. It was a minute after twelve. She walked faster, hoping, *praying* that Aminah was not agitated. When she finally reached their building, it was seven minutes after twelve. Hurrying, she unlocked a side door with her key and skipped the steps two at a time. She walked swiftly down the hall until she reached her room door. Sighing with relief, she unlocked it and opened it, trying to catch her breath at the same time.

Stunned, Tamika stood at the door of the apartment staring in disbelief.

"How are you?" he asked, smiling politely then looking to the ground, kicking nervously at the floor.

She forced a smile to Sulayman as her heart sank. "Fine," she mumbled, glancing away. *What? He was coming too? Dee had not told her that!* If she had known Aminah's brother was coming, she would have waited until next week. And it would have been worth it.

"You ready?" Aminah inquired, suddenly appearing in the living room, dressed and ready to go, a bag over her shoulder, its straps pulling at her *khimaar* awkwardly.

"Yeah," Tamika replied good-naturedly, concealing her true feelings. "I have everything," she told her, patting her shoulder bag.

"Okay then," Aminah said finally, looking at her brother. "You ready?"

He nodded, eyes on the floor in front of him. "Let's go."

Embarrassed, Tamika slowly followed the siblings out of the apartment. In the hall, she glanced cautiously about her, hoping no one would see her with them. She could only pray that she would not run into Makisha, who would never let her hear the end of it, God only knowing what Makisha would assume happened to her best friend. Makisha would probably think Tamika befriended Aminah and Sulayman, especially since she had been asking a lot of questions about Christianity. Makisha had already begun to talk to Tamika less since it had recently become the norm for Tamika and Dee to be together on campus, Makisha thinking Tamika's friendship with Dee was somehow mutually exclusive with the one Tamika shared with her. This, Tamika did not entirely mind, because, deep inside, she enjoyed Makisha's displeasure. It meant that she and Dee's friendship was becoming known among the student body, which meant Tamika's popularity was on the rise. However, being seen with Aminah and Sulayman would not only fail to contribute to her image, but it would take away from it, especially if Makisha had anything to do with it. Makisha would most certainly seize the opportunity to prove that Tamika was losing her mind.

Recently, although she spoke to Tamika less, Makisha had begun to telephone the apartment to see how Tamika was doing, asking her about her health and if she had gone to church lately. Tamika felt awkward, aware that Makisha felt obligated, now viewing Tamika as going astray. Makisha's uncle had even called that week, asking Tamika how everything was and if she still had questions. She had brushed him off, assuring him that she was fine and that everything was now clear. Although Makisha's uncle believed it, Makisha was not convinced. Her conversations with Tamika were more subtle warnings about the state of her soul than they were friendly exchange. At times, Tamika wanted to turn the tables, warning Makisha about her soul, telling her that she was committing a sin by worshipping a man, but Tamika was not strong enough yet. She had not yet even become a Muslim. But she planned to. When? That was another story entirely.

"I'll sit in the back," Aminah told Sulayman after he unlocked the doors.

"No, it's okay," Tamika told her roommate, feeling awkward, knowing that Aminah was only offering to sit in the back to keep her company. "Go ahead and sit in the front. I'm fine."

"I don't mind."

"It's okay, truly," she told her sincerely, not particularly excited about sitting next to Aminah in a car for forty minutes. "I like sitting in the back by myself." At least, today she did.

"You sure?"

"Yeah."

"Okay."

"But thanks."

After everyone climbed in the car and situated themselves with their seatbelts, Sulayman started the engine and pulled out of the school's parking lot. Tamika stared out the side window from her seat, which was behind where Aminah sat on the passenger's side. Staring out the window, Tamika was relieved that, with every hundred feet that were driven, they did not pass anyone she knew.

As Sulayman drove, making his way down the campus streets, Tamika's eyes fell upon the campus buildings, now seemingly foreign structures erected for the elite. She did not belong here, she felt suddenly. The school buildings stood in their architectural perfection and carried an air of sophistication. The students who went in and out of them were the intelligent members of society, the future leaders. They belonged. They wanted to be there, and they had a purpose. What was Tamika's? To please her mother? To get it over with? She doubted she would last very long. She was determined nonetheless, at least for the moment.

The first ten minutes of the drive were silent. Everyone was immersed in private thoughts. Aminah was the one who broke the silence. Turning slightly in her seat so that Tamika could hear her properly, she explained, "When we get there, the women will all be covered. And if you want," she offered, "I can give you a scarf to wear on your head."

"Do I have to wear it?" Tamika wanted to know. She was already dressed in a long dress, which she had chosen specifically for the occasion because she knew Muslims had to cover modestly. She was not particularly thrilled with the idea of putting something on her head.

"No," Aminah replied slowly, letting Tamika know that she probably should wear it, "but all the women will have it on, and you'll, uh, kinda stand out if you don't have one on."

Tamika shrugged. *Why not?* she considered, entertaining the possibility that it could add to the experience, giving her something unique about which she could write in her term paper. "Okay, that's fine."

"It'll start off with a two-part sermon," Aminah explained, "and this will probably last no more than forty five minutes or so, and then everyone will pray."

Tamika listened.

"You may want to just sit in the lobby near the door where you can see everything, unless you want to sit in the back."

"Whatever's best." She did not care one way or the other.

"It's up to you."

"I guess I'll just sit in the lobby." She figured that would give her the most comfort, seeing as though she would be a stranger and not know the proper etiquette for the mosque, and she did not want to disrupt anything.

"I'll show you where you can sit," Aminah offered, "and afterwards, if you have any questions, feel free to ask anything."

They were silent for a few minutes.

"Oh yeah," she remembered. "Are you still coming to my house afterwards?"

"I think so," Tamika replied, inside groaning at the reminder. "That's what Dee told me. Is that okay?" she asked, hoping she sounded as if she wanted to go.

"Yeah, it's fine. I just wanted to make sure."

"Oh, okay."

The remainder of the drive was silent, strained, at least for Tamika, who was counting the minutes until they would arrive at the mosque. At least then she would have a moment to breathe, as she would be alone, at least for about an hour. She hated the feeling of suffocation she felt during the drive, trapped in the back seat of a vehicle in which Sulayman Ali was the driver and his sister next to him. It was almost humorous that Tamika was actually sitting there, but her disappointment and discomfort prevented her from laughing. She would have never imagined that there would ever come a day like this, when she was voluntarily in the same room, let alone car, with Sulayman. Her dislike for him had often been expressed to Makisha and others, including family members. It was not uncommon for Tamika to discuss with them the bold articles he would write that reeked of arrogance and self-righteousness. Presently, she wanted to get the day over with, all of it, hoping that it would pass more quickly than the car ride. The only thing that calmed her was the mental reminder that she was only enduring this for the sake of her grade.

After what seemed like hours, they pulled into a large parking lot, which was filled with many cars. Other vehicles were pulling in and parking when they arrived. Women dressed similar to how Aminah dressed (some wearing face veils) and men dressed in Arab garb emerged from the cars. People of different races and ethnicities eagerly greeted each other, some shaking hands, others hugging.

Tamika felt as if she were in another country. She had never realized that such communities existed in America. She had heard of Muslims and had seen them on occasion, even in Milwaukee, but she never thought much about them, because they were not a significant part of her life. Her knowledge of them was limited to what her family shared, which was mostly stereotypes and mention of them going to Hell. But now she was actually in their midst, present at their most important gathering of the week. She had not even known they had any weekly sermons, her ignorance now rearing its ugly head. Before conducting the interview with Aminah, she did not even know what they believed really, aside from that they did not worship Christ.

She felt weird as she got out of the car, as if she did not belong, suddenly becoming aware of her appearance. Before leaving, she thought nothing of her short sleeves, but she now felt as if she were naked, her bare arms out in the open, exposed, a cruel announcement to all around her of her lacking belief, of her ignorance. She kept rubbing her arms, their bareness now disturbing her. She wished she had thought to at least wear a jacket.

"You want an *abiyah?*"

"A what?" Tamika asked, unaware of what Aminah was talking about.

"An *abiyah,*" Aminah repeated, tugging on her large dress.

"Uh," Tamika considered it, realizing that her discomfort, if not improper dress, must have been obvious.

"Here," Aminah offered, not waiting for a reply, opening the trunk with a key from her chain. Luckily, Sulayman left, waving to them and mumbling something to Aminah as he made his way to the building.

Tamika heard the sound of something unzipping, and she realized Aminah was opening her bag in which she had packed her clothes for the weekend. A moment later, Aminah was closing the trunk, now holding a large navy blue dress in her hands.

"You can just slip it on in the bathroom," Aminah told her, handing her the dress that appeared too big for Tamika.

"What's this called again?"

"A lot of people call it an *abiyah.*"

"*Abiyah?*" Tamika repeated slowly.

Aminah nodded. "Yeah, you'll hear it called that, like I just used, but most people call it a *jilbaab.*"

"A what?"

"*Jilbaab.*"

Tamika nodded.

"But it's not really a *jilbaab* though, because a *jilbaab* is really a one-piece outer garment that starts from your head and goes down to your feet covering your entire body."

"Even your face?"

Aminah nodded. "Yeah, in general." They were walking to the building now.

"Then why do they call it *a jilbaab?*" Tamika inquired more for conversation than genuine interest.

Aminah shrugged. "Custom, I guess. But I don't like to, because *jilbaab* is mentioned in the Qur'an when God tells the women to wear it when they go out. So it's not good to refer to something as a *jilbaab* if it's not," she went on, as if Tamika wanted to know. "Because that poses the danger of people misunderstanding the Qur'an, especially if they don't know the original meaning of the word." She shook her head, chuckling. "And you're in for a war if you're gonna tell some people what it really means if they already think it means something else. But anyway, it's not a *jilbaab.*"

In the bathroom, after putting on the *abiyah* and a head covering that Aminah had given her, Tamika followed Aminah to the area in which the sermon would be held.

"You can sit here if you want," Aminah told her, pointing to a few seats that were at the lobby doors, which were all glass except for the wooden trim, enabling Tamika to see what was happening inside. "You can hear everything from here, because they have intercoms in the lobby."

"Thanks," Tamika told her, sitting down, her attention now fixed on the crowd of Muslims. She did not know that they sat on the floor for the sermon. Tamika would never have imagined that. She also noticed that the women were sitting in the back while the men were sitting in the front.

"*Allaahuakbar! Allaahuakbar!*"

The sudden sound through the speakers startled Tamika, but she listened, curious, waving mindlessly to Aminah who disappeared into the crowd after walking through the doors. The man's voice continued for a few minutes then stopped. Tamika could not help but wonder what he was saying, as she noticed men and women murmuring something after each pause in his words. Also, she noticed that throughout the mosque various men and women were praying individually, after which they would sit down with everyone else.

The crowd, Tamika could not get over that. Droves of people had come for the occasion. They were tightly packed in the large room, sitting so close to each other that each person almost touched the other. People continually moved forward, back or sideways, whichever direction was necessary, in order to accommodate the others who would arrive.

A woman passed and smiled at her, saying, "*As-salaamu-'alaikum.*"

Mortified that she had no idea how to respond, Tamika replied, "Hi," immediately regretting the reply as the expression of the woman's face changed from pleasure to puzzlement. But Tamika was grateful that the woman did not inquire further, because she was not prepared to explain who she was and why she was there.

"*In-alhamdulillaah,*" the strange words echoed through the lobby. Tamika then remembered why she had come. She opened her notebook, prepared to write down what she was seeing and hearing, although she had no idea of the latter.

She was grateful a few minutes later, when the man began to talk in English. She would not know what to report on if she did not understand what was being said. At first, her mind drifted, paying little attention to the speech, and her eyes inadvertently fell upon the glass door. She mindlessly studied its finger and handprints, and she noticed a small lip print. A child must have been pressing its small face against it. The glass needed cleaning, some vinegar would do it...

"...we look at the non-Muslims," the words jumped out at her, throwing themselves into her ears.

Tamika's heart raced, and she nervously pulled on her clothes, adjusting them, hoping no one knew.

"No, we can't be like that," the man said. Tamika's ears perked and her mind raced in search of what he had said before that. "We don't have a religion in which we come once a week, looking and dressing like we love God, then stripping that identity the minute we walk out of here."

Oh, that.

"No!" the man stated emphatically, as if angry with the congregation. "That's not what this religion is about. Allah has pulled us out of that and gave us sense. We're not part-time Muslims, ID card Muslims, Muslims only when it's convenient, or only when we have to be, when everyone else around us is and when it's safe to say we are too. And then we turn around and go to work and school wearing a different face.

"No, brothers and sisters, it's not like that," he continued. "It's not like that at all. We don't believe we're 'saved,' somehow guaranteed reward for nothing but a decision to say, 'I believe.' No, this statement comes with conditions. How can we be Muslims and sit around and look to this crazy world for direction in our lives? How can we have the only religion worth being affiliated with and we do this? We're gonna look to *them* for our answers?

"Some of you think that's where the success lies, don't you?" he taunted. "Some of you have probably said that the reason why Muslims are so behind the rest of the world is because we don't have enough doctors, enough lawyers, enough scientists, enough whatever." He paused. "So is that it? Is that it!" he challenged them, scolding like a strict parent. "Is that our problem? Do you think that's what our problem is? Do you actually think that Muslims are being killed, murdered, *raped,* because we need more professionals? Do you!

"And some of you think that Muslims are so oppressed, so mistreated because we don't have satisfactory numbers on election day!" He paused, and his breathing, like his emotion, echoed through the intercom. Tamika realized then that he was indeed a powerful speaker. "Some of you even go as far as to blame the problems of this *ummah* on this! Not enough Muslims showed up at the rally, eh? Not enough Muslims are voting, eh?

"Well, I'm here to tell you, no. No! No, that's not it!" He paused. "Certainly, *certainly*, this is *not* the sum total of our problems. And even if *every* Muslim did whatever each of you thinks he should do, we're still in a pitiful, *pitiful* situation.

"And if our problems were as you think, brothers and sisters, then the Prophet, *sallaahu'alayhi wa salaam*[26], and his companions would not have only been unable to be our examples, but they would have been the epitome of our failure! And we, *we* would have represented progress.

"'Cause I'll tell you right now that, *yes*, I know we need doctors, and I *know* we need engineers, and yes, I'm no fool, I know we need Muslim professionals.

---

[26] "May prayers and peace be upon him."

"But I'll tell you something. We don't *need* Muslims in voting booths, we don't *need* Muslims at rallies, and no, brothers and sisters, we don't need one Muslim politician, not one Muslim politician!" He paused, calming, and the sound of pages ruffling filled the mosque.

"Some of you don't wanna hear that, eh?" his voice lowered. He chuckled. "Snatches away all your opinions, your goals, huh? Snatches away the foundation you've built for yourself? Well, isn't that a shame? Isn't that a *shame*? That you feel like you have nothing, *nothing*! Nothing, without getting a piece of that political pie!

"And no, I'm no fool, I know there's benefit in these things, especially given our treatment in jobs and schools and how we're portrayed on television. But certainly, we can't classify these things as *needs*, let alone as the cause of our problems in the world.

"You want proof, don't you?" he taunted them. "How can this be? We need empowerment, you cry! We need a voice, you scream! We need our problems solved!

"Do we?" he whispered challengingly. "Do we?" his whisper grew louder. "You really want empowerment, you really want a voice, you really want your problems solved?" still a whisper. "Then wake up!" he cried.

Even Tamika began to feel shamefully self-conscious at that moment.

"*Wake up!* Quit averting the blame from yourselves! Quit looking to the *cause* of your problems as the solution!"

No one said anything.

"No," he clarified, "I'm not telling you to go sit at home and *dhikr*[27] all day and everything will be okay. And no, I'm not saying shut yourself off from society. But certainly, *certainly*, no sensible person would believe that you can successfully remove ill from a society by becoming ill yourself! By becoming a *part* of the problem that needs to be solved!

"You have a direct message, written message *and* human example from the Lord, Creator of the heavens and earth, in your very hands, in your very reach, and you abandon it, throw it behind your backs, and turn to the world for guidance, and you think that we need more *dunya*[28] to solve our problems!

"Do we need more brothers and sisters discarding their Islamic identity? Is that it? Do we need more of our brothers and sisters abandoning Islam to solve our problems? Reinterpreting the religion? Is that it? You know something Allah doesn't know, do you? *Do you!*

"Well, you have another think coming. If you *think* that Allah revealed the Qur'an and sent His Messenger, *sallaahu'alayhi wa salaam*, to play

---

[27] Literally, to remember God, but in this context, in means to recite the name of God repeatedly using various praiseworthy terms.

[28] Anything that pertains to the present world as opposed to the Hereafter

games, to be a part of your lives only when what they say agrees with your opinion, then you're not only ignorant, you're duped. *Duped*, tricked, shackled! Shackled by the world! Slaves by choice! And you may as well stop fighting." He lowered his voice. "'Cause they already won. They already won. Because," he whispered loudly, "because the game is over, the bug is trapped, entangled in a web he didn't even see!" He paused. "Or that he *refused* to see.

"No, brothers and sisters, your answer is not there, not anywhere except in doing what Allah and His Messenger, *sallaahu'alayhi wa salaam*, said, and that's it. That's it!

"Sounds too simple, huh? Too easy?" he asked, his voice lowered again. "No, that can't be it, you tell me. That's simplifying the problem.

"Well, then if it's so easy," he raised his voice again, challenging. "If it's so, so *easy*, why don't you do it? *Why don't you do it!* Stop prostituting your wives, your sisters, and your daughters—yourselves! Turn off the television and open the Qur'an! Go to the masjid shopping for your religion instead of Blockbuster shopping for movies! Turn off that silly music, that recitation of *Shaytaan*[29]and turn on the Qur'an! Get the latest singer out of your lives and let the Prophet, *sallaahu'alayhi wa salaam*, in!"

He grew quiet, pausing to allow the enormity of his words to sink in.

"Not so easy anymore, eh? Not so simplistic, eh?" He chuckled, but that he was not happy was apparent. "Don't wanna give up your desires, do you? Instead of changing your lives to fit Islam, you want to change Islam to fit your lives!

"Don't wanna give up your *riba*[30], so you make it *halaal*[31]! Don't wanna give up your music, so you make it *halaal*!"

He grew silent, and the sound of his breathing filled the microphone.

"And you call yourself educated," he said, voice lowered. "Educated! You have a million degrees behind your name! But not an ounce of Islamic knowledge! And what's worse," he told them, "what's worse is you don't care. You don't care if you don't know your religion. And those who pretend to care, you change the religion, and then follow *your* interpretations wholeheartedly." He paused. "How convenient for you." He laughed. "How convenient.

"Look to the Qur'an and *Sunnah* so it can give you guidance," he suggested. "Not so *you* can give *it* guidance." There was a long pause. "Don't know what I mean, huh? Do you? Give it guidance? Huh?" he repeated, mocking what most of them must have been thinking. "How many

---

[29] Satan
[30] Usury
[31] Permissible

of you have shed your clothes of *jahiliyyah,* of ignorance, and put on the garb of Islam! Not half of the garb, but all of it! How many of you truly look to Islam to bring a change in your life! Or do you look to Islam to change it to fit your life that's full of desires?"

Silence.

"How many of you fear Allah before you sign your name on a *riba* loan, a mortgage, a credit card! How many of you encourage your sons *and* daughters to marry? How many of you point to *yourselves* abandoning this religion as the cause of Muslims' problems around the world! How many of you take your daughter, your son, and open up the books of the Companions, of the Prophet, *sallaahu'alayhi wa salaam,* and say, 'You should be like *that'!* And *not* like that in theory, or symbolically, but in practice! How many of you have said from your mouths that we live in modern times, that the Islam of the past is no longer applicable! That we are somehow exempted from fighting oppression and defending our lands! How many of you have uttered this from your mouths! And then you turn around and say, 'I follow the Qu'ran and *Sunnah.*'

"No," he told them emphatically. *"No.* I'm here to tell you, no! If you want some progress, look to what your Lord has to offer, not the world! Not the television! All you have to be is a *believer*!

"Notice," he was whispering, cautioning again. "I didn't say a Muslim. I said a believer! A *believer*! Listen to the words of Allah! Will you argue with Allah! Your Lord says of the believers," he told them, reciting something that Tamika did not understood. He then translated, "'The believers, men and women, are protectors one of another. They enjoin what is just, and forbid what is evil. They observe regular prayers, and obey Allah and His Messenger. On them will Allah pour His Mercy. For Allah is Exalted in power, Wise.'"

He paused.

"Let me ask each and everyone of you, and you can raise your hand in your heart, because Allah knows you better than you know yourselves. How many of you protect one another? How many of you know the Muslims in your city? How many of you care? How many of you rush to give charity, looking at the needy Muslims as a *mercy,* an opportunity to expiate sins, instead of as a burden? How many of you hate to see your Muslim sister on welfare?

"Not many," he answered for them. "And I don't even have to conduct one research. The answer is in the state of the community." A pause. "How many of you command the good, forbid the evil, and obey Allah and His Messenger, *sallaahu'alayhi wa sallam*? How many of you can even accept when good is commanded, without criticizing your Muslim brother or sister, without shooting him or her down, saying look at him, look at her, who are they to judge? How many of you are like this, hate being told what's right, hate being told of the evil in your lives? And how many more of you won't even accept, won't even admit what is good, what is evil! How many of you command the *evil* and forbid the *good*! How many of you *hate* to see a Muslim not hanging pictures, not listening to music, not intermingling with the opposite sex, not dressing like the world, not going into *riba*? How many of you! How many of you backbite them, talk about how *they* are confused, *they* are extreme? While you, *you*, the so called 'balanced Muslim' sit around eating *riba*, watching R rated movies and sick television shows, and know more music than you know Qur'an! How many of you! If the Prophet, *sallaahu'alayhi wa sallam*, was alive today, which one of you would he think is extreme! Which one of you would be considered 'balanced'?

"Wake up, O Muslims. Wake up! If you are like this, then you *hate* at least some of what Allah has revealed. And this, *this* is a characteristic of the hypocrites! The hypocrites!

"So then," he asked, almost whispering, "who is your example?"

He paused again.

"Allah says," he recited again then translated, "'O you who believe! Obey Allah and His Messenger, and turn not away from him when you hear (him speak). Nor be like those who say, 'We hear,' but listen not. For the worst beasts in the sight of Allah are the deaf and the dumb…'

"So here is your success, O Muslims, if you want it! If you really want it! And no, this is not an allegorical or symbolic message. It's real, *real!*

"But if you have ideas on how to help Islam, do it. So if you want to write a letter to the editor, if you want to attend a rally, go ahead. Go ahead! But don't forget your Islamic duty! Don't *ever* let these things, like rallies or voting, replace what you have an *obligation* to do in the first place! And that is to *return* to this religion and protect your brothers and sisters everywhere in the world. But the first step. The *first* step is implementing Islam in your own lives."

After the Muslims prayed, the lobby was suddenly swarmed with Muslims, making it difficult for Tamika to move about. She sat where she was, and her neck and underarms warmed with perspiration from the body heat emitted by all of the people. Around her people talked and laughed. Some women stopped to shake her hand, hug her, and say, "*As-salaamu-alaikmu.*" She was grateful that they did not wait for a reply. She had no idea what to say in response, although she had heard the greetings exchanged between her roommates each day. She felt awkward, out of place with each embrace, unfamiliar with such friendly contact between strangers. But she could not help but admire it, reflecting on how strong the bonds of sisterhood must be between these people.

As she had watched the women pray a few minutes before, she was almost mesmerized by their unity, how they stood shoulder-to-shoulder, foot-to-foot, as the men did. Women of all ages and races together, praying in one place to one God. It made Tamika sick with desire as she witnessed even children bowing humbly before God next to their parents and friends, and she longed to be a part of that power, that strength, that sisterhood. The sound of the congregation saying "Amen," recited in unison after the prayer leader's recitation, melted her heart. Its song-like utterance incited in her a hunger to be amongst them. She had felt ashamed at that moment, sitting in the lobby, deep inside knowing she belonged with them, next to the other women, praying too. How could she have even thought to delay becoming Muslim?

But even then, even as she was inspired by the sermon, even as she admired their unity, even as she envied the powerful message, still, there were desires pulling at her. She wanted to be a singer. She wanted peace in her family. She wanted to keep her image, her friendships, despising the idea of being a stranger, a sore thumb in a crowd. Although inside she knew there was nothing wrong with any of it, even being different, she was not particularly excited about covering her body and hair. She was now convinced that Aminah was right, that the earliest religious women did dress in that manner. But, no, not Tamika, she could not do it. How could she? How could she dress like that, when years before she had mocked it, had laughed at it, sitting with friends and family discussing how confused those women were to dress like that? Would that not make her a hypocrite? And what would her mother say? Her aunts? Her friends?

"There you are!" Aminah said, relieved, now standing in front of the chair where Tamika was still sitting. "I thought you were outside."

Tamika forced a smile and shook her head, immediately reminded that she had to go to Aminah's house. She hoped the time would pass quickly.

"You ready?"

She nodded, "Yeah."

"Sulayman's already in the car."

Inside, she groaned at the reminder.

Like a lost child, Tamika followed Aminah out the exit and into the parking lot, sometimes having to push through the crowd in order to oppose the force of the people upon her.

"Aminah," a woman's voice called as they walked swiftly to the car where Aminah's brother was waiting.

Tamika turned and found a woman a few steps behind them, completely covered in a light gray— *jilbaab?* A small slit was barely opened enough for her eyes, just enough for the woman to see, and her hands were gloved. No part of her was exposed. The woman reminded Tamika of pictures of Arab women she had seen, the ones for whom she felt pity. She had assumed they were oppressed, cruel men having made them dress in that manner, men forced by their "oppressive" religion.

At that moment, Tamika realized her ignorance, as she had never even heard a veiled woman speak, unexpectedly surprised to hear the woman talking, and so casually—so content.

"Oh! *As-salaamu-alaikum!*" Aminah eagerly greeted the woman, turning to embrace her warmly. "I didn't know you were coming!"

"Well, what can I say?" the woman said good-naturedly, chuckling. Tamika was still adjusting to the reality that there was actually a person—a personality—behind all of those clothes. "I needed some inspiration."

There was a brief pause.

"And who is this?" the woman inquired politely, turning to Tamika, Tamika suddenly feeling self-conscious.

"Tamika," Aminah told her.

"Oh," the woman's voice said in pleasurable surprise, as if she had heard of Tamika.

Tamika felt uncomfortable, unsure where to look. She was accustomed to looking a person in the face, but the veil created a barrier between her and the woman. It was difficult for Tamika to relax and casually greet her.

"How do you like living with Aminah?" the woman asked.

Tamika forced a smile. So Aminah had discussed her with this person. "It's pretty good," she lied. She actually enjoyed living with Dee.

"Good, good," the woman commented, her clothed head nodding. "I hope my daughter's treating you well."

Her daughter? She was Aminah's mother?

"You're coming to visit us, I hear."

"Yes," Tamika replied, eyes diverting, unsure where to let them fall.

"Well," Aminah's mother said finally, "I better go on. I don't wanna keep your father waiting."

A few minutes later, Tamika was in the car again, suffocated and uncomfortable. But she could bear it, she told herself. The drive to Aminah's could not be as a long as the drive from Streamsdale. But, still, she was likely to be counting the minutes, the time likely to drag, especially if she had to spend too long at the Ali residence.

Chapter Ten

The heavy rain fell against the firm glass of Tamika's bedroom window in thuds, its rhythmic pounding a just complement to her contemplative thoughts, as she reflected on the events of that day. The night was dark and cold, a sharp contrast to the warmth of earlier, when she had gone to the Friday sermon and visited Aminah's home. She had learned a lot, more than she had expected, more than she had wanted. Her stereotypes were swept away like dust after a brisk wind, removing all doubts from her mind as to what she should do.

"I was clueless," Aminah's mother had recalled her life before Islam, laughing.

Listening, Tamika had stared at the woman, amazed. She looked like an ordinary person. Tamika could not get over that. The sprinkle of freckles across the bridge of her nose, the large brown eyes, the thick blond hair that fell loosely around her shoulders. If Tamika had not seen her at the mosque earlier, she would have never guessed that the woman who sat laughing and joking before her, comfortably dressed in a buttoned blouse and jean skirt, was the same woman who was covered from head to toe with a thin slit barely enabling her eyes to be seen. The same woman who appeared "oppressed."

"Practically atheist," Sarah, Aminah's mother, had shared. "If you would've told me about God, I would've told you to prove it." She shook her head, chuckling. "I guess I was just turned off by the Christian church."

"For me," Dee's mother had interjected, her accent strong and thick, "I guess I was a little different. I was really religious, but when my husband told me about Islam, I fought it. I didn't want it to be right, you know, because of all the stereotypes and things I'd heard."

As the women spoke, sharing their stories, Tamika realized for the first time that these were average women, regular people, ladies whom Tamika had likely seen at the grocery store, stood behind at the bank, and waved to during a stroll through the neighborhood. They were not oppressed. They were not even introverts. Rather, they were opinionated, strong women, who loved who they were and what they had chosen. No one had forced them into anything. No one had asked them to cover, told them they had to. They had simply done it, because God wanted them to.

Dee's little sisters, all four of them, the youngest being four and the oldest fourteen, had drilled Tamika with questions.

"You don't pray?" the four-year-old had asked her, eyes wide, blinking with innocence.

"She's not Muslim," the fourteen-year-old rebuked, as if the question had been out of place.

The four-year-old, Naimah, stared at Tamika in disbelief. "You're trying to go to the Hell Fire?" she asked, gasping. "Are you scared?" she inquired before Tamika could respond, eyes intent, almost whispering.

"Naimah," the fourteen-year-old stopped her, eyeing her, correcting. "You shouldn't say that."

"But she's not Muslim?" the little girl was stunned, terrified, eyes wide, wanting answers. She found it hard to believe.

"Now," Dee's mother had interrupted, looking at her daughter, "you know everyone's not Muslim, don't you?"

"But she's going to the Hell Fire?" the girl kept asking, looking as though she was about to cry, the information paining her.

"We can't say that," Dee's mother gently corrected.

"But she's not Muslim!" the little girl exclaimed in desparation, as if she wanted her mother to know in case she misunderstood, or in case she could help Tamika's poor soul. "Mom," she pleaded, begging for her mother to listen.

Embarrassed, Dee's mother lifted the child, forced a smile and said, "I'm sorry," and left the room.

At the moment Tamika had felt dirty, as if she was a heathen, a monstrous spectacle for the entire family. Tamika understood they did not intend it to make her feel that way. But it was too late. The little girl had spoken, her innocent words vocalizing what everyone else was thinking but knew was impolite to say.

"You thinking about becoming Muslim?" Aaesha, the fourteen-year-old, inquired kindly, trying to make up for the unwanted interruption from Naimah.

Tamika had shrugged and exchanged friendly conversation with the family for the remainder of her time there. She had spent the entire time at Aminah's house listening to Aminah and Dee's mothers talk about Islam and answering questions from Dee's little sisters, who found it strange that Tamika was not Muslim.

Tamika, on the other hand, was in awe of everything she saw and learned. She was not only amazed at the striking differences between Dee and her mother and sisters. Tamika was also surprised by the striking contrast between how she had viewed Muslim women and Islam and what she witnessed was reality. She never imagined that there were others who felt as strongly about their religion as she had. She had never dreamed that there were little children—Muslim children—sick with worry about the lost souls of those who had not accepted Islam.

How ignorant, how stupid Tamika had been, she realized regretfully. She should have known that there was another world different from hers, another perspective other than what she had seen, and another Islam different from what she had perceived. How was it that she had lived eighteen years, now officially an adult, and still have harbored childish stereotypes about people who were unlike her? Hadn't it hurt her, the mistreatment and assumptions by others based upon the color of her skin? Yet she held similar ideas, baseless views, about Muslims.

Just then, she understood, the painful realization stinging her. She now understood what it meant to be racist. And it scared her, terrified her—she could actually relate. She had, albeit unintentionally, accepted the images of Muslims that she had seen on television and accepted as fact that Muslim women were oppressed, never having verified the information. Why did she need to? She had a television, books, and what she heard from friends and family—just as racists were unfamiliar with blacks, whether by circumstance or volition.

Did she dare, could she possibly say, that she was like Jennifer, a person who had carelessly flung a filthy, racist word at her, tearing at her heart?

No.

But it was possible, definitely possible that she had viewed Muslims the way Jennifer had viewed her.

If it were not possible, then why was she so amazed by Aminah and Dee's parents? Why? Why was it shocking that they spoke, laughed, had fun—*chose* to cover and be Muslim? Why was it so amazing to find a white woman and a Cuban woman sitting in a room with their families, reminiscing on their lives, their lives before Islam? Why did Tamika find it strange, unreal?

Was she a racist too? Had she too been reared upon ignorance and unfounded beliefs? Prejudice, although she claimed to be a victim of the same thing? Was she a hypocrite? ...*Was her mother?*

"Hey, Tamika."

The voice was soft, whispering, as if uncertain if Tamika was awake.

Tamika sat up. "Yeah?"

Dee smiled, her dimples small shadows in the dark room, the dim light from the window making her face glow. A sweet scent of perfume filled the air around Tamika's bed, and Tamika realized Dee was dressed to go someplace.

"You tired?"

Tamika forced a smile. "No, just thinking," she replied, her mental exhaustion detectable in her voice. "What's up?"

Dee turned on the light, Tamika blinking as her eyes adjusted. "I wanted to know if you felt like singing tonight."

Singing? Now? Tamika shrugged. "If you want to."

"No," Dee laughed, realizing what Tamika thought she meant. Tamika noticed the small gold leaves dangling from Dee's ears as her thick hair moved with the laughter. "I'm talking about going to the studio."

"The studio?" Tamika repeated, unsure if she had heard Dee correctly.

"Yeah."

Dee was dressed in a cream colored dress that hung just above her ankles, a small slit on the side, and patent leather shoes adorning her feet, Tamika noticed, admiring how the color of the dress complimented Dee's tan skin.

"That's where you're going?" Tamika inquired.

"Yeah," Dee replied, "but I wanted to see if you wanted to come." She paused, hesitating, and then added, "My recorder, um, he kinda wants to hear you too."

"Me?" Tamika was excited suddenly. "The producer?"

Dee shook her head. "No, my recorder. The producer won't hear us until the formal."

"Then, uh," Tamika searched her mind. "Who's this?"

"Remember I told you I was recording some tapes?"

"Oh yeah."

"Well, he records them."

"Oh, I see," she understood. "But why does he want to hear me?"

"Because I told him about our plan for the formal."

She wrinkled her forehead, puzzled.

"He's the one who talked to the school and set up everything for the formal."

Oh. She nodded. "So he wants to approve my voice?" she joked, chuckling self-consciously, her question more serious than her inquiry suggested.

Dee shrugged, forcing laughter. "I suppose. Probably just to know who's getting up on stage, you know, because he's responsible for the program and everything."

"You think it's okay?" Tamika inquired, for a second scared that she would be unable to perform.

"Yeah, yeah," Dee told her, waving her hand. "It's no problem."

"Okay then," Tamika said, thinking aloud, glancing around the room to see if she needed to take anything. "Should I bring my songs?"

"He has them."

Her eyes widened. "He does?" Tamika now became nervous.

"Yeah, and he likes 'em."

She could have fainted from excitement. This was not happening. What if this was her first step to making it big, to having her own recordings—*professionally!*

"So you gonna come?" Dee asked, hands on her hips, teasing.

"Yeah, girl!"

She laughed at Tamika. "Then let's go!"

Tamika jumped from the bed, hurrying, slipping on her shoes and frantically brushing her hair in the mirror. "Is this okay?" she asked Dee after finishing her hair, referring to the floral dress that she was still wearing, tugging on it gently so that Dee could see what she was referring to.

"Uh," Dee replied, uncertain, her eyes tracing its wrinkles that had developed from Tamika lying in bed. "You probably want to run an iron over it."

"I'll change," Tamika decided quickly, turning to open the closet, fumbling through each of the outfits, sliding the ones she did not want to the side. A few seconds later, she pulled a dress from the hanger and quickly changed, too excited to feel ashamed of undressing in front of Dee.

"How's this?" she inquired, now wearing a white cotton blouse and dark blue rayon skirt.

"A lot better," Dee told her honestly.

"Okay then," Tamika said, slipping on her shoes again. A moment later, she and Dee made their way into the living room.

"It's raining cats and dogs out there," Dee commented, walking over to the front closet. "You better wear a rain coat."

"I have an umbrella."

"You'll need a coat too," she suggested.

"Where'd you park?" Tamika inquired, removing a rain jacket and umbrella from the closet.

"Right outside the side door."

"You found a space?" she asked in surprise. Parking was normally difficult to find.

"It's Friday night."

"Oh," she chuckled, nodding. Most students left for the weekend by Friday afternoon.

Dee opened the door, and she and Tamika left the apartment. Dee locked it with her key before they made their way down the hallway.

"Don't be nervous," she advised Tamika, grinning, knowing Tamika was probably dying of nervousness inside.

"That's easy for you to say!"

Dee laughed. "Don't worry, he's really nice."

"I hope so."

"Trust me."

"She seems nice," Sarah commented that night in reference to her daughter's roommate.

"She is," Aminah admitted, arranging the plates in the dishwasher of her family's kitchen. Although Dee had picked up Tamika several hours ago, Dee's family had left Aminah's house only thirty minutes before. Aminah and Dee's parents had talked for several hours while the children ran through the house, enjoying themselves as usual. "It's just that," she started to say, then sucked her teeth. "I don't know."

Sarah was quiet for a few minutes as she wiped the cabinet. She paused to glance over her shoulder at her daughter, whose expression was distant and concerned as she loaded the dishwasher. "You're worried about Durrah, aren't you?"

At first Aminah declined to reply, feeling as if she would be betraying her friend to share what she felt. But a moment later she gave in, tired of holding it all inside, unable to vent, now needing to have a listening ear, one that would understand. She sighed sadly. "Yeah."

Sarah frowned, suddenly feeling sorry for her daughter. She could only imagine the pain that Aminah must be going through to see her childhood friend struggling with serious issues, especially in the religion. Sarah rarely discussed Durrah with Dee's mother Maryam. She realized that Maryam, if not in denial, was not completely aware of the things in which her daughter was involved. In a way, Sarah understood her friend's ignorance. Only a few years before, Durrah was like the twin sister of Aminah. She was outspoken about Islam, hosted Islamic events in the masjid, and held study circles for the sisters. Before they graduated from high school, Durrah and Aminah were even discussing the *niqaab* a lot, seriously considering covering their faces with the veil.

Sarah could only imagine how difficult it would be to come to terms with reality if one day Aminah came home uncovered and involved in public singing and beauty pageants. Such a circumstance was almost unthinkable, if not outlandish, given Aminah's dedication to the religion. But the scary part was that Durrah had been the same, no signs of weakening faith apparent to anyone, until she slowly began to uncover her hair before college. What possessed her to do it, no one knew, but whatever it was, it took a toll on Durrah's religious commitment. Seeing that occur terrified Sarah, pushing her to pray voluntary prayers regularly instead of every now and again. She now woke for *Tahajjud*[32] each night, crying and begging Allah to keep Aminah on the Straight Path and to guide Durrah back to it. She also asked Allah to keep her, her husband, and Sulayman strong. It tore Sarah apart to hear Maryam talk about Durrah. Maryam often made references to speeches Durrah had delivered and literature she had compiled about Islam before going off to college, a hint of pride still in her voice. She was living in the past and holding on to it. She knew Dee's lifestyle was a phase—at least she had convinced herself that it was.

"Just make *du'aa*[33]," Sarah advised, not knowing what else to say.

"I do," Aminah told her, almost whining.

Sarah was silent, now rinsing the dishcloth in the sink. The sound of water running heavily and pounding against the metal sink replaced the awkward silence and relieved the women from having to speak, at least for the moment. When she turned off the water, she squeezed the cloth in her fists. The water slid through the spaces between her fingers, and she began wiping the counter again. Her mind was far from concentrating on the food that had fallen there. "Just keep on her."

"That's the thing," Aminah sighed, complaining. "I do that all the time, but—."

"Does she listen?"

"Sometimes." She sighed again. "But recently, she's been real resistant and irritable."

"Do you know why?" Sarah guided a small pile of food droppings into her palm, its side pressed gently against the edge of the counter to catch it.

"She doesn't talk to me." Aminah felt like she was spilling her heart out.

Sarah was silent.

"I don't know what else to do."

"Just keep trying."

Aminah groaned. "I do."

"Don't stop."

She sighed again. "But I'm tired. I don't have time to think about it anymore."

"You have time," her mother corrected, secretly empathizing with Aminah. She herself was unsure what her daughter should do.

"She's just not Durrah anymore." Aminah was not certain if it was a necessary statement, wondering if it was considered backbiting. She hoped it was not.

---

[32] The voluntary night prayer, best when prayed in the last third of the night before dawn.

[33] Informal supplication to God for something one wants.

Earlier that day, as she listened to Durrah's sisters talk to Tamika about Islam, she was reminded of Durrah, who once had been energetic, lively and dedicated to the religion. Even Naimah's concern about Tamika going to the Hell Fire reminded Aminah of Durrah when she was a child.

"You think they're scared?" Durrah had asked once, her *s* sound a whistle through the large gap where her teeth had fallen out. There was a hint of a budding tooth barely visible on her top gums. Durrah and Aminah were sitting on the swing set in Durrah's backyard, rocking slightly and gently kicking the soft dirt as they talked.

"The *kuffaar?*" Aminah asked. The non-Muslims was a subject that was mind-boggling to them both, the concept of them going to Hell Fire eternally being their most popular topic. At the age of six and seven, the girls were inquisitive and very imaginative. Everything they read was real, vivid, as if right before them. They read in the Qur'an about the lasting torment of Hell and how its flames burned the skin. The skin would be restored, only to be burnt again. The flaming fire would be fueled by people—the disbelievers. The girls were terrified, haunted. It was as if they were reading a horror story. At their tender age, they could not understand how anyone actually chose to go there by not being Muslim.

"Yeah."

"I don't know," Aminah replied, contemplating. "Maybe."

"You think they don't know?" Durrah wanted an answer, needed an answer, much like her sister Naimah had.

"About the Fire?"

"Yeah."

"I don't know, but Ummee says most know," Aminah said in her childish tone referring to her mother.

"*Really?*" Durrah asked slowly, stunned. It made no sense to her. How could they know and not be Muslim?

"Yeah," Aminah said confidently, more because her mother had told her than her own certainty and knowledge, although she was making it appear like the latter.

"Maybe they forget?"

"Probably 'cause they can't see."

"But they see."

"No," she had told Durrah, correcting, her desire to be knowledgeable ringing in her voice. "The thing over their eyes is invisible."

"Invisible?" Durrah repeated in amazement. "So they can't see it?"

"No."

"Really?"

"Yeah, and Ummee says it's called a veil."

"Like what my mom wears?"

"Yeah, but its not made out of the regular fabric stuff."

"It's not?"

"No," Aminah told her, her childish voice becoming authoritative. "It's made out of something else."

"Invisible fabric?"

She considered it. "I don't know," she admitted but quickly added, "but they can't see anything with it."

"They can't?"

"No, not the good stuff."

"So they see all bad stuff!"

"Yeah," Aminah told her, convincing herself at the same time. Her explanation sounded logical.

"I don't ever want to wear one," Durrah stated emphatically.

"Me too."

"You never gonna wear it, 'Minah?" her eyes asked, scared, as if she needed a promise from her best friend.

"No, I won't," Aminah promised.

"You think we can take it off if it comes on us?"

She considered Durrah's question. "It's a real strong fabric, I think, too strong to come off."

Durrah shook her head. "Then I don't ever want to wear it."

Presently, Aminah shook her head, unable to get the striking similarities between Naimah and her older sister Durrah out of her head. Both were terrified of everything they read and could never understand anyone actually choosing a path other than that of Islam.

"But she'll come around, *inshaAllaah*[34]," Sarah told her daughter, consoling.

"Yeah," Aminah agreed slowly, wanting to believe her mother.

"A lot of Muslims who were born into Muslim families go through many changes before coming back to Islam," Sarah comforted. "It's common."

Aminah nodded slowly in agreement, her thoughts distant. "That's true."

"So don't worry about it," Sarah advised. "Just keep on her, and keep making *du'aa*. She'll see one day."

"But she already knows," Aminah pointed out.

Sarah was silent momentarily. She sighed. "I think that's the case with most Muslims who were born into Islamic households but get caught up in the world," she replied thoughtfully. "They know, but they just don't act."

"But that's scary."

---

[34] God-willing

"I know," she agreed, sharing her daughter's sentiments. She was suddenly worried about her own soul, realizing how easy it was to go astray.

"I just don't know how long I can stand living with her." Aminah knew it sounded cruel, but she wanted her mother to know that she was tired of babysitting. It was beginning to take a toll on her own faith and ability to practice Islam.

Sarah sighed. She was afraid Aminah would say it. It had concerned even her for quite some time, and she was afraid for her daughter. Sarah understood how association led to assimilation and how each person was on the path of her friend, and this frightened Sarah. But she was too shy, too ashamed, to share her gut feelings with Maryam. She was afraid to offend her, hurt her—afraid to bring to Maryam's attention what she did not want to admit. But Sarah was worried about Aminah, aware that college life was fast paced, alluring, especially in the social arena. And Aminah was human, like anyone, and she was not immune to temptation. Although she firmly believed Durrah would come around, Sarah was afraid that, in the meantime, some of her bad habits and desires would rub off on Aminah.

"And," Aminah continued, sighing, feeling comfort in talking to her mother, "I wanna do *da'wah*[35] to Tamika, but," she shook her head, "I can't even get a chance with Durrah around. She's such a—."

"Be patient," her mother cut in, implicitly warning her daughter to not go overboard in expressing her frustrations. Sarah did not want the conversation to be directed at tarnishing Durrah's character. "Allah guides whom He wills. If Tamika's meant to be Muslim, she'll be Muslim, no matter what Durrah does. So just focus on them both, but try to be an example. That's the most important thing."

The rain's pounding lessened until it became a drizzle, sprinkles that the wind blew into Dee and Tamika's faces, tickling their noses and cheeks gently like a light shower. They stood outside the door to Dee's recorder's home. It was a small house, Tamika noticed, and not too far from the school, the drive having been no more than five minutes.

"He lives in Streamsdale?" Tamika inquired in surprise. She had no idea that any recorders lived close by.

"He's a graduate student studying music."

"At the university?"

"Yeah."

The door opened and a tall, handsome young man dressed casually in a T-shirt and jeans stood in the doorway and invited the students inside.

---

[35] An Arabic term meaning to teach someone about Islam.

Tamika could not tell what race he was. He could have been American, Hispanic, or perhaps even had some Asian in him, but his dark hair was cut low, too short to derive any hints from its texture. He smiled. "Come in, please."

He had no accent, Tamika noticed.

"You must be Tamika," he greeted, extending his hand, and Tamika accepted it, shaking it, placing her small hand in his large one.

"My name is Kevin."

The house was quiet except for the soft sound of music playing from a stereo. The house smelled of a pleasant, fresh scent that Tamika could not identify.

"I'll take your coats," he offered as they took them off, accepting them in his hands and hanging them on a coat rack behind the door.

"Is anyone hungry?"

Tamika shook her head. "No thank you." She had not eaten in several hours, but she was so nervous that she doubted that she could stomach anything at the moment.

"I'm fine, thanks," Dee declined politely.

"Okay, then I guess we can get started," he smiled, clasping his hands together and leading the roommates past the living room and opening a door.

"I work out of my basement," he explained to Tamika as they descended the carpeted steps.

"He's got the whole place set up," Dee told her, grinning.

As they entered the basement, Tamika glanced around her, admiring approvingly. The basement was carpeted, neatly arranged with tape and CD shelves along the walls. Along one wall was a recording studio, fully equipped, appearing professional. In a small, enclosed room that was likely meant to be an office were a few microphones, lined up and plainly visible through the glass. He was definitely a recorder, Tamika noted. He was fully equipped for the job.

"I'm ready whenever you are," Kevin told them, taking a seat behind his electric piano and other equipment.

Dee cut a glance at Tamika, smirking teasingly and nudging her.

Tamika nudged Dee too, letting her know that she had better come to the microphones with her.

Dee shrugged, giving in, and Tamika followed her friend to the room. Dee shut the door, and a moment later, Tamika heard Kevin's voice through an intercom.

"Now, you both can sing," he told them, as if making a deal, "but I need to hear Tamika alone first."

Tamika's heart raced, and she tried to calm herself.

"Are your microphones on?"

Dee tapped hers and its sound echoed. Tamika did the same for hers then lowered it to suit her height, which was a few inches under Dee's. As she did so, a piercing sound screeched from the movement, startling her.

"It's okay," Kevin told her, chuckling a bit, embarrassing Tamika.

Dee eyed her friend, grinning teasingly. Tamika rolled her eyes at her playfully.

"We're gonna do a little ad-libbing," he explained. "So just sing whatever comes to your mind, and I'll add music later, and then you'll keep singing."

"Me?"

"Yes," he replied, smiling and laughing lightly at Tamika's nervousness, causing Dee to giggle.

Tamika cleared her throat, stalling, and cleared it again, chuckling nervously. "I guess I'll just sing the same thing I sang for Dee."

"That's fine," Kevin told her. "After I get a feel for it, I'll add music to it."

He must be real good then, Tamika admired internally. She cleared her throat again and forced a cough. She then shut her eyes and began singing, her voice shaking somewhat at first then becoming stronger, "I don't know how, and Lord knows I don't know why, but I can't stop thinking if I'll ever have a chance not to cry..."

In the middle of her singing, the music began, complementing her song. It seemed to belong with the words. Unsure what to do, she started the song again, singing as if she had written it in this manner. But she sang it slightly different to add to the appearance that it was longer than it actually was. As she sang, she relaxed, now comfortable, the music encouraging her, its melodic sound enveloping her, its beauty intoxicating, causing her to wish it would never end.

But it did, and she sang her last words, dragging them out, her voice powerful and captivating.

Dee clapped profusely, laughing and nodding at Kevin, who also clapped, their encore embarrassing Tamika, whose face became warm, unable to relax with the attention.

When Kevin asked her to sing again, the nervousness was no longer there. She wanted to keep singing, not wanting the night to ever end. Song after song, she sang, and finally she and Dee sang a song together—not the one she wrote though, because it was not quite finished.

"I think we have a budding artist on our hands," Kevin commented late that night after they had finished. They were now sitting at his kitchen table nibbling on chips and drinking grape soda from cans.

"I think so," Dee agreed emphatically, her smile large, spreading across her face. "You think she can go professional?" she asked Kevin, the inquiry more friendly teasing than one that needed an answer.

"Definitely," Kevin nodded, laughing and playing along. "The T.D. Sisters," he added jokingly, giving the two a stage name.

Dee burst into laughter. "That sounds like a disease!"

"What? T.D.?" Kevin repeated, considering it, then laughing himself. "I suppose it does."

Tamika chuckled uncomfortably, sensing the two were close friends and that she did not belong, but she was enjoying the moment nonetheless.

"You should just stick to composing and recording," Dee teased sarcastically. "And pay someone else to name the group."

"Hey, hey," he warned playfully. Chuckling, he pointed at her. "Watch it."

"But it's true," she insisted, turning to Tamika. "Don't you think so?"

Caught off guard, Tamika shrugged and forced laughter. "Don't ask me. I'm not in it."

"Hey, c'mon, I need support here!"

"She's smart," Kevin told Dee humorously.

"She's on my side anyway," Dee announced proudly, kidding with him. "We're women."

"Now that's not fair," Kevin complained playfully.

"Too bad," Dee sang as she laughed and threw her hands up in the air to indicate finality.

"Fine, fine," he gave in. "I'm outnumbered."

Tamika smiled, unsure if she was supposed to participate in the exchange.

They went back and forth for a while more, Dee and Kevin, Tamika merely chuckling every now and again, until Kevin mentioned that Tamika might be tired.

"Oh yeah," Dee replied apologetically but still smiling from her exchange with Kevin. "I'm sorry," she told Tamika, standing. "Let's go then."

Tamika stood, relieved, having begun to feel uneasy. She felt as if she were intruding.

Kevin also stood, and the roommates followed him to the door. He handed them their coats and helped each one put hers on. Tamika felt awkward with the friendly gesture.

"Drive carefully," he advised them with sincere concern, opening the door, the cold night air stunning Tamika's body, which had grown accustomed to the warm house.

"We will."

"We'll be in touch," he told Tamika, who nodded. "You got a good voice there."

She smiled uncomfortably.

"Give me a call, okay?" he told Dee, who nodded and waved, making her way out the door.

"Have a good night," he told them, his refined manners becoming apparent to Tamika, impressing her.

"You too," she mumbled at the same time Dee replied.

The door shut, and they were suddenly outside in the cold. Tamika's mind was filled with curiosity. There were questions she wanted to ask but would not. Dee was smiling and shaking her head, still enjoying the conversation of that night.

The drive was silent. Both women were engrossed in their thoughts, Dee's pleasant, a smile frozen on her face, Tamika's contemplative, reflective. She was trying to make sense of everything but was unable to because she could not justify her mental inquiries, suspicions. But she decided finally to put them out of her head, because they were not important. Curiosity often led a person to places that reality would not take her once she discovered the truth.

Chapter Eleven

Tamika slept soundly for quite some time into the night, but something woke her, and at first she was uncertain what it was, and she lay still listening intently for what it had been. A moment later she heard the muffled murmurs, and in sleepy delusion she instinctively thought the sound was the voices of intruders, her heart racing with fear at the thought. A second later, she came to her senses as she recognized the voice. It was Dee, her voice low and unintelligible from where she spoke in the living room. Instinctively, Tamika glanced to where Dee usually slept, the faint glow beneath the door barely lighting the room but enabling her to see her surroundings. The bed was empty and disheveled, as if Dee had been sleeping but awoke, for Tamika had never seen Dee's bed unmade if she was not in it.

"I don't know what to even say," Dee's voice rose, carrying through the house, apparently unaware that her roommate was awake.

Tamika's ears perked, Dee's concerned tone capturing her attention, curiosity enveloping her once again, her questions from earlier that night filling her head again. Kevin? He had told Dee to call. But why would she be talking to him at this time of night? ...Oh... Tamika stopped herself, mentally scolding herself for making assumptions and delving into that which was none of her business. Her mother had taught her better, and she knew better.

"It doesn't matter though," Dee's voice complained helplessly, her despair a sharp contrast to her bubbly behavior early that night. Tamika listened again, lying still, wondering if she was wrong, then justifying her eavesdropping by convincing herself that she was simply overhearing, not prying.

"I don't even know what to say," Dee said again, whining, her voice lowering, Tamika now unable to make out everything Dee was saying. "...letter is good but..."

For several minutes, the words were unintelligible again, but Tamika could tell by the murmurs that something serious was upsetting her roommate.

"Okay, okay," Tamika heard Dee agree to something, Dee's voice becoming clear again. "That's probably best."

There was a long pause.

"Okay," Dee said finally, her tone indicating the conversation was ending. "Okay, okay, yeah. Okay." A pause. "You too," she said more gently, more compassionately, Tamika's curiosity now restless with a desire to know. "Bye bye."

The house grew quiet, and, ashamed, Tamika pulled the covers over her head, anticipating that Dee would enter the room at any moment, and Tamika did not want her friend to think she was snooping. Tamika heard the sounds of footsteps but none nearing the room. Perhaps, Dee was going to stay up all night.

But why? What could be troubling her that much?

Tamika shut her eyes, trying to force herself to go back to sleep, but she could not. She was no longer tired. She tossed and turned for sometime, hating herself for being unable to coach herself to sleep. She groaned, adjusting her position for the umpteenth time, becoming frustrated with her sleeplessness. She lay still with her eyes closed, determined to sleep no matter what. Tamika loved sleeping, and she hated it when she was unable to get it. But luckily, she remembered gratefully, the next day would not be a school day.

About ten minutes had passed when Tamika felt the urge to go the restroom. Initially, she tried to hold it, convincing herself that she could wait until the morning, especially since she was starting to feel tired again, having begun to drift to sleep. But after shutting her eyes and trying to relax, the urge became stronger, almost unbearable, and inside she groaned, as she mentally prepared herself to get up, for she was going to have to relieve herself whether she liked it or not.

Sighing, she climbed from bed, purposefully letting her feet fall softly on the floor, careful not to make a sound. She walked slowly across the room floor, hoping Dee was not sitting anywhere from which she could see or hear Tamika when she emerged from the room. At the door, she cautiously twisted the handle, grasping the cold metal and carefully turning it so as to make no noise. She tried to remain quiet and calm, but she was barely able to hold her bladder any longer. She opened the door slowly but more quickly than she wanted due to her dire need to relieve herself. From where she stood, she saw no one sitting on the couch, but as she emerged from the room, she and Dee's gaze met, and Tamika's jaw dropped slightly, immediately concerned and embarrassed for Dee.

Dee's eyes were red, and tears were rushing down her cheeks. She sat on a far end of the couch, hugging her knees, her polished toenails peeping from under the large pajama top that she wore. Dee's head rose slightly from where her chin sat on her knees, and her eyes grew large with shame. She started to say something to Tamika, to explain, to clarify, but could not.

Immediately, Tamika rushed to the bathroom, quickening her steps, unsure what to say, to do, her heart now pounding, feeling as if she had violated Dee's privacy. After using the restroom, Tamika washed her hands, letting the water run on her hands much longer than she needed, her eyes staring at her reflection with uncertainty. What should she do? Wait there for

Dee to leave or go to sleep? But she decided against the former, because that would mean she would be in the bathroom for an indefinite amount of time.

After a few minutes of pondering, Tamika felt her eyelids growing heavy, and she realized she needed sleep. She would have to pass Dee quickly and pretend as if she did not care, she planned. She felt sorry for Dee, ashamed that she had seen Dee in such a fragile predicament. She wanted to hurry back to the room, hoping Dee would think Tamika was too exhausted to remember the eye contact—the tears.

Taking a deep breath, Tamika opened the bathroom door and exited, intending to avoid eye contact with Dee, but she inadvertently glanced to one side, meeting Dee's gaze, but this time Dee just looked away, her expression one of nonchalance, no longer caring that Tamika saw. What did it matter? Tamika had no idea what was wrong, and wasn't it normal for every person to have a bad day?

Tamika forced a friendly smile as she passed through the hall from the bathroom and returned to her room, her mind racing as she gently closed the door. Dazed, she climbed into bed and settled under the covers staring at the ceiling, doubting she would sleep anytime soon, as seeing Dee crying heightened her curiosity and made her sympathize, although she had no idea what was troubling her friend.

Tamika blinked and squinted, the sun's warm rays reaching through the room's closed blinds, greeting her, informing her that she had slept, although she had not realized it until just then. She sat up, rubbing her eyes, the room too quiet that Saturday morning. Immediately, she thought of Dee, whose bed she noticed was tousled, as it had been the night before, suggesting that Dee had not returned to it since then. Concerned, Tamika climbed from bed and left the room, entering the living room, where she found Dee sleeping on the couch, still sitting up but with her head to one side and her arms dangling pathetically beside her, her palms facing up and her mouth slightly ajar. Tamika glanced away, embarrassed to see Dee in this manner, and walked softly across the floor to the kitchen, trying not to wake her friend.

In the kitchen, after washing her hands with the dishwashing liquid at the sink, as she had grown accustomed to doing as a child, Tamika began to make breakfast for herself, dishes clanking, although she was trying to avoid the noise. Perhaps, she would make French toast, she considered, removing a carton of eggs from the refrigerator, placing it on the counter, then removing a glass bowl from a cabinet. She heard movement in the living room. So Dee was awake now. Tamika felt guilty, thinking she had disturbed her, but she continued to fix the food as if everything was normal.

"Good morning."

She turned to find Dee leaning lazily against the doorway, forcing a smile, her long hair disheveled, sleepiness in her voice and appearance.

"What are you fixing?" Dee asked, her scratchy voice slowly becoming clear. She walked into the kitchen and peered in the glass bowl, which was empty.

"French toast, I suppose." Tamika shrugged, chuckling, removing an egg from the carton and cracking it on the side of the bowl. "That's all I feel like doing."

"Mind if I have some?"

"If you want," she offered but warned, "I'm not a great cook."

"It doesn't matter to me," Dee assured. "I'm just hungry."

"Okay," Tamika warned jokingly.

Dee patted her on the shoulder. "Don't worry. I don't say what I think."

Tamika laughed. "Gee thanks."

Dee laughed, now exiting the kitchen.

The apartment grew quiet again after Dee left the room. Tamika moved about the kitchen thoughtfully, her mind on Dee. She was still curious as to what had been wrong the night before, though her desire to know somewhat waned after seeing Dee at least appearing cheerful.

She dipped a slice of bread in the slimy batter and dropped it in the hot frying pan that had been waiting, the sizzling sound popping and crackling throughout the house and its steam floating in front of Tamika's face. Mechanically, she took the spatula and teased the sides of the toast, loosening its grip on the hot surface. She dipped another and did the same and repeated this routine until several toasts were done, stacked on a plate next to the stove. After turning off the stove, Tamika carried the glass plate to the small round table that stood in the middle of the kitchen and set the breakfast down, returning to the refrigerator for butter and syrup, which she liked chilled. Then she opened the drawers, removing the necessary silverware, and closed them. Less than a minute later, she was sitting at the table serving herself some French toast.

A few minutes after Tamika had begun eating, Dee entered, now dressed in a loose, sleeveless summer dress, her hair pulled back in a pony tail and her face bright, no signs of exhaustion or sadness traceable behind her tan skin. She sat down, her cheerful expression still there, making Tamika momentarily wonder if the night before had actually occurred.

Dee took a bite and smiled, nodding at Tamika. "You're a good cook."

Tamika smiled uncomfortably and shook her head. "You're just trying to be nice."

Dee chuckled. "How'd you know?"

Tamika laughed, shaking her head, enjoying the moment.

"No," Dee said more seriously now, still laughing lightly. "You're just too hard on yourself."

"Maybe," Tamika considered. "But rightfully so."

Dee smiled again, and the kitchen grew silent, the only sounds the clanking of forks against the plates and the occasional suction of the syrup bottle after someone served herself some. They ate in silence for some time, until it became an awkward, polite atmosphere, neither roommate knowing what to say to the other, memories of last night creeping into each one's mind, threatening the fragile tranquility of the moment.

"You finish the song?" Dee inquired, a friendly attempt to break the strained mood.

"Pretty much," Tamika replied, relieved that they had found something to discuss. "I should be done today."

"Really?" Dee's arched eyebrows raised in anticipation.

"I hope," Tamika corrected, laughing.

"Then let's do it."

"But I haven't finished."

"When you're done."

"Oh, okay. Why not?"

"Kevin might want to hear it."

Kevin. Tamika's mind returned to the young man she had met. She did not want to discuss him, not now, as it brought back too much confusion in her mind. She did not understand her roommate, her ways, her life, last night the realization having come to her, raising questions in Tamika's mind concerning Dee. Who were Dee's friends? Her foes? Who was *she*? *Muslim?* Tamika doubted it, the label now appearing more like a family name than a belief system. But strangely, still, she admired Dee.

Tamika knew Dee must be going through a lot—at least Tamika assumed so. But whatever Dee's struggles might have been, Tamika did not care. Dee was strong, a fighter, this Tamika could tell, and she liked that in Dee. Everyone had some obstacles in her life, but what made another more impressive than the other was how she dealt with them, tackled them and moved on. And Tamika was impressed with the way Dee was able to go on, strive for her dreams, despite all of the obstructions in her path. Tamika loved the way Dee was easy-going, always one for a good laugh, able to change a sorrowful or tense day into one of cheer and relaxation just by a clever word or remark. And Dee was so kind, Tamika marveled. She had never heard her say a negative word about a soul, ever eager to brush someone's faults aside, even if the person outwardly scorned her. Why couldn't Tamika be like that, she wondered about herself? Why couldn't she put aside ill feeling for someone and focus on something else, something better? How could it be that a person actually did not care, was not phased or moved, by another's anger towards, or criticism of, her?

Tamika was a very observant person, one to notice even the smallest of things, and she had studied Dee intently since they began to talk and go out, and whenever Tamika would bring up a person, Dee made excuses for him or her, constantly looking at the bright side, offering another perspective, one that always resulted in the mention of a positive character trait. Once Tamika had made a comment about Aminah, about how annoying she was, remembering the several occasions in which Aminah was behaving like a pest, nagging Dee, admonishing her for not praying, as if Dee was her child. And although Dee's displeasure with Aminah's actions was undeniable, as this was often apparent on her face and in her words, she would not allow Tamika to attack her, having brushed it aside, stating that Aminah was only trying to help her in the way she felt was best. Tamika remembered thinking that if it were she who was being nagged, she would likely have cussed the person out, especially if it was a roommate, with whom she had to live and face the harassment every day. How Dee was able to laugh much of it off and maintain a smile and her composure, even with Aminah, was a mystery to Tamika.

"Why?" Tamika inquired with a laugh. She appeared to be joking, but she intended to learn as much as she could. The questions were flooding her mind again, and now was likely the only chance she would have to get some answers. "Didn't he hear enough of me last night?"

"But he likes your voice," Dee shared. "He really thinks you could go professional." She paused and added a moment later, "Seriously."

Tamika laughed, the logical response to Dee's words. "Yeah right."

"You underestimate yourself," Dee told her again sincerely. "You're good."

Inside, Tamika hoped Dee was correct. She wanted nothing else but to fulfill her lifelong dream. She was filling with excitement, anxious to see how far she could go, hoping and praying she could truly make it big. She was determined, and if it meant going to Kevin's everyday, Tamika would go, even if it meant sacrificing her academics. But she could not let Dee know this, not wanting to appear desperate.

"Kevin's even thinking of talking to the producer about you."

"Really?" Although ecstatic inside, this did not prevent Tamika from putting two and two together, concluding that it must have been Kevin Dee had been speaking to. Kevin had not mentioned any such thing last night, which meant Dee had to have spoken to him after that.

"Yeah," Dee nodded. "He might even suggest we team up."

"As a duo, a group!" Tamika's eyes were now wide with hope.

"That's what it sounds like."

"You don't mind?"

"No!" Dee replied emphatically, sucking her teeth and waving her hand. "I don't care either way. Anyway, it might make us a bit more marketable."

Tamika nodded in agreement. "But what would we call ourselves?"

"Not T.D. for sure!"

She laughed, agreeing. "I second that!"

"Then why didn't you say so last night!"

Oh, yeah. She laughed harder. "Hey! My career was on the line!"

"Well, my neck was!"

"Poor thing," Tamika commented, referring to Kevin, shaking her head. "T.D." she repeated.

The roommates laughed hysterically, thinking of how Kevin must have been serious when he said it.

"He should stick to recording," Tamika agreed aloud now.

Dee nodded emphatically. "You got that right."

They calmed themselves a few minutes later, sighing and shaking their heads.

"But I gotta give it to him," Tamika commented sincerely. "He's a natural for music."

"That's true," Dee agreed. "He's already written over a hundred songs."

"He has!"

"Yeah, can you believe it?"

"That's amazing."

"He's a genius."

Tamika was silent momentarily then asked, "So he plans to study music?"

"Now," Dee replied, her expression more serious. "But he was a double major in math and music as an undergrad."

Tamika chuckled. "Strange combination."

"I know," Dee agreed, too chuckling. "But you never know what kind of talents are out there."

"So he's not gonna do math anymore?"

She shrugged. "He's gonna see how the music goes and go from there."

Tamika nodded. "I see."

There was a long pause.

"Where's he from?" she inquired.

"Kevin?"

"Yeah."

"His mother is from Mexico, and his father is Egyptian and white."

"Really?" Tamika was surprised. She would have never guessed.

Dee laughed in agreement. "I know. It's strange huh?"

"Yeah, it is."

There was brief silence.

Tamika started to ask about him, but Dee stood before she could.

"I better get to studying," Dee said, picking up her sticky plate and carrying it to the sink.

"Yeah, me too."

"But let me know when you finish, okay?"

"The song?"

"Yeah."

"Okay."

Aminah sat on the couch in her living room studying, a book lying open on her lap. She had just finished praying *Duhaa,* a voluntary morning prayer that she had grown accustomed to praying since high school. After reading of its immense rewards, she did not want to miss the prayer, so it had become a regular practice for her. There was a time when she would slack, missing the prayer as many times as twice a week, but that was before college. Before Durrah had changed.

Seeing Durrah change so abruptly, so unexpectedly, terrified Aminah. She had never before seen a person on one path one day and literally on an entirely different one the next. She remembered as if it was yesterday she and Durrah's conversations they would have everyday after school, expressing their shock about and disappointment with the lifestyles of most non-Muslims. She and Durrah had gone to public school because no Muslim high school was in their area, which was a small suburb of Atlanta. This experience was one that Aminah would never forget. The promiscuity and carelessness of the students unnerved her.

"They're crazy," Durrah would often remark about their behavior, sharing Aminah's sentiments.

Their faith was high then, and although up and down as everyone's was, it was never so low as to incite them to abandon major parts of their religion. Covering had been one of the most important things to them, and they were the only Muslim students who actually dressed according to Islamic requirements. There were a few other students who were Muslim, but none were openly, the Muslims students having been influenced by the attractive lifestyle of those around them.

But not Aminah, and definitely not Durrah. They were strong, the spearheads of all Islamic activities in their school, Durrah more outspoken about the religion than Aminah. In fact, Durrah was Aminah's strength through much of high school, as Durrah's confidence was higher and her shyness much less, and Durrah had no problem arguing with others about religion and telling them what she believed. Aminah had admired Durrah then, had wished she could be like her, strong-minded, not caring what others thought of her. But Aminah had been somewhat timid, self-conscious about her dress, though she was a strong Muslim and wanted to be nothing else. But still, she felt uncomfortable in the public school environment, dreading each day of school, and although she loved talking about Islam, she did not have enough guts to strike up a conversation with non-Muslims—unlike Durrah, who would go to even teachers and initiate a discussion about Islam, no care given to the fact that she was outnumbered, not phased by the fact that on-lookers supported the teacher.

But what happened? This question pained Aminah even today. She had searched her mind for any indication, any warning that she may have overlooked, but she had found none. But when she had woken that morning, she had thought of something, the memory of the day vague but becoming more vivid as its significance heightened.

She and Durrah had been on their way to lunch one day during their senior year, and Aminah had to go to the restroom. As usual, they stopped at the women's restroom that was down the hall from the cafeteria. Durrah was waiting for Aminah to finish when some other girls had entered the restroom. The girls had greeted Durrah, who had become quite friendly with many students during the course of the year. They exchanged polite conversation as the students combed their hair until one of them said, "Let me see your hair."

At that moment, Aminah emerged from the stall, smiling politely at them and giving a gesture of a wave as she approached the sinks to wash her hands.

"No!" Durrah laughed, holding onto her white cotton *khimaar*.

"Just let me see!" one student begged, laughing, touching the white cloth.

"I thought you said women can see your hair," the other reminded.

"They can," Durrah confirmed.

"I won't tell anyone," the first promised.

Aminah had glanced at Durrah to see how she would respond, wondering how she would brush the students off and tell them no. But Durrah's expression had surprised Aminah, it having been one of thoughtful consideration, as if she saw no harm in it.

"Pleeeeease."

"Just let me see," the other tugged on the cloth.

"Fine," Dee finally gave in, shocking Aminah, who said nothing while watching the exchange more curiously now. "But you can't say anything."

The gasps and awes of the women were exaggerated in Aminah's view as they gawked at Durrah's hair, which fell down her back from under the *khimaar*, under which it had been tucked with a hair clip.

"It's so long!"

"You should show it!"

The suggestions were greeted by a shy shake of the head as Durrah returned her *khimaar* to her head, Aminah finishing washing her hands at that moment.

Presently, Aminah wondered, was that it? Had the students' comments affected her so much that she was drawn in, taken by the attention to which she was unaccustomed? Had it been intoxicating, their words? So intoxicating that Durrah needed—*wanted*—more, more attention, more praise?

But why? Had she not stated on several occasions that she cared nothing about what the disbelievers thought? Had she not asserted several times that she only cared what her future husband thought of her beauty? And had she not told Aminah that she, like Aminah, felt that it was not good to show them her hair?

But what now? Had that all changed, her view now the exact opposite?

But even if that was it, why the extremity? Why the modeling, the singing, and the male company? Was uncovering not enough? Psychologists would probably deduce Durrah was in need of attention, attention she had not received at home, but Aminah knew better. Durrah's parents were full of warmth and affection and were constantly showering compliments to their children, about their Islam, yes, but also about the physical beauty Allah had given them.

So, no, that was not it. There was no void. Rather it was an influence of evil, which likely began as a whisper. But Durrah had succumbed, shocking everyone, perhaps even herself.

Could she too be like that? Aminah? Could Aminah be vulnerable to the attack, the temptation? Did she have buried cravings for the unlawful, for evil, lying in wait to plant itself inside her heart? If so, how would she respond?

As Durrah did?

She hoped not.

Tamika spent much of the morning and the afternoon writing the song, after which she and Dee practiced it, Dee loving it very much and insisting that they do it over again. Tamika enjoyed the attention. Dee's company was addicting, which was why Tamika felt so comfortable with her, so relaxed. Being with Dee freed her of her burdens, whether academic, mental—or spiritual.

"What are you doing for Spring Break?" Dee inquired after their rehearsal.

"Spring Break?" Tamika repeated, having forgotten completely about it. "When is it?"

"The week after next."

"It is?"

Dee laughed. "Yeah, you didn't know!"

Tamika wrinkled her forehead, then relaxed it as she remembered seeing it on the calendar, and March was a few days away. What was wrong with her? She usually kept up with school vacations and made plans well in advance. "I know," Tamika agreed, chuckling self-consciously. "I don't know how I forgot."

"You wanna go camping though?"

"Camping?

"Yeah."

"Where?"

"There's a resort not too far from here," Dee told her. "A few of us are going, and we're gonna stay in some villas there."

"I don't think I can," Tamika told her honestly. "I don't have any—"

"I'll pay for it."

"No, no," she interrupted emphatically. "I can't let you do that."

"Don't worry about it," Dee told her, shaking her head, waving her hand. "It's not a problem."

"No but still—"

"I insist," she interjected, grinning, arms folded, as if she was not going to let Tamika turn down the offer.

"No, Dee, not this time," Tamika stopped her, laughing. "I'm not gonna let you."

"Then it's a gift."

She laughed again. "You just thought of that."

"How do you know?" Dee challenged playfully.

"I know," Tamika assured her, smiling and shaking her head.

"Well, it's a gift," Dee told her, more convincingly this time. "Besides, it'll be fun if you come. We can make up songs and stuff," she suggested.

Tamika bit her lip, half smiling, staring at Dee. Dee was serious, Tamika could tell. How could she turn her down? "Who's going?"

"Alright!" Dee exclaimed, slapping Tamika playfully on the shoulder as she realized victory.

"Who's going?" Tamika repeated insistently with a chuckle, as if daring Dee.

"About ten people, but eleven now."

She shook her head, smiling, amused by Dee. "Like who?"

"You'll meet 'em there," Dee told her with a wave of her hand. "Most of 'em are just friends, but a few of 'em go here."

"To Streamsdale?"

"Yeah."

"Well, I suppose," Tamika said slowly, thinking it probably would not be half bad. "If it's really not a big deal—"

"It's not," Dee assured her, still smiling.

"I hope everyone doesn't look at me funny."

She laughed. "No, girl," she assured her. "Everyone's inviting friends anyhow."

"Then it's more than ten."

"It started off as three," she told her matter-of-factly. "But people kept inviting others."

"I see."

"Anyway, it's not a big deal. Trust me."

"If you say so." Tamika shrugged, flattered that she was invited and excited at the idea.

"Then come with me shopping for some stuff," Dee told her, glancing around for her shoes.

"It's not for another week though."

"But we're leaving Friday after classes," she explained. "So this is the only weekend we have before we leave."

"Okay."

Dee slipped on her shoes and Tamika did the same.

"It'll be quick," Dee promised. But they ended up staying out for several hours, going out to eat afterwards and Tamika having suggested going to a movie. But they had fun, so Tamika did not mind. The time had passed quickly, most of it having been spent laughing and joking with Dee.

Chapter Twelve

Spring Break turned out to be one of Tamika's most memorable college experiences, having been filled with excitement after excitement, and afterwards, she was grateful that she had gone. She had not realized how relaxing camping could be, the waterfalls, the lakes, the grass, and the trees, all giving Tamika tranquility, a much needed peace, an escape from the world. During the relaxing trip, reality became a shadow, a whisper fading in the distance, going away gently with the sunset. And although they stayed in the villas most nights, rendering the trip more a luxury than true camping would be, they had slept in tents a couple of nights, just for the experience, and stayed up most of those nights telling kiddy ghost stories with antics and drama that Tamika never imagined adults had. The stories actually ended up seeming a lot less kiddy than they were when they were coupled with the dark night and uncertainty inspired by the movement of trees and the occasional passing of an animal, not to mention that the students were almost a hundred miles from campus.

It was strange, peculiar, how growing darkness changed moods, how reality and imagination became jumbled, indistinguishable, and one's sense of security lost, as if a person's comfort waned as the sun's brightness dimmed. Tamika had been terrified, but she would not have admitted it to anyone. The stories of the campers were frightening, although she knew most of them were fictitious. Even Dee's "what if" stories haunted her, making her sleepless, and Kevin's stories of wild bears and cougars possibly being near captivated her, as she was almost believing, nearly convinced, leaving Tamika attributing every blow of the wind and passing animal, even if a squirrel, to some ominous monster of a creature who was lying in wait for her.

On one of the nights, which was Saturday, their last night there, Tamika retired to her tent, which she shared with only Dee, because their tent was uncomfortably small, barely able to hold even them.

"They're crazy," Dee commented after they settled in their tent, Tamika lying in her sleeping bag, Dee sitting up, hugging her knees, the light of the lantern making their faces glow and shadows large.

Tamika chuckled uncomfortably, still recovering from the vivid descriptions. "Yeah, I know." She lay on her back with her hands folded behind her head, staring at the tent's ceiling, wishing she could return to the villa that she was sharing with Dee and a few other women. She could not sleep out there, not tonight, it was too much, too unbearable. She felt that there were actually likely dangerous animals out there—somewhere. But she did not tell Dee of her trepidation, ashamed, fearing that she would seem like a spoiled child who thought monsters were in the closet and insisting to sleep in his parents' bed.

Dee sighed, scratching at a toenail with one hand, the polish breaking and falling on the ground. Her eyes became intent, and she hugged her knees again, letting her chin rest comfortably on them, a position that Tamika noticed Dee assumed whenever something heavy was on her mind.

Tamika shut her eyes, but sleep would not come, this she knew, because the action was due more to not knowing what else to do than to any sleepiness on her part. She was not going to sleep tonight, she was determined, even if she felt herself growing tired. She had to remain alert, just in case—in case an animal did come near. She knew she was being paranoid, but she could not shake the feeling of anxiousness, fear that there could be some validity to her feeling, to the possibility that wild animals were actually out there.

"You awake?"

She opened her eyes abruptly, heart pounding, immediately realizing that she had drifted to sleep. For how long, she did not know, but she would have to do better at remaining awake. "Yeah," she told Dee, her tone suggesting that she had not slept at all. She turned on her side facing Dee, propping her head with a hand. Perhaps, changing positions would keep her alert. "What's up?"

Dee wore a faint smile, her gaze far off.

Outside, crickets had been chirping, Tamika remembered, but now she heard light tapping upon the tent. It was raining, Tamika observed, realizing she must have been sleeping for a quite a while. It was colder than before, she noticed, pulling the covers up to her shoulders.

"I was just thinking," Dee said contemplatively, her words slow and measured, reflective. She started to go on but stopped herself, considering it first, her smile fading as her eyes fell on Tamika. "You ever have something that you need to do but you're afraid?"

Tamika thought about it briefly, silence filling the air for a brief moment, the gentle pounding of the rain creating a cozy atmosphere for the friends. "All the time."

"I mean, like," Dee sucked her teeth, deciding to phrase it differently. "Is it easy for you talk to your mom?"

Tamika's eyebrows rose slightly as she nodded, now understanding. "Sometimes," she replied honestly.

Dee was silent, nibbling at her lower lip, thoughts elsewhere.

"When it's something we agree on," Tamika added.

Dee smiled, but it was not due to happiness, this Tamika could tell. "Same here."

"I don't ever talk to her about my singing or anything like that."

Dee forced laughter, waving her hand. "I don't even wanna get into that."

Tamika was silent for a few minutes, listening to the pattering of the rain upon the tent, wondering what was bothering Dee. Dee's mood reminded her of the one Dee had had the night Tamika had seen her crying, and she could not help thinking that whatever had been troubling Dee then was troubling her now.

"You have something you want to tell your parents?" Tamika inquired.

Dee had heard the question, but she was delaying the answer, her eyes looking up for a moment then down. She took in a deep breath then exhaled, wanting to explain but not knowing how. "I suppose you can say that."

Tamika felt sorry for Dee, only able to imagine what she was feeling right then. "You don't think they'd listen?"

Dee shook her head. "It's not that." She sighed. "Just how they might take it. That's what I'm worried about."

"What, your singing?"

She shook her head again. "They pretty much know about that, but I suppose I'll have to talk to them about that too."

Tamika nodded, listening, knowing Dee would explain further, Tamika not needing to inquire anymore.

"It's everything," Dee went on, confessing. "My singing, my modeling, my—." She stopped herself.

"Is there something else though?" Tamika asked. "I'm not saying to tell me, but, I mean, is there something besides those things that will make talking to them harder?"

Dee thought for a moment then nodded. "Yeah." She sucked her teeth. "But I don't know what to do."

"Sometimes I just have to tell myself, just do it, and get it over with," Tamika offered.

"That's what Kevin thinks."

Tamika's expression changed, her forehead creasing, puzzlement apparent on her face as she stared questioningly at Dee, although she had not intended to.

Inside, Dee groaned. She had said too much. She had not meant to mention his name. But it was too late.

"Kevin?" Tamika repeated. "You talked to him about it?"

What the heck, Dee thought, suddenly not caring. What did it matter? Tamika did not know her family. "Yeah," Dee replied, chuckling self-consciously. "'Cause it concerns him."

Tamika sat up, half-smiling, staring disbelieving at Dee. "What is it?" she inquired, an expecting smirk on her face.

"Don't say anything to Aminah though."

She waved her hand as if the thought was ludicrous.

"Nobody."

"Fine," she agreed hurriedly, leaning forward, anticipating.

Dee sighed, a smile spreading across her face, letting Tamika know what she was about to say before she even spoke. "He asked to marry me."

Tamika shrilled in excitement, hitting Dee playfully. "What!"

Dee laughed. "Shhhh," she told her, pressing her finger against her lips.

"What's wrong with that?" Tamika inquired, voice lowered, pleasurable surprise still detectable in her tone.

Dee's eyes widened, and her smile faded. She stared at Tamika with her forehead creased, surprised that she did not understand. "My parents'll never go for it."

"But did you say yes?"

She giggled. "Of course!"

Tamika laughed, filled with excitement for her roommate. "Just let them meet him then."

Dee shook her head. "My dad'll say no."

"Your dad'll say no?" Tamika repeated, confused.

"He has to give his permission first."

"Oh." She had not realized that. "But—"

"It's a rule in Islam."

"But can't you—"

"It's not so much that I'm stressed about the rule or anything," she explained, interjecting. "'Cause I don't even know if it matters sometimes."

Tamika listened.

"Some days I wake up and wonder if I'm even Muslim." Dee paused then added thoughtfully. "Or if I wanna be anymore."

The words shocked Tamika, who stared at her in disbelief.

"I know it's wrong," Dee admitted, searching for an explanation, more for herself than Tamika. "But I'm just tired sometimes, all the rules and stuff. I don't know." She sighed, eyes staring off again. "And anyway, I doubt I could marry him if I was."

"Why?"

"'Cause I don't think he'd count as a Muslim."

"Your husband has to be Muslim?" Tamika did not know that.

"Yeah."

Oh.

"But he's practically like me. His grandfather is Muslim."

"From Egypt?"

"Yeah. But his father doesn't really practice, because his dad's mother wasn't Muslim, and she raised him. His parents divorced when he was eight, and that's when Islam left his life."

"Was he ever Muslim?" Tamika inquired, engrossed in the conversation, feeling as if she were uncovering a mystery.

"As a boy," Dee replied shrugging, "when he lived with both parents. But even then, his mother took him to church and stuff. But he prayed and everything, especially at his grandparents' house."

"On his father's side?"

"Yeah, because his other grandparents are Christian."

"I see."

"But anyway, he believed it and everything."

"You mean Islam?"

"Yeah." She sighed. "But he's like me. He knows it's right, but he's not really 'there' yet, you know, ready to be strict and everything."

"So he wants to be strict in the religion?"

Dee chuckled. "Yeah, I mean, you can go to Hell if you're not, but," she let out a deep breath. "But we just have to take it one step at a time. After we get married, we're gonna try to grow together and work step by step." She added, "And we plan to raise our children Muslim."

"So you do wanna stay Muslim."

"Eventually." She paused, removing strands of hair from her face with her index finger. She was silent momentarily then added thoughtfully, "But not now."

The night drew on, the rain's pattering quickening, becoming stronger, its rhythmic pattern almost indistinguishable on the tent's coat. Tamika lay awake reflecting, imagining how Dee must feel right then, her desire to marry burning in her but then her family and religion pulling her another way. Tamika did not know if she could take it, all the pressure, and she too, like Dee and Kevin, knew it was right, but it was a big step, a tremendous step. Becoming Muslim would mean changing a lot of things—a lot of things Tamika did not want to change.

For weeks, Tamika pushed the possibility of becoming Muslim to the back of her mind again, relaxing somewhat, like Dee, taking it easy for the sake of her sanity, not wanting to rush into anything. After she thought about it, it made sense to wait. She did not want to jump into anything she was not ready for. When she became Muslim, she wanted to do it completely, not halfway, and she wanted to have certain things in place before then, one of them being a talk with her mother. Tamika did not think too much about her singing career. She had no idea how she would handle that one. But she understood she would eventually have to give it up, but so long as she was able to sing now, she did not think retiring would be half bad. After all, she would already have all the money and the fame, possibly on the pages of history as one of the best singers of all time. Who knew? And by then, it would not matter to her whether or not she sang.

For the time being, she focused on her classes and preparing for the formal performance. Her religion paper was coming along well, and her study skills were becoming better in her other classes. She actually began to entertain the possibility that she could have an $A-$ GPA that semester. It was looking hopeful. She had even begun to call home often, telling her mother of her progress, and, of course, her mother was excited, taking advantage of her bragging rights prematurely, but Tamika did not care. That was her mother, and Tamika had grown used to her mother's attitude about her education.

Chapter Thirteen

Tamika and Dee spent the week before the Spring Formal in and out of both the mall and Kevin's house, at the mall to purchase last minute accessories like cosmetics and jewelry and at Kevin's house to practice their song. They were both nervous, and each could see that in the other, but neither spoke about it, determined not to get cold feet too soon. But Dee's nervousness made Tamika on edge even more than she would be normally, having never seen Dee flinch at the mention of a performance. But she was flinching now, and this scared Tamika, reminding her that the performance was not only important but monumental. Tamika's nervousness was heightened each time she thought of a producer being in the audience, there for the sole purpose of hearing Dee and her.

At times Tamika felt down, thinking he may not come after all, believing that it was quite possible that all of her hopes and rehearsals had been in vain. Besides, she would think to herself, what would make a record producer want to come and hear her at some insignificant formal, the annual Spring Formal at their small town school? What if he did not show? What would she do? What *could* she do? She should stop thinking about it, she often told herself, trying to force herself to remain level headed. But it was difficult, because this show meant so much to her. It was possibly her foot-in-the-door, the door to fame, the door to being the singer about which she had always dreamed, the singer that her mother and family doubted, the singer she always knew she could be.

Late Thursday night, Tamika completed her final draft for her religion paper and all of the note cards for her presentation, freeing herself for the entire weekend, enabling her to relax and have fun. She slept soundly that night, a huge burden having been lifted from her, and she attended her classes the next morning with a clear mind and caring little about whatever else she had to do. For nothing could be as stressful as her religion term paper had been, and whatever assignments she would receive, she could finish Sunday—if she would even have anything due Monday, which she doubted.

Friday afternoon Tamika and Dee went to their hair appointment, for which Dee paid, and returned that evening to their apartment and found Aminah sitting on the couch tapping away on her lap top computer. Dee had hoped Aminah would be gone by then, gone home for the weekend as was her routine. Dee did not want Aminah there while they were getting ready for the formal, because she did not want her to ruin their fun. This night was crucial for them both.

"You're still here?" Dee asked, laughing, concealing her intentions behind the inquiry.

Aminah sighed, scratching her head then rubbing her hands over her face. "I know," she chuckled, eyes still on the screen then tapping again. "I have to finish this paper."

"You didn't finish?" Dee asked with concern, appearing as if she was worried about Aminah's class.

"I did," Aminah replied rolling her eyes as she recalled the experience. "But when I went to retrieve it, it wasn't there."

Dee's eyes widened with concern. "Are you serious?"

"Yeah." Aminah sighed again and shook her head. "So I just called my mom and told her I'll just have to come next weekend." She forced laughter, but she was not happy. "I'll be here a while."

Dee sucked her teeth, empathizing. "I'm sorry about that."

"Oh well. It happens."

She nodded, now wondering what she should do.

"But don't mind me," Aminah told her, aware that her presence may not be welcomed.

"Well," Dee laughed, not wanting to tell her but felt obligated just then. "Don't mind us. We'll be getting ready and practicing and stuff."

Aminah's forehead creased. "For what?"

"The Spring Formal," Dee replied as if Aminah should have known.

"Oh yeah," Aminah responded disinterested, her disapproval detectable in her tone although she tried to conceal it. "I forgot about that."

"So we'll just be sashaying past in a few hours!" Dee joked.

Aminah forced a smile and let her gaze fall to the screen, not wanting to discuss the inappropriateness of the event, having decided that she was going to stay out of Dee's life. She was tired and drained, too weak to hold the both of them. She had her own soul for which to fend. "When will you be back?" She decided that was a safe question.

Dee laughed. "Don't wait up for us."

Aminah wanted to glare at her friend, but she decided against it. "Tomorrow morning then?"

"Sunday morning."

She stared at her friend, her expression confused and scolding, but she had not intended it to be. "Sunday?" she repeated incredulously.

Dee laughed again, not wanting to argue. "Yes, girl," she joked with Aminah, although she knew Aminah was not enjoying it. "There're a lot of activities going on through Saturday night."

Aminah nodded, resuming her typing but fuming inside. Durrah irked her sometimes. Why was everything so funny? Had she lost her mind? Her religion?

"But we better go on and get dressed," Dee said, starting toward the bedroom. "We don't have that much time."

Tamika followed, saying nothing, but inside she was angry that Dee felt obligated to explain herself to Aminah. Who was Aminah? Her mother? Her overseer? But she did not share her frustrations with Dee, because she understood that Dee liked to avoid confrontation with and ill feelings towards people, even if she felt slighted within.

In the room, Tamika took in a deep breath and let it out, calming herself, trying to focus on what was most important, the Spring Formal, and not what was trivial—Aminah. The last thing she needed on her big night was to be diverted by petty issues and end up being distracted while on stage.

Tamika and Dee spent the next couple of hours in front of the mirror, applying make-up and adjusting their hair and dresses, exchanging little conversation in the quiet room, but neither felt awkward in the silence, not this time, the enormity of tonight weighing heavily upon them, filling their minds. As the time to leave drew nearer, Tamika felt her heart begin to pound, staring at herself in the mirror thinking, this was it. It was actually time. Time to perform.

The friends took in a deep breath at the same time and let it out, and they both laughed. Then they calmed themselves and gazed kindly at each other, each one reading the other's expression of empathy and fear. Dee smiled at Tamika, who was dressed in the long, black silk dress with spaghetti straps, the dress she had purchased for her. She looked beautiful, Dee admired. The gold necklace sparkled from Tamika's neck, as did the gold earrings from her ears. And Tamika smiled at Dee, who was dressed in a long black dress similar to hers but with three spaghetti straps on each shoulder. Dee's hair was pulled tightly back in a bun, small sections of her hair dangling on one side of her face and down her back in soft spirals. She seemed to adorn the gold leaf earrings that she wore instead of them adorning her.

At that moment, Tamika found it difficult to believe that she was actually standing there, there opposite Dee, the Dee about whom she had read in newspapers and local magazines, the Dee whom she admired, the Dee who was a model and a singer, a young woman who had at her young age achieved what Tamika had always wanted to. It was breathtaking to even look at her, but it was even more breathtaking to know that she was her partner this time, Dee no longer a name and picture in the newspaper but also her friend, who would likely walk with her on the road to success.

They left the room, knowing they should leave then to arrive on time if they planned to be there so that Kevin and the others who were arranging the event could explain to them what they needed to know.

Upon seeing them, Aminah wanted to remind Dee to pray, but she stopped herself as she noticed Dee was elegantly dressed, nails polished and make-up perfect. There was no chance that Dee would disrupt all of that by rubbing water on it, and in any case, the nail polish would have to be removed before she could even be fully ready for prayer, because the ablution was invalid if performed with any unnecessary obstruction to reaching the necessary parts, the finger nails being one. So, instead, she just smiled and said, *"As-salaamu-alaikum."*

"Wa-alaikum-salaam," Dee replied, putting on her coat, and Tamika did the same. A second later they had disappeared into the hallway, the door shutting behind them, and the sound of the keys locking was the last sound Aminah heard before she had the apartment to herself for the weekend.

Although sad that Dee and Tamika were going to a formal, full of music and intermingling between men and women, Aminah was grateful that she was alone. She could now focus on her term paper. She imagined that if Dee and Tamika had been there during the weekend, she would not get as much done, because her mind would have been on them, and they would have interrupted her thoughts even if they did not intend to.

Aminah had fallen asleep and awoke glancing around, unaware that she had been that tired but feeling refreshed nonetheless. She instinctively glanced at the clock, and, surprised, she rubbed her eyes, hoping she was reading it correctly. But just as she had read a moment before, it was 10:58. How long had she slept, she wondered?

Just then her mind drifted to Durrah and Tamika, the two friends, one of them who used to be her best friend. But Durrah had found someone else, someone who was not stress-provoking, not pestering—not Muslim. It hurt, Aminah could not deny that, a twinge of envy burning within her. She loved Durrah a great deal. They had been through a lot together, had grown up together and had been friends for as long as she could remember. But she had to let go, their lives having diverged so dramatically from each other, each following a different path, both clinging to it tenaciously. But that was how it was in life, in friendships. They came and went, although many would argue that a true friendship never waned, and if it did wane, this was an indication that it had never been a friendship at all. But Aminah disagreed, for she felt strongly in her heart that what she and Durrah had had was friendship, a genuine friendship. But it had merely faded, brushed away as their desires and goals changed. But it had been there once, and Aminah ached for it again, the late night talks, the sleepovers, the pillow fights, the corny knock-knock jokes. But, most especially, she longed for the religious talks, the ones about Hell Fire and Heaven, the ones about Judgment Day, talks that left them both dumbstruck with fright, determined to never go astray, to never even miss as much as a voluntary prayer.

But as they said, time changed people. Or was it that some people changed with time? Due to the unwise choices of some and the judicious choices of others? One could not blame time for change. Time was merely time, and no fault could be assigned to it based merely upon what happened as it moved on. For time only afforded a person the option, the option to do good or evil. And whoever chose the latter could only blame herself. For time had no will, and it forced no one to think scantily about it. But, rather, it offered each person what they needed...and that was a chance to change.

The master of ceremonies introduced Dee and Tamika so precisely, so eloquently that Tamika momentarily wondered if she knew the young lady, but after studying her, Tamika was certain that she did not. Then her mind was someplace else, although only for a split second, when the master of ceremonies returned the microphone to its place, a signal that it was their moment, their time to shine. The hush of the audience brought Tamika back to reality, her mind racing, fixed upon the presence of the producer, who had definitely come, Tamika and Dee having met him earlier, his beautiful wife on his arm. His eyes were on her, Tamika knew it, as most scrutiny would be directed at her. Dee's ingenuity was already known, the pressure now on Tamika to not disappoint all of those watching, awaiting. The master of ceremonies had mentioned that the words of the song were Tamika's, and at that moment Tamika wished that piece of information would have been saved, saved for the end, if the performance was good. But now her heart pounded so fiercely that she could feel it in her throat, her hands shaking like she never knew possible, and as she ascended the steps to the stage behind Dee, she hoped Dee would take the lead. She needed to be a leech, if only for a moment. Her head was spinning, and she momentarily doubted that any of this was real.

Tamika heard her breath in the microphone as she exhaled, and Dee smiled, the same smile Tamika remembered from the performance she had seen a year before. Tamika felt as if she did not belong, as if there was some mistake, but when Kevin's music began to play, she knew that that was her cue.

"How," Dee almost whispered in her singing voice, and Tamika joined in, grateful that Dee had sang the first note. "How," they sang, stretching out the words so beautifully that it shocked Tamika.

"How can I find the words to describe, to tell?
Tell of my lessons, how I stood, how I fell?

Yes, life is full of learning, they all say
But what of that learning, what of it today?
What is it that I should learn, what should I know?
What is it that I have today that yesterday let go?
Is the knowledge to be lived upon, or just spoken from my tongue?
Does that make me wise, even if my years are young?
So many have stories to tell, for many have walked in my shoes
But who should I listen to, with whom will I win, with whom will I lose?

"Sometimes I lie still, and I hear the footsteps of my thoughts
Pressing against my conscience, what great news it has brought
Another lesson, yet another lesson, in a long line to come
A key to success, a key to wisdom, and wise I shall become
One day I shall learn, the thought tells me,
One day I shall know it too, one day I'll come to see
So I listen, I try to listen, Lord knows I do
But what to make of it, for the lessons are not few

"For I hear voices, oh those voices, echoing in my head
Telling me to go this way, or that way, or another way instead
Each voice screams wisdom, each one praising its own
But they echo, the voices echo, and I feel all alone..."

The friends sang, now each singing alone as the other sang the chorus in a melodic whisper in the background. The voices rose and became more powerful, more captivating as the audience listening intently, awestruck by the duo. Each took her turn to solo, ad-libbing the words. The music came on more strongly as the finale was close at hand. Finally, the song came to a close as the women sang the last words, the music fading with their voices until silence filled the room. Then abruptly, the audience cheered, the applauds exploding, the noise rising in a crescendo of excitement, and someone whistled and shouted at Dee, then at Tamika, praising their performance.

It was over, this Tamika could not believe. A smile grew on her face, and her eyes gazed into the audience. The cheering was like background noise as Dee stood next to her, as pleased as she, both certain that the producer was impressed. Tamika calmed herself, but she could not relax completely. The scene was still surreal. This could not be happening, she kept thinking as she and Dee exited the stage.

The hands shook theirs profusely, startling Tamika, whose body jerked somewhat with the eager handshakes, and many arms embraced, congratulating them, some introducing themselves, and other showering undying praise. Tamika was so joyful at the moment that her cheeks were sore from smiling, and she kept laughing and laughing as each person greeted her, many commenting that they had no idea she was so good.

A warm hand held Tamika's, a grip that was unlike the others, and she looked up to find Makisha, who grinned at her and playfully told her, "You go girl." Tamika laughed and hugged her friend, holding her for a few seconds before letting go. Then Makisha moved on, but still grinning admirably at Tamika, allowing the others to have their turn.

The dancing continued, the Spring Formal's disc jockey interrupting the audience's greeting of the singers, reminding the attendees that today was not a talent show but a party. The producer walked up to them grinning, as the other students slowly went their separate ways, finding their places on the dance floor, enjoying the remainder of the formal there.

"Let's set up an appointment," the producer suggested, nodding commendably, his approval detectable in his tone. He shook their hands, congratulating them warmly, and Dee glanced over her shoulder to Kevin, who winked at her, letting her know he knew. The producer then gave the students his business card and told them to call as soon as they could, and when he walked away, Dee grabbed Tamika's hand and pulled her into the hall.

The music faded, its melodious, rhythmic sound muffled by the closed doors, and Dee grinned at Tamika, hands on her hips. Tamika laughed at her stance, not knowing what to say. Tamika calmed and smiled in return, their eyes locked with each other's for a moment. Tamika noticed Dee's eyes watering, which evoked tears from her own eyes. They embraced, sobbing from happiness, the gesture sealing their friendship. They both knew this was the first day of many days to come. They would be popular singers very soon. After they finished embracing, Dee jumped up and down, and Tamika did too. Both looked like little kids as they shrilled and cried in their jubilance, at a complete loss for words. Tamika had no idea how long they stood in the hall, but the time passed quickly, she enjoying the moment, engrossed in her dreams, which were now becoming a reality. When they did return to the party room, they danced and danced, laughing and grinning at each other every few seconds, wishing the night would never end.

Aminah curled her fingers into a fist then relaxed them, trying to ease the soreness that had come from typing too long. She was determined to get at least half-way finished before Saturday morning, because she wanted to be finished with her paper by Saturday night. She hated cramming and had never done it, at least not on purpose, having been one to plan things in advance. Whenever she was given an assignment, she would start it right away, even if it were not due until months later. But now—she sighed at the thought—now she had more than fifteen pages to type in two days, a feat to which she was unaccustomed. Her papers were normally completed at least a week before they were due.

She typed some more then felt herself becoming tired again, but she wanted to push herself. She had less than two pages to go before she was half way done. But her exhaustion got the better of her. Her mind began to wander, and her head began to nod from heaviness. After fighting sleep for a few minutes more, she gave in. She could not last any longer, and even if she could, her work would be sub-par. She should go to sleep, she decided, shutting down the computer, but only after saving her work on three floppy disks, determined not to lose her work again.

After brushing her teeth and praying the last prayer for the day, she climbed into bed and recited *Ayaat al-Kursee*[36] from the Qur'an, which she normally did before bed. Before drifting to sleep, she lay awake on her side, her eyes staring off in the dark room, which was too quiet and still. She was not accustomed to being by herself, having never lived alone. So the night was strange, eerie, and she longed for company, wishing she were in her bed at home, where her mother and brother were then.

The alarm sounded, and Aminah awoke suddenly, her mind and eyes searching her surroundings, momentarily thinking she was at home but then remembering she was in her apartment at school, her heart sinking as she was reminded of her paper. Groaning, she dragged herself out of bed, feeling as if she had slept too little, but she would not let herself think of sleep. Murmuring the *du'aa* for waking, she turned off the alarm, and, again, the house grew silent, too silent, as it had been the night before. This morning there were no sounds of breathing coming from the other beds. Durrah and Tamika were off having fun. But then again, she considered, they were probably asleep now, exhausted from all of last night's excitement at the Spring Formal, which Aminah imagined must have been a stress relief for them both. The event was the highlight of the year for most students.

She flicked on the room light, blinking at its piercing brightness and rubbing her eyes as they adjusted. She then made her way to the bathroom, dragging her feet, to prepare for prayer. She turned on the faucet and let the water run for a bit until it became warm, stalling as she enjoyed the liquid tickling the palms of her hands. She mouthed "*Bismillaah*"[37] and began performing ablution for prayer, unhurriedly rinsing each hand with the water,

---

[36] Literally, "The verse of the Footstool" (2:255), traditionally recited by Muslims before going to bed.

[37] "In the name of God"

careful to let the water spread to each part of her skin that required purification.

After Aminah prayed, she sat on the floor for a few minutes, and her mind drifted to Durrah and how beautifully she was dressed the night before. Unexpectedly, she felt tears swelling in her eyes at the thought, and she blinked, fighting the tears as her heart ached for her friend. She missed Durrah, who had found a different life, a life unlike hers. For Durrah no longer woke for prayer and read the Qur'an. She no longer went shopping with Aminah for Islamic head coverings or outer garments. She no longer discussed Islam with Aminah, the religion little, if any part, of her life now. Durrah no longer loved what Aminah loved—and she no longer wanted Aminah as her friend.

Aminah swallowed. Unable to contain them any longer, she let the tears ease out of her eyes and slide down her cheeks. And for the first time since Tamika moved in, Aminah admitted to herself that she was jealous of Durrah and Tamika's friendship.

Sometimes Aminah felt sorry for Durrah, who was lost in the fast paced world, mesmerized by all of its glitter and amusements. Durrah was happy, Aminah guessed, but Durrah could not be entirely, not with the double life she lived. Who could be truly happy if she wore one face at home and another at school? Who could relax completely if her actions conflicted with her beliefs? No, Durrah was not happy, Aminah decided. Rather, she was distracted, distracted by her desires, unable to feel her pain, unable to appreciate the happiness that her life had already once offered, through Islam.

And Aminah's friendship.

Aminah missed Durrah, this she could not deny. But she was telling herself to let go, weaning herself from her attachment to her childhood friend. It was difficult to grow accustomed to the change, although Aminah was accepting it, albeit gradually. Sometimes she would read an inspirational passage in an Islamic book and instinctively want to share it with Durrah. But then she would remember that Durrah had changed, now "Dee." But there was hope for Durrah, Aminah knew. Many Muslims went through similar struggles, as her mother had stated before. Aminah would just have to be patient and let Durrah come around. But Aminah wanted to help, to assist in some way, but she needed patience and wisdom, two traits she did not yet possess, at least not fully.

At that moment, as she sat alone in the apartment sulking and reminiscing on her past friendship with Durrah, Aminah decided that she would handle things differently with her friend, the idea coming to her just then. She would be subtler in her Islamic reminders so that Durrah would again appreciate Islam—and Aminah. No, Aminah reflected, she would not compromise her religion, but she would compromise her desire to vent. She would no longer pester Durrah, she planned, because this seemed to turn her friend away. Perhaps, Aminah would go shopping with Durrah some days and even listen to her songs, the ones without music, and encourage her to do Islamic songs for Muslim women. Durrah would actually probably like that idea and welcome it since it was a constructive rather than critical suggestion to include Durrah in Islamic activities. Aminah planned to initially overlook any shortcomings on Durrah's part in a desire not to push her farther from Islam. Aminah felt excited at the idea, and the ideas kept coming, rushing through her mind. Yes, she could laugh with Durrah, enjoy Durrah's company, could she not, and just be a friend? Couldn't Aminah just accept who Durrah— Dee—had come to be, and work from there with the intention of being an example so that Dee would return to Islam? Shouldn't Aminah spend more time complimenting instead of scolding her, letting Dee know she cared— still? Letting her know that she remembered their friendship and wanted to rekindle it, that she had not forgotten all the good times? Yes, she could do that, couldn't she?

Why not?

Aminah even felt better at the thought. It could work, she was confident. Many people had come back to the religion by God guiding them through a patient, loving friend. And she could be that person, Aminah decided, now inspired and hopeful, two feelings she had not had since Durrah's change.

Chapter Fourteen

The moist steam from the teacup warmed Aminah's face as she lifted the cup from the table. She sat in the quiet kitchen, her mind now on her paper although she did not want it to be. The phone began ringing in the living room, but Aminah did not move, wanting to relax and enjoy the moment without interruption. She sat still until the ringing ceased, after which she raised the cup to her lips again. The sweet aroma of crushed peppermint leaves filled her nostrils, the bag in which they were enclosed darkening the hot water to a golden brown with each second that passed. Aminah's thin fingers cradled the cup, which warmed the palms of her hands. She sipped the honey-sweetened liquid, its heat shocking her tender lips, which adjusted to the heat a moment later, as if realizing it was not too hot after all. It was late Saturday morning, a few minutes passed eleven, and she was taking a break from her typing. She had been working on her term paper since she had woken at dawn.

From where she sat, she could see the sun's brightness illuminating the apartment's living room, the luminosity from the lamps appearing like a dull glow against its overpowering light. She had not even realized that she had left them on. She had been typing the entire time, and her head now ached from staring at the screen so long. After allowing herself a few more sips, she set down her cup of tea and took in a deep breath and exhaled. She had a long day ahead of her, and she did not want to be deterred. She was determined to finish her paper, as she had been last night, when she decided she would answer no calls until Saturday afternoon, when she planned to return any calls that were for her. She normally answered the phone, but she told herself that she would not this time, having previously found herself talking for several hours before she even noticed the time.

Aminah shut her eyes for a moment, letting her mind drift to home and fade into nothingness as she stole a moment of rest, not caring whether or not she deserved it, the rhythmic pounding in her head pushing her to seize the opportunity for relaxation, for peace. She was almost finished with her paper, less than five pages to go. She could not stop then. Otherwise, she may not finish in time.

A knock at the door interrupted Aminah's moment of stolen rest, and she abruptly opened her eyes. Mechanically, she stood, searching her mind for who it could be. *Durrah? Tamika?* Had their weekend ended earlier than expected? But, even so, they had keys. Or had they forgotten them?

The person knocked again, this time more forcefully, as if certain Aminah was there. Instinctively, Aminah touched her head as she hurried to the living room, realizing that she was uncovered, eyes searching the room for something to cover her hair. Then she spotted her *khimaar* that she had worn for prayer, the white cloth tossed carelessly on an arm of the couch. She quickly retrieved it and threw it on her head, tossing one end over her shoulder, the head covering now hanging loosely around her head.

"Who is it?" she called a few steps from the door as she approached, hoping the person had not gone while she was covering.

There was a pause, as if the person was hesitating, then Aminah heard the person reply, but she was unable to make out what the person said.

"Excuse me?" Aminah said, her ear now to the door.

"Uh, it's Megan," the young lady said again.

Megan? Aminah repeated the name in her head, searching her mind for any recollection of who she might be. Then she remembered, almost laughing to herself. Megan was one of the students who lived next door. Aminah had spoken to her on occasion, having met her at the beginning of the year, but they did not speak extensively. They had little in common, and their interaction was limited to a polite exchange of words when they passed each other in the hall or on campus. Megan most likely wanted to borrow something, Aminah figured, a pan, a blender, or some other household utensil. It was commonplace for students who lived in close proximity to swap items, even if they were strangers otherwise.

Aminah opened the door, her head peering out, she forcing a friendly smile. "Yes?"

Megan forced a smile in return, but her expression suggested her mind was elsewhere, as she nervously rolled the newspaper that was in her hands and tucked it under an arm a moment later. "Uh," she said, looking past Aminah into the apartment. "Is Tamika home?" she inquired, her eyes hopeful, anxious—concerned?

"No," Aminah replied slowly, shaking her head, uncomfortable with Megan's seeming insistence, as if she needed Tamika right away. "She and Durrah went to the Spring Formal, and they'll be back tomorrow."

Megan's expression changed, her eyes now on Aminah, puzzlement on her face. "You mean Tamika and Dee?" she repeated, as if translating what Aminah had said.

Aminah nodded, "Yes." She was still uncomfortable with students referring to Durrah as Dee, and it was even more discomforting for her that most students were unaware that "Durrah" was actually Dee.

Megan's eyes glanced away, ashamed, as if she wanted to leave but could not. But she looked up at Aminah again, taking in a deep breath then exhaling slowly, disappointment on her face. "So you don't know?"

"When they'll be here?" Aminah inquired, confused. She had just given Megan that information.

"No," Megan told her, her eyes sympathetic. "What happened."

Aminah felt herself stiffen, and she blinked, staring at Megan blankly. "N-n-no," she stuttered, searching Megan's face for an indication of what she was referring to.

Megan's eyes widened somewhat and she opened her mouth slowly. A moment later, she spoke, eyes darting. "There was an accident."

Aminah felt her heart racing suddenly, fear almost numbing her. "An accident?" she repeated, staring at Megan, waiting for an explanation.

"Yeah," Megan told her with marked concern. "Tamika and Dee were in a car accident last night."

What? Before Aminah could muster a response, Megan went on.

"Tamika's okay, but," she breathed, sighing regretfully with the word, "Dee didn't make it." The words parted from her lips swiftly, the information difficult for her to divulge.

Didn't make it? Aminah felt her legs weaken and her ears filled, sound momentarily escaping them and returning a second later. What was Megan saying? *Dee? Durrah?* She shook the possibility from her mind. No, it was not possible. She had just seen her friend the night before. She must not have understood Megan correctly. "Wh-what are you saying?"

Megan's gaze lowered, suddenly feeling sorry for Aminah, handing her the newspaper. Aminah accepted it in her numbed hand, her head seeming to spin. She felt sick. She needed to sit down.

Unsure what else to say or do, Megan hesitated then walked away, returning to her room. Megan's door shut too quickly, leaving Aminah to her thoughts, her confusion...her pain.

The apartment door shut slowly until it was finally closed. Dazed, Aminah forgot to lock the door as she dragged her heavy body to the couch, where she collapsed, and leaned her head back on the headrest.

There had to be some mistake.

"So we'll just be sashaying past in a few hours!" Durrah's voice echoed in Aminah's head, her dimpled smile so real, as if before her, her tan face smooth, appearing almost exhilarating behind the perfect make-up and carefree expression. No, nothing had happened to Durrah. Aminah was going to talk to her when she returned. They were going to be friends again, like they had been before, as children. Aminah was going to use wisdom and kindness to show Durrah back to Islam. They were going to go out again, laugh again, and have late night talks again, maybe even pillow fights. *Yeah,* they both still had that kid in them, and Durrah still had that dynamic personality she always had had, and that humor. She was always one to make you laugh, even if you didn't want to...

Aminah forced herself to unroll the rough-textured paper, and before she could decide if she wanted to read, the headlines screamed, "Spring Formal

Ends in Disaster, Car Accident, Four Injured, One Dead." She swallowed, the last word stinging her, abruptly disturbing her peace of mind, her sanity. Irrational, she checked the date of the paper, hoping it had been a hoax, a back issue, a cruel joke. But the day's date stared at her, confirming what she did not want to believe. Her heart raced as her eyes skimmed the page, not wanting to read more than she needed,

"Friday night ended tragically when a car collided into another, killing one and injuring four others, two seriously. Authorities say that Streamsdale sophomore Robert Samuels, 18, had been driving while intoxicated after leaving the school's Spring Formal when his car that was carrying two friends hit the driver's side of a vehicle belonging to Streamsdale junior Durrah "Dee" Gonzalez, 19, killing her and injuring passenger Tamika Douglass, who is hospitalized, though no serious injuries have been reported...."

Aminah read the words again, a lump developing in her throat, but, still, she did not believe it, as she could not—would not—believe that the ink on this page was telling the truth. She would call Durrah's mother, who would laugh and say Durrah was fine and say that Durrah had called this morning to say she was all right.

No, it could not be true, none of it, Aminah concluded, thirsting for mental relief, realizing then that, if it had been true, Aminah would have heard from her mother or Durrah's mother. They would have called if anything—

...Called. Someone had called, not once, but several times, and someone had called last night, but she did not answer, wanting to concentrate on her paper.

Panicking inside, Aminah's heart pounded so profusely she could barely breathe, pulling herself from the couch and picking up the phone. With the receiver to her ear, her heart sank, the stuttered dial tone telling her what she rather not know. Feeling helpless, heavy, she dialed the voicemail, impatiently waiting for it to inform her who had called. Three new voice messages—and each from home. Her parents rarely called her once a week, let alone three times in less than twenty-four hours.

She swallowed hard, hands shaking, regret engulfing her, suffocating her. But what did she regret? She pressed the button to listen to the message, but as soon as her mother greeted, she hung up, as desperation was traceable even in those short words. She covered her face with her hands, frantically searching her mind for what to do. Call a taxi? Call home?

The phone rang.

Aminah groaned, dreading picking it up. It rang again, and, still, she did not move. It rang again, then again, the last time it would ring before going to the voice mail. She picked it up hurriedly and calmed her voice.

"Yes?"

"Thank God!" her mother's voice said, relieved, too distracted to remember to greet her daughter. "I've been trying to call you all night."

"I know," Aminah mumbled, her vision blurring, at that moment knowing it was true.

"Well, I'm sure you've heard by now," Sarah said, her voice fading, sad.

"Yeah," Aminah replied, her voice cracking, not wanting to say that a stranger told her only moments before.

"Sulayman's on his way to pick you up. The *janazah* is this afternoon."

Janazah. The word had meant little to Aminah before, having been merely a word on the page of a book. Why did that word sting her, pierce her heart, today? She had learned it years before as a child, having been unaffected, unmoved by its implications, its meaning—its enormity. Yes, she knew it meant that a funeral would be held for a Muslim, and she had even attended one. But she had not understood then, the person having been a stranger, not anyone close to her, not a friend—not Durrah. Durrah had even sat beside her that day, her mind wandering as had Aminah's, their immaturity now sickening Aminah, as she remembered how they had been staring at the clock the entire time. They did not want to be there, Aminah recalled. It was their parents' friend, a man, a woman, Aminah could not recollect; it had been insignificant at the time.

She had heard the word death almost everyday, it having been a normal part of the Muslim's vocabulary. After all, was it not the only reason the Muslim lived? Was not every moment of a Muslim's life in preparation for death? Every prayer, every word, every breath was spent hoping that one's soul would be taken while he or she was in the state of Islam.

Islam.

Had Durrah died in that state?

Who knew? Definitely not Durrah's parents or her family or even Aminah's own mother. None were aware that Durrah no longer prayed. Aminah could not bring herself to say it…to backbite…to break Sister Maryam's heart. Sister Maryam loved her daughter, Durrah having been a source of pride and joy for her—until Durrah left to school. But no one really spoke of her drastic changes, the knowledge an invisible thorn in the side, the pain felt, but no one able to see it there—able to admit it there.

There was another knock at the door, but this time Aminah knew, having come to know her brother's method of pounding on a door, especially when he was in hurry and had no time to wait. Mechanically, she stood, her body weight…or her heavy heart…weighing her down. She did not think to pin her *khimaar*, but she removed an *abiyah* from the front closet, slipping it over her head, too dazed to notice it was wrinkled.

She opened the door, her eyes cast down, replying to her brother's mumbled greeting with a weak motion of her lips and then followed him down the hall. It was a quiet walk, one that needed no sounds. They were at a loss for words, and their minds were at a loss for thoughts. For what could they think about but dumbness, as awe filled their brains, blocking all other information, rendering it insignificant at that moment?

Durrah.

Aminah still pictured her alive and well, laughing and joking as she normally did.

Durrah.

No, death was not a synonym to that name. For Durrah had come to mean a strong-minded young lady, a beautiful woman...Aminah's friend.

Durrah.

No, it was not she, could not be she who had been discussed in the article.

In the car, Aminah sat in the passenger seat resting her head against the glass. Then she remembered, but it was probably too late, because patience was at the shock, the initial strike of the pain. But she murmured the words anyhow, ashamed that she had forgotten, remembering so late. *"Inna lillaahi wa inna ilayhi raji'oon,"* she mumbled what meant, "From God we come, and unto Him is our return."

The drive was silent, a delicate, strained silence, Sulayman's eyes fixed on the road but his sight elsewhere, Aminah's eyes staring off into the distance, looking at nothing, feeling as if she was too weak to concentrate on anything. She was too shocked to cry, the reality having not yet set in, although she was now aware it was true. But, still, it was too unreal. Durrah? *Dee? Dead?* No, the words did not belong together in the same sentence, at least not now. There was hope for Durrah, Aminah had believed. Durrah would come around, back to her senses, back to Islam, Aminah was certain she would. Most other Muslims did.

But did she come around?

Dead.

Could it be?

But didn't everyone have to go sometime?

But still...

Durrah? Dead?

But how?

The *janazah* was this afternoon.

But Durrah? Could there have been a mistake?

She glanced at Sulayman, whose eyes were fixed, his expression tense and fragile.

No, there was no mistake, she realized somberly. Durrah was gone— gone forever—now about to go to the grave.

The grave.

The thought terrified Aminah, sent chills down her spine.

The dark grave, the questioning, the angels...

Angels.

Years ago Aminah had thought of angels like most other people did, as nice, gentle, human-like creatures who resembled a beautiful white woman or a cherubic child, adorned with dove-like wings, and appeared only in a person's life to bring them good. They were always smiling, always glowing in happiness, and ever bringing joy by their mere presence.

But she later learned that she was wrong.

Dead wrong.

No, angels were not bringers of glad tidings, at least not always. Each of them had a role to fulfill, each role different, God having assigned them different responsibilities. There was the angel who was in charge of rain and others who assisted him. Then there were the angels in charge of recording the actions of a person, one on the right of each person and another on the left. And there were angels who diverted from humans those things that were not fate. There were various angels in charge of many of humans' affairs. But they were not beautiful women, nor were they children. In fact, they were not human at all. Rather, they were a special creation of God, created from light, who fulfilled their duties to God without protest or question. They were creatures without choice. And in fulfilling their duty, they did not always bring good news, and they were not always smiling. And they were not always gentle. For there were those who were in charge of seizing the souls of humans at death.

...And they had already seized Durrah's soul.

Durrah was now going to the *Barzakh*—the Barrier—entrapped. And there was no turning back. She was on the first part of her journey to Heaven—or Hell. Now likely about to experience the torment of the grave, the agonizing torment about which she and Aminah had studied years ago, the torment that had once petrified them both, kept them up many nights, inspired them to fast and pray as much as they could.

And, still, several years later, the words of the Prophet (s) filled Aminah's mind, the memories of what she had learned returning to her, the words strangely poetic, uncanny, the soundless words like taunting lyrics humming in her mind.

As for the disbelieving (or corrupt) man, when he leaves this world and enters the Hereafter, stern and harsh angels come down to him from heaven. Their faces are black, and they bring with them sack-cloth from Hell. They sit around him, as far as the eye can see. The Angel of Death comes and sits at his head and says, 'O evil soul, come out to the anger and wrath of God!'... The soul will be dragged out of his body with as much difficulty as a many-

pronged skewer being pulled through wet wool (the veins and nerves will be destroyed by it). He will be cursed by every angel between heaven and earth, and by every angel in heaven. The gates of heaven will be locked and the people of every heaven will pray to God not to allow his soul to ascend through their domain. He will take it and immediately put it into the sack-cloth. It will stink like the foulest stench of dead flesh ever witnessed on earth. They will take the soul up, and whenever they take it past a group of angels, they will say, 'Who is this evil soul?' They say, 'It is so-and- so the son of so-and-so,' using the worst names with which he was addressed in the world (They will go on) until they reach the first heaven. They will ask for it to be opened to them, and it will not be opened. '...No opening will there be of the gates of heaven, nor will they enter the Garden, until the camel can pass through the eye of the needle...'[38] God, may He be glorified and exalted, will say, 'Register his book in Sijjin, in the lowest earth'

Then God will say, 'Take him back to earth, for this was my promise: I created them from it, I will return them to it, and I will resurrect them from it again.' So his soul will be thrown down from the heaven until it reaches his body. '...If anyone assigns partners to God; he is as if he had fallen from heaven and been snatched up by birds, or the wind had swooped (like a bird on its prey) and thrown him into a far distant place.'[39]

So his soul will be returned to his body. [He will hear the footsteps of his companions when they leave him (in the grave)]. Two stern angels will come to him, rebuke him, and sit him up. They will ask him, 'Who is your Lord' He will say, 'Hah-hah [due to excruciating pain], I don't know!' They will ask him, 'What is your religion?' He will say, 'Hah-hah, I don't know.' They will ask, 'What did you say about this man who was sent among you?' He will not even know his name, but he will be told; 'Muhammad,' and he will say, 'Hah-hah, I don't know! I heard the people saying such-and-such.' He will be told, 'May you never know!'

Then a voice will call from heaven, saying, 'He has lied; so furnish his grave from Hell, and open for him a gate to Hell.' So some of its heat and venom will reach him, and his grave will be constricted until his ribs are crushed together. There will come to him a man with an ugly face, badly-dressed, and foul-smelling. He will say, 'I bring you bad news.' This is the day that you were promised.' He will say, 'And you, may God give you even worse news! Who are you? Your face brings bad news!' He will say, 'I am your evil deeds. By God, I only ever saw you reluctant to obey God and ever-eager to disobey Him. May God repay you with evil!' Then there will be sent to him one who is blind, deaf, and dumb, who will carry in his hand an iron

---

[38] Al-A'raaf, 7:40
[39] Al-Hajj, 22:31

rod which, if he were to beat a camel with it, would turn it to dust. He will beat him with it. Then God will restore him, then he will be beaten again. He will emit a scream that the whole of creation will hear, except for men and jinn. Then a gate will be opened for him to Hell, and his grave will be furnished from Hell. He will say, 'My Lord; may the Hour (of Judgment) never come!'

From the window Aminah's eyes fell upon the passing trees, their leaves budding, the bright green a sharp contrast to the yellow, orange, and brown of several months before. The colors had dried to a dark brown then and had been scattered about on the grassy lawns, leaving their respective trees barren, lifeless and naked, appearing almost helpless, their branches like aching arms outstretched, begging for life. But they were greeted with the cold of winter, doomed, their silhouettes ominous structures against the pale glow of moonlight, suggesting a lurking death. Yet they had been restored to life, their arms now adorned with coats of green, hinting to budding flowers whose heads would soon blossom in their fullness.

How was it that so many could not understand, could not see? That God could give life to the dead, the lifeless creatures that lie under and upon the earth. Did He not create the trees, take away their life of luscious greenery, dry them to brittle brown, and flawlessly restore them next season? And was that not easy for Him? And could He not return humans to life after death, restoring them to their very finger tips and call them to Judgment?

Then how was it that so many humans were heedless, irresponsible, walking about the world carefree, oblivious to the signs around them, the leaves, the grass, the trees—death? Were those not signs for all to see, to ponder? Or did people think they would live forever, that death would not come to them? Did they think they could do whatever they pleased, what they wanted, satiating every carnal appetite, committing evil after evil, and would never be called to account? Did they think their selfish desires, their opinions—their arrogance—would benefit them in the End? Would their lifestyles of feigned wisdom and so-called freedom come to their rescue when the Angel of Death seized their souls? Would their foolish questioning of God and His laws fill their puny minds, or would they submit then—finally— when it was too late? Or perhaps, they had grown so accustomed to waking each day that they had begun to believe that tomorrow would always be there, that ambiguous tomorrow, when they would change, when they would be better, when they would submit, the promises of someday always wetting their tongues.

Durrah, poor Dee, what of her life now? What of her not praying? Her singing, her modeling? Did it matter anymore? Was she singing any longer, in the grave? And were any more eyes gawking at her beauty, admiring, praising, and wanting to be her?

Our Lord, Aminah silently prayed, *let not our hearts deviate now after You have guided us, and grant us mercy from Your presence, for You are the Bestower!*

The day dragged on slowly. Words were thought but not spoken in Aminah's home that day, her mother, father, and brother moving about as if in slow motion, not sure what was right to say, what was wrong. Should Aminah dare to say, 'May Allah forgive Durrah,' when she was unsure of the state of her friend's soul, when the last time she saw Durrah prostrate in prayer was months ago? Perhaps, Durrah was just a sinner and no more, Aminah wanted to believe. But something eerie pricked at her conscience, taunting her senses, her heart. Aminah tried to think of the Durrah she knew before college, before the music, before the singing, before the modeling, before the male friends. But, with each thought, came the memory of a windy day when she and Durrah had been playing in the sand, grabbing handfuls from the sandy piles, giggling innocently as they opened their fists and watched the dust fly from their hands, disappearing in the wind.

That day, why had it come to her mind just then?

A moment later, she knew.

They had learned in Islamic Studies class, the one they attended in junior high school, that leaving Islam was like that, like holding a fistful of sand then letting go, each grain of golden dust representing a good deed of the Muslim and the brisk wind the consequences of disbelief. And just as the wind swept it all away in one gush, leaving the palms of one's hands bare, so it was with disbelief, leaving the disbeliever with nothing, his works disappearing, vanishing, as if they had never been there. And like the palm of a child's hand whose fist let loose the sand, so too was the person left bare. A life of work, of sacrifice, of good works, all rendered useless, the painful price to pay for turning one's back on God. For even if a person had lived a life of Islam, it would benefit him nothing if the Islam was absent at the time of death. For what mattered was not so much how one lived but how one died.

But that was just it, how did one know? How could one prepare? Who knew the moment at which his soul would be taken, the moment of death? It could come as one reclined on a couch, or decided to go to one last party before pulling himself together and living right.

It was scary, frightening—chilling—how suddenly it occurred, its unexpectedness being its most prominent and terrifying trait, never ceasing to leave shock, even with one who heard of it each day and knew that one day it would be him—or her. Then why the surprise, the despair? Why the pain? And why did so few prepare?

At the masjid, Aminah stood in one of many rows of Muslims gathered behind the body of Durrah. As she stood there, her mind wandered, unsure if she belonged...if anyone belonged...behind her friend. But she could say nothing, for doubt did not warrant a verbal confirmation of the state of one's death. She listened to the imam speak of forgiveness and the hope of Paradise, of great reward. And all Aminah could think about was the body wrapped in white sheets—Durrah, her friend, her poor friend.

There would be no more of her jokes, of her laughter, of her dimpled smile. No more of her "sashaying," her modeling, or her exhilarating style. There would be no more days of pondering in the backyard on a swing. There would be no more days of inspiring conversations...about anything. There would be no more time for Aminah to even admonish her friend. For Durrah's days of hope were over, her chance to do better having come to an abrupt end.

As Aminah left the prayer area, she could not help but notice the expressions, the puzzlement, the confusion on the faces of Durrah's classmates, of her friends, not because of Durrah's death, for they already knew of that, but of the fact that Durrah—Dee—was Muslim. Who would have known? They were baffled, troubled, disoriented. For how could it be?

What a shame, Aminah could not help but think despite her own sorrow. What a shame that those who knew her well had no idea, no clue that this Dee, the superstar, the beauty queen, the singer, was Muslim. How sickening a reality, and how much more painful her death. They were crying, yes, Aminah having heard their wailing even as she prayed. But what did their tears matter? They did not understand. For what did the knowledge of Durrah's death do for them now? How did it change their attitude, their life? Did it move them to submit, bring them back to their senses and inspire them to fear God? Or was the moistening of their eyes indicative of a selfish sadness, one that cared little of what this all should mean? What did they miss of Durrah, of Dee? Her intoxicating singing voice, her breathtaking smile? Her glittery clothes, her sense of humor? What? And what did it matter, any of it, if they went on with their lives, heedless and careless, only to be like her before long—dead—gone, another period at the end of a sentence, the sentence of life. Another in a long line of periods, periods that did not move its readers to ponder, to reflect, or even care, except to say they missed her, and *Oh how sad*. But did they really know how sad it was? Or were they blind, their hearts veiled and sealed, they doomed astray, a just recompense for their arrogance, their refusal to submit?

Oh, what did polygamy matter now, or how Muslim women dressed, or the rule on music and singing, or the man as the leader, or Islam's view on jihad? Who cared now? Who would? For now was a time of regret for those who had been lost, contaminated—spiritually sick in the world, in need of a healing that only submission to God could give.

Aminah felt the pull of the car and the hum of its engine as she sat in the back seat next to Sulayman, their parents in the front. Still, no one spoke. But what could they say if they did? Perhaps, her father would talk to them later, or maybe her mother, and calm everyone, advising them to just pray for Durrah's forgiveness, for her soul...

The drive to the Muslim graveyard was long, too long. It seemed like hours before the car finally came to a halt, but Aminah knew it had not even been forty minutes, having looked at the clock.

The burial ground was plain, its dirt showing little signs of green, small patches of grass barely visible in far off spots, suggesting the grounds must have been recently acquired. From the car window, Aminah could see the graves, piles of dark dirt slightly raised about ground, the length of human beings, mostly adults, but a few were no more than a couple feet long. For a second, her heart ached at the thought, small helpless children under ground, their little lives over, probably having not lived long enough to even talk, to run, to play. But then there came a reminder, a gentle tug at her brain, her senses, as she realized that there was nothing sad about their predicament, nothing distressing about the death of a child, not the death of a child born from a Muslim womb. For there was no torment, no pain, no stress, and there was not even the need to ask forgiveness for its soul, for Paradise would be his or hers. It had no time to slack, to sin.

How different things would have been had Durrah's soul been taken while she was a child, and how much stress would have been lifted from Aminah's own soul if hers had been taken then too. Then she would not be worrying, fretting over how her life might change, how her views might shift or how her belief may disappear. Or how what was so clear today could be so foggy, even unimportant, tomorrow, Islam possibly becoming a trivial word in the wind, its meaning lost, its beauty hidden and its strength weakened from her heart. That was what she feared the most—being dead before she died.

Sulayman and their father left the car, leaving Aminah and her mother sitting in their seats, the women uncomfortable with joining the crowd of people that had gathered on the burial grounds, unsure if it were correct, proper for them to follow the people to the grave. But from where she sat, Aminah could see the heavy, lifeless body clad in white sheets being carried to the grounds, its dense weight weighing its carriers down.

Durrah.

That was really Durrah in there.

At the grave spot, they lowered her, the weight of the body striking the ground with a thud as it slipped from their grip before they could gently place it down. Then they placed her in the grave, her home for now, the white sheet disappearing underground and the dirt thrown on top of her, burying her, burying Aminah's friend.   Aminah imagined the clumps of dirt hitting the sheet with each toss, each scoop from the ground...

"Can you imagine?" Durrah's eyes had widened, sparkled that day, years ago when they were both ten, having just begun wearing *hijaab*[40].

They were discussing the grave, having studied in class the angels' questioning of a person.   "No," Aminah replied, eyes scared.   She was frightened at the mere thought, as was Durrah.

"But can you imagine answering the questions and not knowing what to say?   What if you don't answer them right?" Durrah had asked, awestruck.

Aminah had not responded, terror having filled her.

"That's scary," Durrah had said that day, gaze distant, hugging her knees. "That's scary..."

---

[40] The Muslim women's Islamic covering of her head and body.

Chapter Fifteen

Aminah's soft voice rang strong, filling the apartment, demanding, as if inviting others to join in, to share in her feelings, to share in her prayer, the last prayer she would pray before going to bed. Outside, the Sunday night was cool, its breeze gently moving the strips of the vertical blinds, the cool air brushing against Aminah's cheeks. She had opened the patio an hour before, when she had returned to her apartment and needed some fresh air. She normally did not open the large glass sliding doors because of the rowdy college students who had chosen to hold shouting conversations on their balconies rather than in person or on the telephone. But tonight Aminah was undisturbed by students, not because they were not there, but because their voices had faded in the background, like muffled whispers behind a closed door.

As she prayed, her mind was filled with thoughts of life and its brevity, and death and its abruptness, and how so few caught on. How was it that so many lived life but did not understand? How was it that so many cared about paltry wealth and status, distracted by the passing pleasures of this world? And why was it that Islam had brushed the lives of so many yet so few accepted it? And worse still, how was it that some of those who had accepted it and bore witness to its truth turned away, choosing a life of negligence, negligence of one's soul? How could a person choose blindness after he had seen the life of Islam? How was it possible that a person could shed tears of happiness, his heart moved by Allah's Words in the Qur'an and then live another moment and just turn away, the words now halting at his ears, their inspiration unable to pierce his heart, as if a stubborn, unmoving barrier were there forbidding any trespassing to the soul?

Was that how most Muslims lived, the words of Allah trivial when compared to their life of wealth, status, and petty desires, whether for some sin or an opinion they did not wish to change? Yes, that must have been it, the summary of the Muslims' downfall, explaining their tremendous failure, why their lives bore little resemblance to the Muslims of old. What was it that the Muslims of today lacked? Sincerity, dedication, faith itself? Was that it? Was Islam missing from the lives of those who claimed it, the entire world suffering from their weakness, the lives of Muslims now the laughing stock of the human race as Muslims paraded the streets as wannabes, fumbling pathetically for an identity, any identity but that of Islam. Was Muslims' weakness so great, so profound, that Islam, the most prized possession one could have in life, was not a source of pride but one of shame? But what was there to be ashamed about, Aminah wondered? That they were to worship God alone and associate none with Him? Did they prefer a life of ignorance, of paganism, of sinfulness? Was that it? Was that what caused a Muslim woman to shed her *hijaab* in preference for sharing her body with the world and cake her face with make-up and rub perfume on her skin, inviting strange men to gawk, to desire, to lust? Was that what caused Muslim men to abandon their responsibilities and sit content in their homes, content because they "did their job," which was nothing more than carry a sign in protest and shout words of anger, scolding the aggressor for being aggressive? Was it weakness in faith, a lack of belief in the Hereafter that caused Muslims to abandon their religion and replace it with foreign ideas, rendering them free of their obligation to teach Islam as the only path to Heaven and rendering them free of practicing Islam?

Yes, that was it. And it was heartbreaking. It was heartbreaking that the holders of truth abandoned truth in an effort to be more pleasing, more appealing to the compelling falsehood of their time, constantly found apologizing for, when not abandoning, religious mandates that were distasteful to those who did not obey their Lord. But it was terrifying too, Aminah could not deny that, the possibility of her slipping having always hung over her head. Life was short, and no one knew what tomorrow would bring, piety or disbelief, success or failure, happiness or grief—life or death.

Had Durrah—Dee—seen it coming? Had she been prepared? Or had she filled her life with somedays, thinking she would do tomorrow what she was too weak to do today? Had she even considered, thought, that maybe, just maybe, this would be it? Had it even occurred to her as she dressed that night for the Spring Formal that she would never return? Did she have a clue? As she painted her face and adorned her body, what was she thinking? How wonderful was God or Islam?

And how had Dee died? In a car on its way to another gathering of desires, of fun. Wouldn't be back till Sunday? *O Lord,* she had no idea! She had made her plans, filled her schedule with activity after activity. But none had been her death. Oh, how terrifying that was, Aminah felt, shivering at the thought, to fill your day with appointments and not see the angel of death coming to fulfill his.

Aminah allowed the meaning of each verse she recited to penetrate her heart, giving it life, causing her heart to overflow with love, hope, and fear of her Lord. At that moment she did not care about a soul, feeling ready for anything, prepared to do anything, anything for the pleasure of God. Why should she care about what others thought? What did it matter if others thought it "uncool," unappealing to be Muslim, to worship God as He asked? For they, like she, would one day die and wake in the grave, questions asked of them, questions that only few would be able to answer with firmness. So what if others laughed? So what if others stuck to the false path of their family and friends? Aminah was on a path of truth, and she was not going to give up—at least she prayed she would not.

Her voice cracked as she recited from God's Words what meant:

> *Until when they come (Before the Judgment Seat),*
> *(God) will say: 'Did you reject My signs though you*
> *comprehended them not in knowledge, or what was it you*
> *did?'*

As she recited the words, Aminah reflected on the people, some who were Muslims, who proudly lived only according to that which they claimed to understand. Haughty and arrogant, they turned against definitive proofs, refusing to humbly submit to God, filling their brains and wetting their tongues with opinion after opinion, question after question, frowning upon those who blindly obeyed their Lord. What a shame they were, Aminah thought, a shame to the human race, their foolishness too vast to encompass in words, their actions like that of a wayward child who only obeyed his parents in those commands with which he agreed, in his ignorance thinking his disobedience was a mark of wisdom, awhile he was the laughing stock of the sane world.

> *And the Word will be fulfilled against them, because of*
> *their wrongdoing, And they will be unable to speak (in*
> *plea)*

> *See they not that We have made the Night for them to*
> *rest and the day to give them light? Verily, in this are signs*
> *for any people who believe!*

But did they heed? Did they reflect upon the signs? Did they submit?

> *And the Day that the Trumpet will be sounded—then*
> *will be smitten with terror those who are in the heavens and*
> *those who are on earth, except such as God will please (to*
> *exempt), and all shall come to His (Presence) as beings*
> *conscious of their lowliness.*

How magnificent it was, God's wisdom in how He planned things. He let the arrogant wander the earth lost and confused, filling their lives with choices and opinions that opposed His command, their state of arrogance preventing them from bowing down, they too haughty to accept truth. But that same arrogant person, the same one who averted his face in disgust when called to the religion and command of God, would come on the Day of Judgment in a state of humility, submitting to God. But his submission would come when it was too late to benefit from the surrender, for his life on earth had been the only time to do that.

But did not the arrogant see that their life was short, that when compared to the grave and the Day of Judgment, this life was nothing, its brevity pathetically insignificant in comparison to the Hereafter, yet the deeds committed in it determined the abode of a soul? The Day of Judgment was akin to 50,000 years in this world's terms, and this time frame did not even include the time spent in Heaven or Hell, a time immeasurable for humans, as there, there would be no death, the bliss of Heaven and the torment of Hell ongoing, never to come to an end.

When viewing matters from that perspective, who would dare to not submit, and who would dare to sin? Was it worth it to succumb to temptation for a moment when it could have everlasting results? Would that moment of pleasure be worth it when more than a lifetime of consequences awaited? Was it worth it not to be Muslim due to fear of family and friends when tomorrow you could wake in the grave, family and friends nowhere in sight?

You see the mountains and think them firmly fixed but
they shall pass away as the clouds pass away: (Such is) the
artistry of God; Who disposes of all things in perfect order.
For He is well acquainted with all that you do.

And how many lived their lives, conscious that everything would soon pass away? And how many fewer lived their lives oblivious to God watching and the angels recording, God well aware of everything that they did?

If any do good, good will (accrue) to them therefrom,
and they will be secure from terror that Day. And if any do
evil, their faces will be thrown headlong into the Fire, 'Do
you receive a reward other than that which you have earned
by your deeds?'

For me, I have been commanded to serve the Lord of
this city, Him Who has sanctified it and to Whom (belongs)
all things.
And I am commanded to be of those who bow in Islam
to God's Will

*And to rehearse the Qur'an. And if any accept
guidance, they do it for the good of their own souls. And if
any stray, say, 'I am only a warner.'*

*And say, 'Praise be to God; Who will show you His
Signs, so that you shall know them, And your Lord is not
unmindful of all that you do.*

Aminah completed her prayer after nearly thirty minutes. While praying, she had spent extra time reciting and reflecting during her standing and stayed long in prostration, as her heart was filled with humility and hope, her tongue moving with supplication after supplication, praying for her soul and the souls of her family, praying that none would go astray. After she finished, she sat silently, her mind focused, her body humble, tears still glistening in her eyes, her mind drifting to Durrah and what she must be going through now...

A soft knock at the door startled Aminah. For a moment she doubted that she had heard it, but seconds later, she heard the knock again. Who would be visiting at this time of night? She stood, her mind back to reality as she walked curiously to the door. She asked who it was, but the reply was too faint. Aminah asked again, but still, she could not make out anything, except that she heard the voice of a woman.

She hesitated. She normally did not open the door unless she was certain who it was. She unlocked the door and cracked it, peeping through. After recognizing the face, she opened it wide.

Tamika forced a smile, her weakness apparent on her tired face. Her hospital wristband was still fastened on her thin wrist, a couple of inches below the white bandage that covered the place where her IV had been. She walked slowly, appearing older than when Aminah saw her last, her make-up no longer visible, now replaced by slight paleness on her face, and her hair was pulled back, slightly disheveled.

Tamika made her way to the couch and sat down. Aminah did not know what to say to her roommate. Both were at a loss for words. Aminah shut the door and locked it, these the only sounds heard at the moment. Aminah stole a glance at Tamika whose gaze was now toward the blinds, Tamika staring past them, although what was beyond them was only darkness. Aminah had heard that Tamika had made it through the accident with barely a scratch and that the hospital had held her more for precaution than necessity, but she appeared to have been through a lot.

Tamika had not known about the tragedy until a couple of hours before, and it was still surreal to her. The hospital workers had told her visitors not to tell her, at least not then. Tamika had constantly inquired about how Dee was doing, having been told, "She's fine," each time. But for some reason, the answers had not been enough, and she sensed they were not telling her the whole truth. Tamika could not shake the feeling of intense concern for Dee. The last thing she had remembered before waking in the hospital was a piercing shrill from her friend as bright lights filled the car, the sudden impact shocking them both. The scene was somewhat like a movie, except it had been real.

Tamika had had no idea, no clue, that Dee had died until the information was revealed to her by Makisha, who had taken Tamika home after she had checked out of the hospital earlier that day, when the doctors saw no need to keep her further. After informing her of her friend's death once they arrived on campus, Makisha had taken Tamika to the school's chapel for a program that evening that had been dedicated to Dee. The ceremony had been filled with eulogies, the choir singing, and the playing of some of Dee's songs. Slides had even been shown of some of Dee's performances, while video clips were shown of some of her shows, each clip followed by the playing of one of Dee's songs from her tapes, her singing tapes, likely supplied by Kevin, who sat on stage, face firm, strong, then breaking finally, tears gushing from his eyes, setting off sobbing from the audience, many of whom were moved by this phenomenal young woman who they had not even known.

"How would you describe yourself?" the man asked Dee during a beauty contest on one of the video clips.

"Hmm," Dee had said, her humor detectable even with that small sound, as she looked into the camera, a perfectly polished fingernail tapping on her chin and a grin developing on her smooth face, her dimples creasing, illuminating her beauty as she smiled. "Am I supposed to reply honestly or just tell you what you wanna hear?" she inquired jokingly, tossing a glance at the questioner, who laughed.

"Whichever you choose."

"Well, I'm perfect, what can I say!"

The audience on the tape roared with laughter as the chapel audience roared with tears, as many remembered Dee's down-to-earth personality that would easily win hearts, even from foes.

"So is there any word to describe your perfection?" he had asked. The other contestants had chosen perfectly scripted responses that they had given, and he patiently waited for Dee to do the same.

"No," she replied simply with her confident smile, as if that were a satisfactory answer.

"No?" the man repeated, chuckling. "What do you mean?"

"Words can't describe me!" she joked, throwing up her arms, the reply more indicative of the comedian in her rather than any conceitedness.

Then they played the clip of her singing, her strong voice rendering even the chapel audience speechless as she sang the seemingly simple song, "You are so beautiful..."

Even Makisha's eyes had become flooded at that point, her hands covering her face in sadness, in shame, Tamika only able to imagine what her best friend was feeling, thinking at that moment. Tamika's mind was elsewhere, her tears spilling down her face for a different reason, remembering what Dee had been doing before the shrill and sudden crash. Dee had been singing, being silly during the song, letting her voice deepen for the man's part and singing squeakily for the woman's part, when that suddenly ended with a bang, and a shrill so piercing that Tamika could still hear it then.

"Aminah," Tamika almost whispered, her eyes still staring off into the distance, intent.

"Uh, yes?" Aminah, who had made herself busy in the kitchen, replied, now appearing in its doorway.

Tamika then met Aminah's gaze. Tamika's eyes were serious, no smile even faintly traceable on her face, her expression causing Aminah discomfort, her eyes dancing, unsure if she wanted to meet Tamika's gaze. "Can you tell me what to say?"

For a moment, Aminah was thrown, unsure what Tamika was referring to, but when her eyes met her roommate's, she understood, Tamika's vulnerability, her fear, her desperation, detectable behind her softened eyes.

Aminah took in a deep breath, having never done it before but knowing how, *"Ash-hadu...,"* she spoke the Arabic words.

Tamika repeated slowly, her voice weakening with each word, sensing their meaning, although she did not understand the foreign language.

Then Aminah translated, Tamika repeating the statement in English, "I bear witness."

"I bear witness," Tamika repeated firmly, softly, determined.

"That none has the right to be worshipped but God alone."

"That none has the right to be worshipped but God alone."

"And I bear witness."

"And I bear witness."

"That Muhammad is the Messenger of God."

"That M-m-m," she tried to say, but her voice cracked, interrupting her, tears filling her eyes, her voice now more a whimper than intelligible speech. She pulled herself together. "That Muhammad," she said through tears, pausing to sob, "is the Messenger," she cried, covering her face in shame, as she began to feel free, not caring about anyone or anything else except the enormity, the power of her words. "That Muhammad is the Messenger of God."

No one spoke, and Aminah too cried, tears flooding her eyes, her mind on what had pushed Tamika to do it then. Both of them knew, but neither spoke about it. It was understood. Their sobs filled the house, their crying likely heard by neighbors, but right then they did not care. A moment later, Aminah felt a hand on her, and she looked up to find Tamika before her, as if asking for something. A moment's gaze told her, and she complied, embracing her roommate, each of their shoulders shaking, trembling as they cried.

That night Aminah led Tamika in prayer, the first in many of their prayers that they would pray together. The days and months following, Tamika surprised Aminah a great deal. On her own, Tamika began to cover in Islamic garb and memorize Qur'an. She even gave up public singing and made her newfound faith the subject of most of her songs, intending to one day sing for Muslim women.

But the day Aminah never forgot was the Monday following Tamika's entrance into Islam, the day of Tamika's presentation, which Aminah had been invited to attend. Dr. Sanders had given Tamika the option to delay it, he being sensitive to what she had gone through during the accident. But Tamika had insisted, having come to class prepared, more prepared than Dr. Sanders or any of the students would have expected. She was wearing a *khimaar* and *abiyah,* and the teacher and students thought she was wearing it for effect, a mere costume for her report. But Tamika had been clever, having only mentioned that she was wearing the dress of Muslim women. She had gone on to deliver a thorough and insightful presentation on Islam, one that even Aminah immensely benefited from. And Aminah could tell that she was not the only one impressed with the speech. Both Dr. Sanders and the students were deeply engrossed in Tamika's powerful words and beneficial information on a religion that was foreign to most of them. After she had completed her speech, she stated, "As we can see, Islam, the fastest growing religion in the world, is a holistic religion, its teachings affecting every aspect of the Muslim's life. Its roots reach back as far as Adam, and given its followers strict adherence to its original teachings, it holds an authenticity that no other religion can rightfully claim. History shows that other religions have changed tremendously, their teachings having been adapted and compromised over time. And although, as we saw earlier, some heretical groups of Muslims seek to adapt the religion, Islam is the only religion that remains in its orthodox form. The teachings of Islam are profound and its message convincing." She paused then added matter-of-factly, as if a logical clincher for her speech, "Which is why I chose the religion for myself."

Copies of this book can be ordered online at
<u>www.al-walaa.com</u>
or by calling Toll-Free:
1(866)550-7839

CPSIA information can be obtained at www.ICGtesting.com
Printed in the USA
LVOW060925310512

283983LV00001B/43/A